THE
Stolen One

THE Stolen One

SUZANNE CROWLEY

Greenwillow Books
An Imprint of HarperCollins *Publishers*

I'd like to thank my agent, Rosemary Stimola; my editor, Virginia Duncan; and everyone else at Greenwillow Books, especially Paul Zakris for his beautiful jacket design and Chris Borgman for the haunting cover photo.

This book is a work of fiction. References to real people, events, establishments, organizations, or locales are intended only to provide a sense of authenticity, and are used to advance the fictional narrative. All other characters, and all incidents and dialogue, are drawn from the author's imagination and are not to be construed as real.

The Stolen One

 Printed in the United States of America. For information address HarperCollins Children's Books, a division of HarperCollins Publishers, 10 East 53rd Street, New York, NY 10022.

www.harperteen.com

The text of this book is set in 12-point Venetian.

Book design by Paul Zakris

Library of Congress Cataloging-in-Publication Data

Crowley, Suzanne Carlisle.

The stolen one / by Suzanne Crowley.

p. cm.

"Greenwillow Books."

Summary: After the death of her foster mother, sixteen-year-old Kat goes to London to seek the answers to her parentage, and surprisingly finds herself invited into Queen Elizabeth's court.

ISBN 978-0-06-123200-8 (trade bdg.) — ISBN 978-0-06-123201-5 (lib. bdg.)

[1. Orphans—Fiction. 2. Identity—Fiction. 3. Country life—England—Fiction. 4. City and town life—England—Fiction. 5. Elizabeth I, Queen of England, 1533–1603—Fiction. 6. London (England)—History—16th century—Fiction. 7. Great Britain—History—Elizabeth, 1558–1603—Fiction.] I. Title.

PZ7.C88766Way 2009 [Fic]—dc22 2008015039

09 10 11 12 13 PHX / RRDB First Edition 10 9 8 7 6 5 4 3 2 1

For Lauren,
who loves fashion
and all things beautiful

I know what I saw that day in Humblebee Wood, aye, I do, and it was no dream. There was a fog that morning—devil's cover they call it, for you never know what lies beneath. I was running to meet Christian when I tripped and fell over a root, ripping my only kirtle. I was looking at the tear, deciding on what stitch I'd use to hide it from Grace, when I saw her. A ghost, dressed regally in red, floating through the swirling fog. She looked at me, her eyes piercing and sad. She wore a crown. I will never forget her.

CHAPTER 1

he wolf is sitting on his haunches under our ancient chestnut tree, his eyes boring straight through me. Grace Bab always said he would come to Blackchurch Cottage, and I never believed her.

I never knew my mother, the mother that birthed me. Nor my father, for that matter. And it's by God's good sense, Grace says, I never knew *him*, for he was the greatest scoundrel the world has yet seen. Still, though, I inherited his high spirit, and my mother's red hair, red as the good Queen Elizabeth's, and if Grace didn't lock the door at night, she fears I'd wander off in the darkness as I did as a child. Wolf's bait, she calls it, my hair.

Grace has always feared the wolves of Humblebee

Wood. They howled in the night like ghosts, making mischief under the cover of darkness. *When a wolf appears at Blackchurch Cottage, we must prepare the winding sheets, for a death is near.* Grace has always been full of dire predictions and tales of omens, loose of her senses some say.

But it was Anna, not Grace, who first sensed something was wrong. Anna who knew when a storm was to come hours before it actually arrived, or the exact hour a babe in the village was to be born, and Grace would appear before ever being summoned, another sign, the villagers said, of the evil doings of Blackchurch Cottage.

Our morning had started out as usual—a breakfast of pottage and crusty bread, then Grace and I washed our clothes in the creek, where I liked to run my fingers through the river stones pretending they were rich jewels, and then straight to our needlework—our livelihood. Grace left the door open, as it was an unusually cool day for the end of August, and the sweet smell of druid's honeysuckle from nearby Cleeve Hill came to us on a light breeze.

God's me, oh how I wanted to jump up and run. Although I love the needle (I'm told it's in my blood, from my mother), I had a hard time sitting still. When I was a child, Grace had to tie me to a baby minder, for fear I'd fall into the fire. And even now she still threatened to tie me to my chair, for it's my stitches and unusual designs that kept us alive. The most beautiful she has ever seen, and the merchant who Grace brought them to on market days at Stow-on-the-Wold agreed. He gave us measurements for customers in London, the rich and wealthy, and who knows, maybe a lofty lord or two.

We sat in our keeping room, which was where we spent our lives, stitching near the fire. I was working on a lady's cloak of sky blue satin, tufted with silver spangles. Along the dark blue collar I'd stitched twining leaves, gillyflowers, and hummingbirds in gold and black. I ran my fingers tenderly over the creamy, soft fabric. I loved my embroidery, aye, I did. And I mourned my creations when they went off into the world. What I would do to own such a garment instead of my one dull-as-day woolen kirtle! But Grace made sure we didn't linger over our finished pieces. They went straight to the wooden chest at the end of our bed. At least till it was market time again, and Grace would leave us for a few days and come back with a pocketful of coins and a not-often-seen serene smile upon her somber face.

But I knew where she kept the key. "There are no

secrets in a house of girls," Grace Bab said, although she was quite good at it herself. Sometimes when Grace went to the village, I'd wear the finery around the house and pretend I was a great lady, strumming the small prized lute Grace kept on a peg near the door, an elegant remnant from her London days that we were never allowed to touch. Anna would watch with worried eyes, fearful I'd be caught. She was too nervous to join in. I was always the naughty one—always.

"I smell wolf's juniper," Grace said suddenly, looking up from her needle. "Do you smell it?" She spoke of a rare, wild weed that was said to guard a wolf's den. A weed she sometimes used to stop the bleeding when a babe came too early.

I could only smell the honeysuckle, which still lingered in the air, sweet and beckoning. Grace looked around, inhaling a bit more, like a rat in the larder. Then she shook her head and mumbled that she had imagined it.

I glanced at my sister Anna, who was twining the thread. She had missed the exchange. Sweet Anna—Deaf Anna, she's known in the village, for Anna is nearly deaf and has been since she was born. Grace taught her to speak, only to you it might sound like a pond frog's croak. Grace and I knew her speech very well—every inflection, every strain for the right pronunciation. No one else did, though. She was a mute to all others, for it was only us she trusted. She hardly ever left the cottage. She was quite content to never leave, you see. She said our valley was the last place God made and it was here she would die, while I plotted escapes of every kind each little minute of the day.

Oh, but she's beautiful, Anna, so very beautiful, except for her ears, which she hides under her glorious yellow-golden hair, hair she inherited from Grace, whose own hair is as white as a Dunn's Hill ghost now. "Happened overnight," Grace claims. "God took it from me for saving them." My cousin Christian and Uncle Godfrey from the plague, she means. Together Anna and I were known as the "vexed twins," meaning we were to be pitied—me with my hair and Anna with her crippled ears. It was often said that neither of us, Anna and I, had a good future in hand, that an unlucky star shone upon us. But I always said *fa*, the future was ours for taking—I'd seize it for the both of us. Someday I'd leave this place, I knew it deep down in my soul. I'd leave.

Suddenly Anna got up and walked to the door, her eyes wide and wild. Her back stiffened strangely. When I saw the pale hair on her neck rise, I jumped up and joined her, my hand on her shoulder. At first I did not see him, as one does not see something that cannot be. I blinked. Yes, but he was there. A wolf sitting under our chestnut tree, strong limbed and fierce—a ghost in daylight. *When a wolf appears at Blackchurch Cottage, we must prepare the winding sheets, for a death is near.*

We seemed to lock eyes for a moment, the wolf and I, for we had known each other before, I think, and then he turned and trotted away. I watched him run along the hawthorn hedgerows that quilt the hills beyond our tiny village.

"What is it?" Grace called from behind us.

I gripped Anna's shoulder and tilted her face to me. "Just a little golden bird," I lied. We'd never hear the end of it, if she knew. And she'd tired so easily of late, her nerves raw. "Must have come all the way from London." Anna dropped the black thread she still held, and it rolled across the floor. I slipped my arm around Anna and pulled her to me. She was shaking.

"Come away from the doorway, girls," Grace said quietly as she continued to stitch. I slowly turned my head back to her as she muttered, "Golden birds foretell an omen."

I tilted my head for Anna to sit back down, which she did. "Did not Kat's mother have a golden bird in a gilded cage, Mama?" Anna said, her voice cracking more than usual. I smiled at her, thanking her for continuing the lie. I quickly turned to Grace, hoping beyond hope that she would answer.

But Grace gently raised her hand, admonishing Anna to hush, as she always did when my mother was mentioned. "Come away from the door, Kat," she said quietly. She never looked up from her needle. She needn't have. She knew what lay beneath my beating heart. And that's why she worried about me so. And for a brief, fleeting moment, I thought I smelled wolf's juniper too; it stung my nose like fire smoke before floating away from our cottage. I narrowed my eyes and looked out at the hills, but the wolf was gone.

"Come back to your work, Wren," Grace murmured behind me. Grace called Anna this in her rare affectionate moments. "And you too, Kat. Quit dawdling in the doorway."

"Work, work, work," I mimicked, rolling my eyes as I stepped back from the threshold. "Morning, day, and night—can we never be free of it?"

"Sit down, Kat," she said as she drew up another stitch and plunged the needle back down in her cloth. "No more prattle from you."

I plopped back down on my stool and picked up the cloak and my needle. I looked out the window again and then narrowed my eyes at Grace. Why had our whole lives been tainted with fear and admonitions? And mysteries? Why should she always be so full of worry and short of temper like a stonemason hag? Still, though, I knew she loved me dearly. When she was close to falling asleep at night in her chair by the fire (I hardly ever saw her abed, so afraid of falling asleep was she), I'd try and thief answers from her.

"Where do I come from? Why me?" I'd asked her one cold winter night.

"I'd do anything for you, my little Kat," she'd answered, her eyes fluttering shut. "No one wanted you. But I did."

When I was a child, Grace hid my hair under a child's coif, hoping by taming it, she'd tame me. "Spirit" she called me, for I was like the wild heather on Woeful Downs. I was only allowed to remove the linen when bathing at the creek. One morning someone saw my hair released from its binding, and soon it was known in the village that I had the hair of a she-demon. "Who shall have you, girl?" Grace had proclaimed then.

And even now, I must hide it under an ugly matron's coif, although I am sixteen years and it is quite proper for a girl to wear her hair down. "How else is the maid to catch a husband if he cannot see what he is to get," Frances Pea, who owns the Pea & Cock, asks when we come to town. "And with that tongue of hers?"

I am known for my outspokenness, and privately Grace sometimes pops my mouth when I prattle too long or say something too sharp. But Grace is also well served in talking out of both sides of her mouth. To Frances Pea, who is hard as a crumpet stone, and who was thrown by her first husband in Old Simon's duck pond for her scolding and unquiet ways, she responds, "Yes, perhaps she will, for a sweet maid who possesses both wit and sense will surprise her husband with daily miracles."

Which is very funny, for neither is the God's truth (I have the sense of Perceval's mare, Grace says, and am prone to rash impulses like my mother), and even more, there is no hope of finding a husband here in Winchcombe except for old Mr. Dar, who is nigh near forty *and* poxed, and the Widower Beachum, who has eight stout girls and only one cow amongst them.

There is Christian. Yes indeed, there is always Christian Dawe. Grace has been singing his high praises from noon to nightfall of late. But I have to laugh, for he is barely a boy, really, and like a brother to me. Ha! And when I remind Grace of her admonition to never buy a horse with a curly mane—for you see, Christian is possessed of the most unruly mess of locks—Grace tells me to shush.

But Grace says I will someday soon have to take a husband, before I lose the sweet blossom of youth that disguises one's imperfections. And it must be someone who can bear me and my meager dowry, and take Anna, too—and for that we can't be choosy. A woman must have a husband; this is her all-abiding goal in life—a husband good or bad. Without a husband, a woman is left to the mercies of this cruel world. Such is a poor woman's lot, and such was mine. I didn't like to think of husbands. And I would not, no matter how much Grace harangued me. I'd dreamed only of what lay beyond our lovely vale, past Postlip Hill, past Nutmeg Farm to the dusty roads that lead to better things.

But it consumed her, Grace, this hope of finding us settled. For some reason she thought God would take her soon, even though she was not of an age to expect it and was always of a strong constitution, just tired of life now, that's all. She'd even escaped the sweating sickness the year before, when it hit nearby Corndean and Grace was called upon to help at Nutmeg Farm. Poor Christian's mother, Agnes Dawe, was taken to the lord on the day of All Souls, only a few hours after falling sick.

Uncle Godfrey and Christian lay near death too, but God spared them, through Grace's magical hands.

Grace did not catch their sickness, which was as virulent as a great flood. Nor did she bring it home to us. Grace is skilled of the hands, you see. Both of needle and healing. It's one of my few early memories of her, those long, tender hands stroking my wolf's bait hair at night and telling me all would be well as long as I stayed with her. They were her crowning glory, those hands.

Something troubled Grace. I'd spot it in her eyes, a devil worry, a worry of the heart. Once as we sat by the hearth fire, she said of a sudden, "They will take my hands." Everyone knew of the old tale of the witch Comfort Woodhouse from Wolfhames Hill, whose hands were taken from her newly sown grave. Years later a one-eyed shepherd plucked a bony fingertip from the River Severn.

But Grace would not say what troubled her or why she might meet an early grave. She told me once when I was very young—too young to know—that she would never lie to me, but she could not tell me the truth. Not yet. Someday. She would know when. Was someday soon, I wondered? What secrets did she keep from me?

We had another visitor that morning. Christian came at noon with a bundle of bane pears, smiling at me as he laid the basket on the end of our trestle table. It was our signal, you see, to meet later at the barrow of Belas Knap. If he had placed the pears in the middle, we would meet at the ruins of Puck's Well. I looked up slyly at him as I worked on a pair of gloves fit for royalty—of soft green kid, with pansies and swans in gold, and glass pearls ruched along the ruffled edge. I tried one on and admired its beauty, then pulled it off before Grace could see.

Christian said hello to her, and she nodded back from the other end of our keeping room. She was making us a crusty tartlet. "Those will do nicely," she said, nodding at his bundle. Even though we seemed to eat pears noon and night, I never tired of them, so delicious were they. Uncle Godfrey had expanded the pear grove, and the pears always sold well at market. According to Grace, Christian was very lucky that he would someday inherit such a good farm. And a year or two before, an old shepherd had left Christian seven little lambs, which he adored and coddled over day and night. And this showed he was an enterprising young man, an additional feather in his cap. But I was irritated by those flea-bitten beasts, who loved to nip at my bottom whenever I visited.

I picked up my needle again. Anna, suddenly clumsy, dropped her spool and it rolled across Christian's foot. He leaned down and handed it back to her, chivalrously, like a knight giving a wildflower to a maiden. Anna, her face aflame, fled from the cottage.

"Why, what's wrong with her?" I asked, taking the spool from Christian's outstretched hand as I watched Anna run across the meadow. I laughed. "Something indeed is in the air."

Grace frowned at me. "And how find you your father today, Christian?"

"His back is laying him low, Aunt, from the picking," he said, winking at me, his head turned from Grace. Four o'clock, he was telling me. "He wants to know if you can come later," he continued.

"Of course," Grace said. "I'll come soon. He'll be right and ready for some ale at the revel tonight."

Everyone looked forward to the revel, where there was much merriment and jollity, a little taste of heaven, you see.

CHAPTER 2

obody comes out to Belas Knap, which means "beautiful hill," anymore since old mumblecrust Bella Wilde told everyone she had seen a row of hooded, wailing monks walking across its summit at midnight. "Crying for ole King Henry they were," she said, referring to the villain who'd pulled down nearby Hailles Abbey. It's actually the ancients, the old ones, who are buried in the barrow of Belas Knap, and why would they have any reason to bother anyone now?

The talk of fairy folk and little beasties that nip at your feet and pull you underneath with the bones of old is not enough to deter me. This is my favorite place in the whole world. I come here as often as I can, and sketch things from nature—the centers of wildflowers, the veins on leaves, the markings of a leopard moth, or the feathers of a golden-crested wren. Later my sketches would find their way into my designs, which Anna would carefully prick onto the fabric with a needle and transferring powder.

After Grace left for Uncle Godfrey's, leaving strict instructions for completing the velvet cloak, I raced through Humblebee Wood, throwing off my cap and letting my hair flow free in the wind. Anna had come back from the meadow after Christian left, pouting, but would not tell me what troubled her when I prodded. She had simply plopped down on our bed to take her daily nap. Unlike Grace, who is afraid to sleep, Anna embraces it like a newborn babe, succumbing to a blissful world where she has no pain. For sometimes her ears plague her mercilessly, a low, dull pain that brings with it strange noises that echo in her head.

Finally I reached the grasslands that converge with the huge, low hill—the barrow. Christian was not yet there, so I climbed the mound and sat in my favorite spot to wait. I had an unobstructed view of Sudeley Castle, the sun making it glow like the golden palace in a tale of King Arthur, the spires and trestles pointing toward the sky. It's here that Grace would find me as a child sitting, watching, still as a ghost. But I have no memories of those night wanderings. Very few memories, really, of my very early years.

A real queen lived at Sudeley before I was born and before Grace tried her luck at a better life in London—Queen Katherine Parr, the last wife of Henry VIII, who was smart enough to outlive him. After he died, she married her true love, a handsome lord. But she died in childbirth, and her baby not long after. "Poorly served, she was," they say in the village. If her ladies had taken better care of Queen Katherine, perhaps she wouldn't have died. "If you had been there," I said to Grace one time, as I watched her prepare a healing potion, "perhaps she would have lived." And Grace had slapped me, and for the entire night I smelled jasmine on my cheek, and wondered why I provoked her so. "Bumble bug," Grace sometimes called me, referring to the bedbugs that bite in the night just because they can.

"Why do you always watch it?"

I startled. It was Christian. He plopped down next to me and rested his head in my lap. I continued to stare.

"I don't know," I said. "It calls to me, I suppose."

He laughed. "You're a dreamer." He tried to tickle my

neck with a blade of grass and I ignored him.

"And why can't I dream of better things? Why must we be poor fools with miserable lives?"

"You best be content with what you have," he said, frowning. It did not sound like him.

"God's me, what have they said now?" I asked, looking down into his honey brown eyes.

He closed them a moment, sighing. "Why do you have to curse? And always talk so? Father Bigg says you will have to do penance for twenty-score years if you don't learn to control your tongue."

"I don't care a farthing for what Father Bigg says." Christian winced. "And since when do you listen to that beetle brain? I do my own penance." I had plenty of time to say my Hail Marys while I stitched the hours away. Stitching and stitching, that's all I seemed to do, yet I loved it with all my soul. Grace said that sometimes the things we love the most were our greatest crosses to bear.

"How could you now," Christian continued, "when Grace has not taken you and Anna to mass in over a year? Why, I think it's been since my mother died."

"You should talk. You are always with your sweet little lambs now, aren't you?"

"When I meet my maker, I'll wear a tuft of wool on my

shirt, the shepherd's mark, and I'll be forgiven. What shall you wear?" And then he blushed deep, and I knew it was because Grace used to say I had so little sense of decorum, I'd probably forget my own clothes when I met my maker.

"Grace says we have our own church in our cottage." I laughed. Our stone cottage was built by a monk who had been thrown out of his order for a sin no one now remembers. We spent Sundays learning to read from the Bible, Grace having been taught when she was young by her gentle-born mother, Jane. Jane had defied her parents and married for love.

Christian rolled his eyes and sat up, turning away from me. "Some say Grace is a witch and that she played with the devil when she was gone." Before Anna and I were born, Grace had disappeared from Winchcombe. Several years later she returned, widowed apparently, with a young one set on each hip and an old, toothless milch cow following her. Hedge-born, they whisper behind our backs, meaning we are lowborn, the lowest of the low. There was never a Mr. Bab, they think, even though Grace, in addition to the feeble cow, had enough coins when she came home to purchase our small two-room cottage after her father passed away. The villagers, being weavers, know when a story has been spun.

I sighed. "People here think London is the devil's playground, but few have actually been there." Grace had, and she indeed had little good to say of it now.

I stood up and moved away from Christian. I stopped atop a limestone ledge. A cool breeze from the direction of Cleeve Hill played with my hair a moment, then moved on down the ridge. Some said there was an eerie feeling at Belas Knap, and I could rightly say I had never felt it until today. Something cold crawled up my spine.

Christian walked up behind me. I could feel him breathing, waiting.

"What's wrong, Christian?" I asked keeping my voice low. "Why all this talk? Why are you being so mean?" For some reason my heart tickled. Christian had always been my greatest admirer, and something had changed.

"I don't like that they talk of you . . . and Anna," he whispered. "Look at me, Kat."

The air was suddenly very still, and my heart began to pound. Grace Bab had warned me, but it was too silly to even fathom. Christian might propose, and you are to say yes, she said to me at the stream a week ago. I had laughed. "Laugh all you may, Spirit, you could do much worse," she'd said. "Much worse."

Please don't. Whatever you think you should say. Please don't say it.

I closed my eyes. He had been my best friend forever. We had run across these hills. . . .

He touched me on the shoulder. I turned and started to speak, but he put his thumb on my lip and shook his head. The sun shone behind him, lighting his dark curls like embers. Only I didn't think of unlucky horses with curly manes this time. Something turned in my stomach. Piper had once said Christian was handsome and I told her that was the best jest I'd heard since the tale of the clod-pate frog who hopped in the alehouse and asked for elderberry ale.

A giggle threatened to emerge. Why was I so nervous? It was just Christian, the boy who once rolled all the way down Postlip Hill just because I dared him.

He stared at me hard, unblinking. "I want you as my wife, Kat," he said flatly. "My wife. I have thought of it for a long time. And I'll take care of Anna, too, after Grace is gone."

I sniggered. I knew it was mean, but I couldn't help myself.

"Grace is not going anywhere," I said, but the words sounded false even to me.

"You have to have seen, Kat, that she is not well," he said, snatching my hands.

"I don't know what you are talking about," I said, pulling my hands away and trying to walk past him. But he grabbed my shoulders and pulled me to him. Our eyes met, and before I knew it, he was kissing me. A jolt passed through me, a pang as our lips touched.

I pulled back. "Christian," I said, looking up at him, way up. When had he gotten so tall? "We cannot marry," I started. "We are cousins."

"You know very well that is not true," he whispered. "And cousins can marry, if they are of a wish."

I pushed away from him.

"Father told me," he continued. "Grace paid a visit a fortnight ago, and they spent a long time walking amongst the pear trees. But I think I have always known that you are not one of us, just as everyone else in the village knows or suspects. No one will have you, Kat," he said. "No one."

No one wanted you. But I did.

"What did she tell him? Who are my parents?" I asked. "Are they alive?"

"I don't know. Father is of little words," he answered. "And I don't care to know anyway."

My heart burned. I walked past him and stood on the ridge looking out past the castle. "I don't have to marry," I said quietly. "I can make a living with my hands," I said, holding them out to him.

"It's not enough," he murmured. "You know it's not enough." Aye, it was true. We barely had enough, and whatever little extra money we made had to be used to purchase the luxurious fabrics we needed. It was an endless cycle, and we barely managed.

I raised my chin. "Perhaps I'll go to London myself and sell my work. It's highly prized."

He just stood there looking at me as though I had lost my mind.

I turned to head back to Humblebee Wood.

Christian caught my hand. "The truth is, I love you, Kat," he whispered, "I always have." I turned to him and stared at his face, as though seeing it for the first time. Yes, he was handsome. Unbearably handsome. His eyes shone—a shiver went down to my toes. But he was Christian. And I didn't want to be the wife of a pear farmer, no matter how delicious those pears are, and no matter how lowly I was born. I shook my head no, broke free, and started to run.

But then I stopped in my tracks when I saw a cloaked

figure amidst the oak trees. One of the wailing ghost monks? Goose bumps went up and down my arms. No. The cloak was my work, an ash-color woolen with star thistles couch stitched on the edge. I knew it well; I had had blisters for a week from working the needle in the thick wool. Someone else knew where Grace kept the key. *There are no secrets in a house of girls.* Then the figure turned, and I saw it was Anna, tears running down her cheeks.

CHAPTER 3

y mother's favorite color was crimson red, the devil's color. Grace never allowed the color in the house, and once when I asked her why, she told me it was a hue that never did anyone any good, especially my mother. Which only deepened the great mystery of my mother, for Grace said she was as far from the devil as could be—pious, so pious that when she made a mistake, it was calamitous. When you live high above everyone else, you fall far.

Some say Queen Elizabeth is pious too, but known to turn on the ones she loves. I didn't believe it, though. I thought she was the greatest sovereign to have ever lived. A peddler came through our village one time, and among his wares he had a fine woodcut of her. While

Grace had her head turned, I gave him a small coin for it (for I knew where she hid our coins, too) and for a small bundle of red taffeta. I kept my treasure from prying eyes, but when I was alone, I'd pull it out and admire her. Oh, her dignity! Her beauty! And her dress! How I wished I could be her! I'd run my fingers over the pleats, the flounces, the rows and rows of pearls and sumptuous jewels, and imagined myself dressed so nobly.

But no, I was vexed to wear my drab woolen kirtle to the revel that night. It had been washed and mended so many times that I feared it would rend in two if I as much as sneezed. None of my infamous stitching here; my stitching would ruin in the hard river water we used to wash our clothes. Coveting beautiful things is a sin, a sin that attracts greater sins, Grace always warned. "Be humble of what you have. It is enough." Grace needed not know what I wore underneath my dress that night—a lovely red taffeta petticoat, stitched secretly and hidden from Grace. It felt wonderful against my skin, devil's color or no. I sighed, and Grace pinched me. "You should be glad you are going, Spirit," she said. "Sneaking off as you did." I glanced over at her and was surprised to see a gentle smile tucked at the corners of her mouth.

Anna, walking on the other side of her, was not so happy. A black raven perched on a faraway cypress cawed, and Anna held her hands over her ears until the noise subsided. She had been pretending to be asleep, no sign of the cloak, when I came home. Grace, home early from her errand to Uncle Godfrey's, had watched me carefully when I walked in, but she hadn't said a word.

I glanced over at Grace again as we made our way down a steep slope guarded by a row of darksome trees. She knew Christian had proposed. She was biding her time. Aye, I knew her well. She would pounce on me when I least expected it. I was a mighty foe in words, she had said many times, using my words to win whether wrong or right.

Ha, then I wouldn't mention Christian at all. Not at all. And the whole cursed episode would be forgotten. I'd probably see him at the revel, and I had a mind to kick his shins. Us marrying—it was silly indeed. Ha. My crimson petticoat brushed against me again, and my legs tingled.

As we reached the town green, Grace turned to Anna so she could see her lips and whispered, "Hold your heads high, maids." Mine was already held high, but poor Anna seemed to bow lower. What distressed her so? Had she seen us kiss? Nay. I touched my finger to my lip and couldn't help but smile.

The village was aglow with candles. It was lovely, like the sky had been turned upside down. In the middle of the village green, a bonfire was lit—a gesture to the old ones who used to light bones to honor their gods. And all along the main road, bushes were pinned to the doors of houses that were serving their best ale, made from recipes handed down through generations and much fought over.

Father Bigg stood on the green, a tankard in each hand. He had learned to let some of the old pagan beliefs slide by and turn a blind eye, although he was convinced there was much mischief that went on behind his back. A group of children danced around him with a garland of daisies.

Grace left us to go add her pear tartlets to the gathering of food set up on trestle tables dragged from the Pea & Cock. Anna peered at me, her eyes reflecting the crimson of the bonfire, and for a moment I thought I saw a sliver of hatred before she ran after Grace.

I drifted toward a group of people laughing and clapping, gathered around some minstrels. Strangers are not usually welcome in Winchcombe, but when the ale has been passed around enough, everyone's a friend, especially if they can play a fine tune and tell a pretty tale. I stood at the back of the crowd and watched, mesmerized by the singers. They had the look of merry travelers, and I wondered where they'd been and what they'd seen. One minstrel in particular caught my eye. He was tall and regal, with long black locks, the contours of his face pitched odd and angular. A Spaniard, perhaps, although I'd never seen one to know the difference. "Spanish romancers," Grace called them, those dark men who talk women off their feet. Had this handsome man ever been to London and had he been to Queen Elizabeth's court? They were singing a bawdy song about the queen and I blushed deeply, as dark as my petticoat, I'm sure.

A lusty wench she be
For she only has eyes
For Dudley,
And when he finds her
At night,
He gives her his sword,
So she'll make him
A lord!

Piper appeared next to me. Even she smelled of ale. "Have you heard?" she asked. She was always ready with some bit of gossip, a flibbertigibbet, Grace called her.

"No," I responded, looking around for Christian. I swallowed. Suddenly my stomach hurt. Grace claimed I had no conscience, like my father. She was wrong on that count, for sure. I truly cared for Christian. I truly did, even if my eyes kept catching those of the Spaniard.

"The minstrels saw a girl fairy on Cahill Road on their travels here today. Imagine that, in the middle of the day! And when they tried to chase it, it screamed like it was mad, and ran over Postlip Hill. Why, it could be headed straight for Blackchurch Cottage!" Piper exclaimed.

I continued to watch the minstrels, frowning at their silly words. "My, but you are quiet tonight, Kat Bab," Piper went on. "You and Christian, Sulky Sues the both of you," she said, and turned.

"Christian?" I grabbed her arm. "You've seen him?" I asked.

She pulled her arm away from me, rubbing it. "Why, he has been sampling the ale at every house along the lane, he has. 'Twill be wearing a violet around his neck tomorrow with all the other fools." She hiccupped.

I looked desperately around, finally spotting a bunch of lads, their gangly arms and legs hanging from an oak tree like snakes. They were watching something. A spectacle. I wondered if perhaps a soothsayer had come, like the one we had several years ago full of wordy wit and saucy jest. He was the only man ever thrown in the duck pond. He had predicted a bad hay harvest. He left before dawn, and sure as salt, the next season a drought hit the farmers hard.

Piper rattled on as I narrowed my eyes on the tree. "I tried to get him to tarry, but no, so ill-mannered he was. He said he was done with women, so fickle and bothersome they are." I pulled my eyes away from the tree. Piper was looking at me carefully, very carefully. "So I told him," she continued, "he should put lad's love in his shoe, like all the other boys, and before sunrise the woman who was meant for him will seek him out."

Over her shoulder I spotted Uncle Godfrey, also eyeing me strangely from where he sat playing dice with old Tommy Mundey. Uncle Godfrey, who has only ever had a kind word and soft hug for me. He crooked his finger for me to come, and I peeked at the tree of gangly snakes again before walking over to him.

Uncle Godfrey stood and nodded to old Tommy. He

threw him a coin and took my arm. "I'll have a word with you," he said, gently walking us away from listening ears.

I couldn't meet Uncle Godfrey's eyes, no matter how kind they were. "I've watched you grow into a young lady and have hoped you'd gain more sense along the way, that I have." He spit. "But my sweet Agnes will come home to me before that will happen, that's for sure." He nodded to the churchyard. "You will marry him, Katherine. You will. How can you be so cruel? To Christian. And Anna? And Grace? You won't give her soul some rest before she goes?"

"She will not die," I said, not meeting his eyes. "She will save herself. And she does not know yet."

"Aye, and she will not know," he said. "By God's grace, if you upset her anymore—" His voice choked.

I looked up and was surprised to see my uncle had tears in his eyes. My sweet, good uncle. Piper had asked me once what secrets he had, for he always went to confession after mass, when everyone else disappeared like summer rain. And after knocking her down, I had told her it was simply because he was good. Isn't anyone wholly good, or are we all full of wormholes where we stuff our secrets and ungodly desires? But it had made me wonder about my uncle—what he knew and what he kept from us. He looked away from me, back to the churchyard where Agnes lay.

"What is my secret, Uncle?" I asked. "If you could tell me, perhaps . . ."

"Perhaps you could accept my good son?"

I couldn't answer him.

"I don't know everything, Kat. Only a little," he said softly. "Agnes knew. Knew everything, but took it with her. You may not be of our blood, but we've raised you as our own. And that should be enough." He shook his head in disgust and started to walk off.

"Uncle Godfrey!" I called after him, but he never turned back, and disappeared into the dark. I took a deep breath, my eyes drawn up to the sky.

Suddenly Anna came running, her eyes wild. She croaked, "I can't find Mama. Come! Come!" She pulled me, and I followed her across the green, around the churchyard. I could hear shouting and yelling, and I saw we were at the oak tree, only now the lads were on the ground surrounding something, taunting. When they saw me, they parted, and the source of their amusement was laid bare.

Christian, bloodied and covered with dirt, was rolling

around with Jossey Boots, the town liar. No one believed a word Jossey said, even when he claimed his father's barn was on fire and the blaze could be seen from every hill from here to London.

I stood there for a full minute, dumbfounded, staring at the rolling fists and feet, while the lads in turn stared at me, grins wide. Suddenly there was a loud guttural roar. Anna.

Everything stopped. Even Christian and Jossey. Anna stood there horrified as all eyes turned on her. There was no laughter, nothing, just shocked silence as she stood there, her hands trembling at her sides. Finally she turned and ran.

Christian stood up. He plucked a handkerchief from his breeches and wiped at his bloody nose. It was the handkerchief I'd given him for his last birthday—his initials were embroidered on it. He seemed to have little care for it now.

Jossey, the worst for wear, rose to his hands and knees, panting. Some of the lads helped him up, and off they went down the lane.

The others wandered off until Christian and I were left, each of us breathing hard. I reached out to touch his bruised cheek, but he knocked my hand away. God's me, but he reeked of ale. "Why, Christian," I said. "You're drunk as Cuthbert Wiggam!"

"Leave it be," he mumbled, sounding just like Grace. He turned to go, stumbling some, from the ale or the blows I was not sure.

"Well, at any rate, you bested him, that you did!" I laughed as I followed. I remembered how timid he was as a child, when Uncle told him to scare the sparrows from the pear trees, and Christian didn't have the heart. He'd given them oats to eat instead, and one had even eaten from his hand.

"Christian!" I called again. He stopped, but would not turn. I walked up behind him. He was still breathing hard.

"What was it? Why were you fighting?" I tried to touch his arm, but he flinched as though I were made of fire.

"He was talking of you," he started. "And Anna. Said you were witches."

"Christian," I interrupted, "this is nothing new. Why would you have a care?"

"Because *if* you are to be my *wife*"—he bit off the words one by one—"and Anna my sister, they cannot talk of you. They will not as long as I have breath."

"Christian."

"Shhhhhh," and at first I thought perhaps it was the wind that spoke, so soft the sound was.

"I have just not ever thought of us in that way," I said quietly. "But I will think upon what you have asked. Truly I will."

He stood perfectly still. And then, "Have you thought at all that perhaps *I* have changed my mind?"

I was still deciphering his low words as he stalked off toward the lane that led to Nutmeg Farm. I reached down and picked up the bloodied handkerchief.

On the north side of the church, away from the churchyard where my aunt Agnes lay, is an old elm tree. Hannah's Elm it's called, and it's said it grew from the stake in the heart of a suicide. A drowned maiden, she was. Underneath the tree's wide, sturdy limbs, paupers and strangers were buried, along with the other suicides who were always buried in the dark, unshrouded and uncoffined.

I walked past this sad ground on my way back to the revel and paused a moment, remembering. Poor Emma Townsend was regularly beaten by her husband, and everyone in the village knew. A bundle of straw was dumped on the Townsends' doorstep as a warning for the man to stop. This, you see, was always done to sinful offenders of this sort, for the villagers always took care of their own. This time the warning didn't stop her husband—if anything it brought on a worse beating—and not long after Emma was found hanging in her barn. Everyone said it was her husband that good as killed her, but still, poor Emma joined Hannah under the elm. The next day her husband was found dead, his head bashed in, on the doorstep of his cottage in a mound of fresh hay. Later, when I'd pulled a single stalk of hay off Grace's back, she'd simply thrown it in the fire. And when I'd shut my eyes waiting for the inevitable slap, it hadn't come.

There are good men and bad, Grace says, but most are of the latter, full of wormholes. As I headed back toward the merriment of the revel, I heard a noise. I turned and froze. I saw a glimpse of something red in the fog, but when I looked back, it disappeared like a will-o'-the-wisp. The hair on my arms stood on end as a cold breeze blew across my cheeks.

CHAPTER 4

I once asked Grace if I was comely. "Alluring, you are," she had answered. "But you might as well be ugly for the good it will do you." We were at the river during the summer I turned thirteen. *Alluring*. I had tried to glimpse my reflection, barely perceiving a flash of my wild red hair before Grace had thrashed the water with her hand. "Your father was vain," she'd said, shaking the water off as though she'd dipped her hand in a manure pile. "And look where it got him. Dangerous is the man with the devil spark in his eye."

As I walked past the Pea & Cock, the minstrels were outside lounging, drinking ale. One of them had his arm around the town slut, Maud Davey. Poor thing. It didn't take much to get the reputation, just being seen doing some kissey-kissey on a moonlit night. And I guess she felt she had to live up to her name, and the only thing worse than having a bad man, Grace said, is having them all. I glanced about for the handsome Spaniard. Aye, he was there. He caught my eye and winked, and I suddenly knew what Grace spoke of. I blushed down to my toes and walked on. I needed to find Anna and see if she was all right.

"Do you have news for me, Kat?" Grace said to me quietly when I found her with the old women, the "old creatures" she called them, by the table laden with food. They were all sitting in a row, like sharp-eyed ravens, with a wide view of the town green. Anna sat off to the side, quietly eating, her eyes purposely not meeting mine. I wanted to go and talk to her, but I knew Anna well. She'd push me away and everyone would see. There was no sign of Uncle Godfrey. I wondered if he had gone home like Christian.

I suddenly realized how hungry I was. There were dumplings with wild plums called heg-pegs, hot mutton pies, shortcakes, and elderberry pies. Grace glanced toward Jane Alden, the maker of the elderberry pies, before pushing them aside and pulling forward her pear tartlets. She then handed me a cup of dandelion ale, women's drink.

I took a small sip. I glanced over at Anna. Behind her on the green was the pack of gangly boys, who were now playing cross and cricket. "Perhaps we should go home," I said to Grace. Piper walked by, and one of the boys grabbed her arm and whispered something in her ear. It wouldn't be long before word of the fight reached the row of ravens. And then Grace.

And sure enough, Piper, head held high, walked over to the table and told Alice Ogilvey, who had to wake the crone next to her, Old Hookey (an unfortunate nose, you see; no one remembers her real name, she's so ancient), and on down the line it went until the last one said straight to Grace, "Your nephew's been brawlin' about your lasses." All eyes were upon us. "Seems Jossey Boots 'as almost lost an eye."

I looked away. I noticed that someone was passed out on the green, feet splayed and shoeless. Father Bigg. He had the biggest feet in the village and, no doubt, next Sunday he'd be preaching about everyone's sinful drunkenness and evil-making.

"Why, of course he did. Sensitive boy, he is. Indeed. And a good son. Agnes would be very proud. He was only defending his intended, my Katherine here." I gaped at her.

The ravens' mouths all dropped open as though they were chicklets ready to be fed a hot hearty meal. And Old Hookey even stood up, dropping her tartlet.

My head spun around to Anna to see if she'd read Grace's lips. Yes. Her face was stricken. And I knew then what my heart had been denying all day. Anna loved Christian.

We walked home in the thickening fog. Grace seemed to be in her own silent world of triumphant dignity. Her face, softly lit by a small candle she held, had the countenance of a corpse who's died a peaceful death. She didn't seem to notice the forlorn figure of Anna, who walked along the other side of me and inched closer and closer till our arms brushed together every other step or so, chafing me with tender regret. Finally I hooked my arm in hers, pulling her tightly toward me. I heard a stifled sob escape her.

Grace jested, "I think Kat would swallow you whole like Jonah's whale if that would make you any closer."

Then she hooked her arm in mine, and the three of us, linked together like Puckleworth sausages, rounded the last hill toward Blackchurch Cottage.

It was the sound of sparrows, clamoring in the birch trees like the bells of Winchcombe Abbey, that told us something was amiss. We slowed our pace and, as we did so, the birds' call dissipated as though someone had said, "There now, you've done your duty, hush and let them see."

A faint light emanated in the fog. Fire? I thought to myself, my stomach dropping. Anna's eyes grew large.

"Pray, God's death, what is this?" Grace murmured. The three of us began to run, Grace's candle fluttering out.

When we reached the cottage, to our relief we saw that it was not a fire, but several of our precious candles, flickering low in the windows, melted wax cascading like icicles. Grace never lets us burn our candles down. We live by the hearth fire at night.

As we walked closer, we saw there were hawk moths buzzing at the window, desperate to get in. And our yew cross, the one the monk had placed on our door over a century ago, representing good luck and a long life, had been pulled from its hook. When I tripped over it, Anna crossed herself. But Grace, with the look of a challenged warrior, walked straight in the door.

Our tidy cottage looked like it had been picked up and turned upside down by a giant. Our cooking utensils were strewn about, our chairs toppled over, yarn untwined and strung across the floor like an enormous colorful spiderweb. And everywhere a thin layer, like fairy dust, of Anna's transferring powder. And God's me, a terrible, sickly sweet odor—the odor of death. I held my breath as my eyes continued around the room. Thieves? Cutthroats, perhaps? A few years ago a thief had traveled unseen through several villages in our area on revel night, making off with a bounty of goods, for although the poor are always crying poor, everyone seems to have some bit of coin or jewel hidden.

I immediately thought of running to Nutmeg Farm for Uncle Godfrey and Christian, but Grace stepped forward to the doorway of our sleeping room like a snake who has spotted its prey. I followed. Anna stood stock-still, frozen in the front doorway. I motioned for her to come.

The first thing I noticed, beyond the odor which was even stronger in here, thick as the butcher's shop on slaughter day (all three of us immediately held our aprons up to our mouths), was that our chest was open and our precious clothes were carefully draped over the sides. It was as though a gentle thief had been sorting through them one by one.

Anna stiffened. She put one hand on my shoulder and pointed to our bed. Someone, or something, was lying in it. And it moaned. Grace walked right over to our bed and pulled the sheets back.

Anna and I stepped forward on our tippy toes, peering the best we could around Grace. Lying in the bed, dressed in a little girl's gown of gold silk edged in pearled lace, one I had but finished last week, was a child-woman sleeping fitfully.

Grace stared at the creature with a strange melding of half puzzlement and half recognition on her face. "Jane," she murmured. "Jane the fool."

And then, almost as if in response, the thing coughed violently, twitching as though invisible hands shook her back and forth. A thin line of vermillion blood ran down her chin and down into the gold of the dress, meandering like the trail of the bloody nose beetle Christian and I used to tease to see it spit its red poison. The creature opened her eyes.

"Why, Grace," she said in a strangely lilted accent, "are you not glad to see me? You owe me the pendant. We made a bargain, aye, that we did. And I've come for it." Her eyes danced.

"Mad," Grace said through clenched teeth. "You are

raving sick mad!" Grace turned to me. "Boil some water!"

I stood stock-still, my eyes on the red *S* that continued to snake down my beautiful creation. The gown was fit for a little princess, and we were hoping to fetch enough for it to last through the winter.

"Go, now!" Grace yelled when I didn't move. "And Anna, you gather the digweed from the weed basket. And linen. We need linen. Leave it all on the threshold. Do not come back in here, the both of you!"

"Shall I go to Nutmeg Farm for Uncle Godfrey?" I asked, still rooted to my spot.

"No, absolutely not." Grace turned to me, her eyes afire. "She's got the plague. If they were to get it, they'd not likely be spared a second time. Go, now!" she screamed.

And as I left, I heard the creature say as sure as daylight, "And that be her? The little babe? Perhaps I'll take her; she'd be worth a queen's fortune now, wouldn't she?"

I lingered, my back to them, my ears prickling. I'd waited my whole life for this. Dreamed of it. Aye, I had.

"Go, Kat; she's senseless. Go. If we are to save her, go, I beg you," Grace said behind me. I turned just my head to see if Grace would meet my eyes. She would not.

Anna busied herself collecting Grace's herbs as I

brought a pot of water to the stone hearth. I hooked it on the cooking rod and pushed it over the fire. My hands were shaking.

Anna looked at me with questioning eyes, frantic eyes. "A fairy demon?" she croaked.

I shook my head no. "A dwarf," I mouthed to her as I hid my hands in my skirt. That's what the creature in our bed was—a dwarf. One had come through many years back with a group of traveling troubadours—a jolly man with bells on his cap who danced a limber jig for coins. And Frances Pea, so enthralled with the little man and his friends, let them drink for free, since everyone had quickly come to town to get a gander at the little fellow. Grace, curiously, was not so enchanted. When she'd found me in town gawking with everyone else, I'd received a swift swat. "Cunning," she repeated under her breath as she hurried me home. "Cunning. Cunning. Cunning." I still don't know if she was talking of me for giving her the slip, or the little man.

Anna brought the herbs and linen and laid them in the doorway. I pulled the pot holder back and, very gently with the warmers, carried the water to the doorway. But Grace sat on the bed in such a way, like an animal shielding its young, that I could not see beyond her.

She motioned for me to lay the water down where I was without turning her head. I did as directed and then turned to leave.

"I want you and Anna to sleep in the larder tonight. Gather the blankets from the cupboards. You'll be warm enough," she murmured.

"But the wolves," I protested.

"We have more than the wolves to worry about tonight."

CHAPTER 5

hen Anna and I were little girls, Grace would never let us bathe together. I was plopped down in the sow's trough, scrubbed with rosemary soap, and then my wild hair washed with elderberries. And then Anna had to bathe in my dirty water. One time Aunt Agnes walked in with news that Christian needed a salve for a badger bite. "If you treat her such, how can she ever be one of us?" And from then on Anna went first. But we both knew that nothing had really changed. What would possess a mother to love a daughter who was not her own above the one who was? Yes, she loved Anna. But I was set apart. I received all the slaps, the reproval, the hugs and kisses. And Anna was never touched for good nor bad.

"You'll never leave me, will you?" Anna asked. We leaned together for comfort, shivering under the blankets in the darkness of the larder. A willow warbler cried out. And then a wolf howled, as if answering its call.

I squeezed Anna's hand. I knew she would not be able to read my lips in the dark.

"Someone will die tonight, Kat," she said, her voice suddenly sounding clear, beautiful, haunting. "I hear hymns being sung. Burial hymns."

I turned to her and shook my head. The fog must have lifted, for the moon shone on us through the cracks, setting Anna's face aglow like a snow-white fairy princess. "No, no one will die," I said.

"I will never marry, will I?" she asked. "No one will have me." I squeezed her hand tighter.

Anna smiled weakly and laid her head down on my shoulder. "I hear them. They're calling me."

"Sleep, Wren, sleep." She was soon asleep. Not long after, I slept too.

I awoke with a start, and it took a moment to realize where I was. Anna had turned away and slept peacefully in the straw, one hand tenderly cupping her ear. I stroked her cheek and then crept away as quietly as I could and crawled out of the larder. It was the middle of the night, the time when God's eyes are closed and anything can happen.

I stood up and immediately felt a presence. Something was watching me. I whipped my head around. It was the wolf. He was sitting under our chestnut tree again, calmly staring at me. I reached up and felt my hair, my wolf's-bait hair, and tried to tuck it into the back of my dress.

He had come for me—I knew it. I closed the larder door and slowly turned to the cottage, looking back several times over my shoulder. He never moved, but his eyes gleamed in the night like dancing stars.

The cottage was completely dark. The candles had been snuffed, except one lone one in the bedroom. I crept to the doorway but stood slightly back in the shadows. Grace sat in a chair by the bed, holding Jane's hand.

"I looked for you all these years," I heard Jane murmur. "I never thought you'd come here where it began, like a fox back in its hole."

"Where else was I to go?" Grace answered as she ran a cloth over Jane's forehead.

"And Agnes?"

"Over in the churchyard," Grace murmured. "Died a year ago now. The sweating sickness."

"And you didn't save her, the sister of your heart?"

"I saved my brother and her son," Grace answered, throwing her head back defiantly. "Sometimes we can't ask too much of God."

Jane laughed. "I think if you could, you would have let that brother of yours die. Just your luck to have it the other way around now, isn't it?"

"You know nothing," Grace said.

"I know enough. I saw you two that time. I saw how you looked at him. You hated him." Jane laughed.

"I have forgiven him," Grace said as she continued to cool Jane's forehead. "It was all many years ago."

"Forgiveness," Jane said sarcastically. "And have you forgiven *him*, for what he did to you?" Then she coughed fitfully, and a horrible rattle reverberated through the hollows of her chest. The death rattle. Grace had described it to me before. Once it sets in, there is no turning death back. "It was our lady who shouldn't have died," Jane continued. "Dirty hands. Dirty hands. Someone should have looked."

I inched forward and bumped something at my feet. The basket of healing herbs untouched.

"You know I did everything I could for her," Grace answered. "I had my own cross to bear that night."

"Aye, you did, didn't you?" She coughed again, and this time she couldn't stop. I turned my eyes away as Grace lifted her head.

"Drink," Grace told her. "It will ease your suffering."

"Will I die tonight?" Jane asked.

"Yes. I'm sorry. It's too late for you."

Jane took a long, languid breath. "What did you give me? I see my mama standing in the doorway."

I stepped back as quiet as a field mouse.

"It's to make you sleep," Grace said to her.

"The girl, she favors her father," Jane murmured, her eyes closing, fluttering.

"Let's not speak of him," Grace said.

"Aye, he was a naughty rogue, wasn't he?"

"Shush. Shush," Grace whispered.

"You can't hide it forever, Grace," Jane said. "They both have it, don't they now? I saw with my own eyes. Aye, I did. Others will see it too, and know the truth."

Grace ignored her. It was silent except for the wheezing of Jane's chest.

"Where is the pendant, Grace Bab?" Jane murmured. "I was a fool to believe you. Aye, a fool indeed. I was, a queen's fool. But you were a whore. And I'd rather die a fool than a whore."

I leaned forward again. Grace calmly stroked Jane's hand as though she tended a child who'd woken from a nightmare.

"You'll never get it, Jane. I'm sorry. No one shall. It's buried forever."

"My mama's waiting for me," Jane murmured. "She's calling me."

"It's time," Grace said. "Go to her."

Then it was quiet. I saw Grace shut Jane's eyes.

I felt as though my heart would beat out of my chest. A full minute went by as I stood there and Grace sat, staring at what I knew not. Then she spoke. "Now you can go to Nutmeg Farm. Just Christian. Only bring him. We must bury her. Uncle Godfrey must not know. He won't understand."

Father Bigg used to say that murderers live eternally in agony, for they are the worst sinners of all. But after Emma Townsend's husband had been killed and left on his doorstep, Father Bigg didn't say a word about it at church the next Sunday, even though we all knew the murderer sat among us.

I wondered what Father Bigg would say if he'd seen what I'd seen and heard tonight. Is it right to hasten a death when death is already waiting?

What did you do, Grace? I asked myself as I ran from our cottage. What did you do? Could you have saved her? I stopped when I saw the wolf under the tree. Behind him in the darkness, the landscape seemed to hold its breath. The wolf knew death had come to our cottage that night.

I ran through the dark night toward Christian. Christian. He would help us. I knew he would.

I ran across the downs, hilltops, and lanes till I reached Nutmeg Farm. Several times I looked over my shoulder, expecting to see glowing eyes in the night. But I saw nothing.

Cowslip Cottage was still asleep when I reached Nutmeg Farm, dawn just approaching. It's said that a centurion dressed in full golden armor still sitting on top of his mount lies beneath Winn Hill. I used to beg Christian when we were children to dig the man up and we'd be able to live richly off our find. But Christian always said no good ever comes of digging up the dead, gold or no.

I found him in the orchard, sitting with his back against one of the pear trees. His lambs grazed nearby. I wasn't sure if he was awake or not, so I crept up to him.

But his hand shot out and pulled me down.

He smelled of the night—of ale, and wool, and something else—something husky and raw. "Christian?" I started, but he pulled me close before I could say anything, and God's me, I tell you, I couldn't stop him. I wanted him to kiss me, even if a dead fool lay in our bed back at Blackchurch Cottage.

I melted into the kiss, reveling in his tender lips, kissing him back. It was Christian who pulled away first. Two of his sheep stood nearby watching, their collar bells gently tinkling, and behind them several of Agnes's geese squawked. "Is that your answer, Kat?" he asked with a small smile.

"Christian," I said, standing up and brushing my skirt off, embarrassed. Piper was right. Why, I was no better than Maud Davey, I was. "Something has happened tonight at the cottage. You must come now and bring a shovel."

"What?" he said, rising. "What has happened?" I watched as he easily picked up one of his sheep as though it were a feather and put it in its enclosure. When had he become so strong?

"We came home from the revel and found a visitor at our cottage. A very sick visitor." I heard a morning sparrow chirping of the coming day. "Oh, hurry, Christian, we must return before the sun is up!"

Christian glanced back at his cottage, thinking of his father. "No," I told him. "Don't wake him. Grace said just you."

CHAPTER 6

here were two now. Two wolves sitting under our chestnut tree when Christian and I made it back to Blackchurch Cottage a little while later. And the new one, a female, growled at us ferociously. Christian started at them with his shovel, but I bade him no. "Leave them be. It's in there." I motioned with my head at our cottage, my eyes still frozen on the wolves.

He started for the door and I called after him, remembering. "Wait, Christian. It's the plague. I'll go." But he had already walked inside. I ran after him.

The hearth fire was in a full-blown blaze. Immediately we were thrown back by its fierce warmth. Grace sat near the fire, clutching something in her lap, her face wet with the heat. Amidst the red flames I caught a glimpse of gold. She was burning the child's gown.

"Where's Anna?" I asked. Christian stood next to me, so close I could feel the warmth of his wool coat.

"Still in the larder," Grace answered. "I wouldn't let her come in." She stood up and I saw that she held the linen from our bed. She threw the bundle into the fire and the flames roared up to greet the new offering. "Have you ever buried a body, young Christian?" she asked. Her eyes shone golden red.

"No, Aunt," he replied calmly. "Only one of my lambs once, last Michaelmas."

"Well, then," she said, looking over at him. "That'll do. You'll be able to bury her." She motioned with her head to our sleeping room.

Christian walked toward the bedchamber. "But the plague," I called. "He can't touch her. He'll get the plague!"

"I have faith. He will not get it again. It's you I'm worried about, Kat," she said as she carefully sat back down on her chair, wiping at her brow. "Go to Anna. You need not see any of this."

Or she didn't want me to see any of it. I suddenly did not trust her anymore. Not after what I had seen and heard. But I held my tongue, for once. I glanced back at Christian, who was lifting the tiny figure off the bed. Grace had shrouded her. At least she'd given Jane that dignity. I turned my eyes and ran from the cottage.

I found Anna huddled in the larder, grasping her knees. "I brought Christian," I told her. "All will be fine." But I was not so sure myself. Something, light as a devil's kiss, went up my back.

"Someone is here, Kat," she said, her eyes glowing in the dark corner. "I can hear her. Aye, I can."

The shivers ran up my arms as I peered around the empty larder. "No, Anna. You've been dreaming."

"She's here, Kat," Anna persisted. "And she's come for you."

"Who? Jane the fool?"

"No. Someone else."

Christian was walking away from the cottage, the shrouded figure in his arms. "Stay here," I said to Anna. His shovel was still by the front door, and I ran for it. I picked it up and went after him.

"What do you think you're doing?" he yelled over his shoulder.

"I want to help you!" I called after him. "And you can't speak to me like that, I tell you, Christian."

"I can speak to you any way I please. You are acting the fool. This is man's work, Kat," he said more softly. "Go to Anna."

"I will not. I want to help you!"

He shifted the bundle in his arms and grabbed the shovel. "Go now!" he said, his voice low and threatening.

I stood staring at his back, my hands still feeling the soft wool of his coat as he walked off into the woods. Finally I glanced back at Blackchurch Cottage. My truth, my destiny, was in there.

I went to Anna first. I lifted her head. "Christian is burying Jane. I'm going to help Grace clean up. You must at all costs stay out here. Do you understand me, Wren?" She nodded.

"I'll be back for you soon, I promise," I said as I left the larder.

A moment later I found Grace, collapsed on the hay of our stripped bed. An arrow of fear coursed through me as I slowly walked to her side. The smell of juniper had returned, intermingling with the sweet smell of death. I stood there watching her heavy breathing. She stared back at me, and for the first time ever I saw that she was scared.

"I saw a ghost tonight, Grace, walking up Sudeley Lane," I told her. She watched me carefully, but her eyes seemed somehow empty. I described the figure and her dress.

"Ahh, it was her favorite. In crimson, her favorite color. Henry gave it to her. She loved that gown even though it belonged to his former wife, who was a little minx and got her head chopped off. It didn't matter to her. She loved beautiful things, and that gown was lovely."

"Will you tell me now, Grace?"

Grace coughed, and spittle ran down the side of her mouth. I grabbed a cloth from the bedside and wiped it away. "Who was my mother, Grace?" I asked calmly. "And my father. Who were they? I've a right to know."

"I've sinned," she said, her eyes starting to roll. "I'm stained with my sins. Can you see them, Kat? My stains?"

I could only see the signs of death marching its way through her body. "Grace, tell me what to do." I grabbed both of her hands. They were icy, dead. "How can I save you?" I pleaded.

"I was already dying, Kat. Of the cancer," she said. "Aye, and I'm glad of it. God is calling me and I will do as he bids." She shivered, and I pulled the remaining blanket up to her. "You must marry Christian immediately or there will be talk. . . ."

I laughed. "There's always talk of us, Grace."

She grabbed my arm with such force that I felt as though a lightning bolt ran through me. "Heed my words, Spirit," she said, trying to pull herself up. "You have no choice. You must marry Christian. He'll make you a fine husband and will take care of Anna. You'll have a good life here, Kat. It's all that I've worked for."

"You said you would tell me the truth someday, Grace," I said quietly. "You promised."

"I made lots of promises in my life, Kat. But I kept the most important one. I took care of you. Loved you as my own," she said.

Yes, I had known that my entire life. But it was a love hued with many things—regret, guilt, and something else I never could perceive. I heard a muffled sob behind me in the shadows of our keeping room. Anna. Could she see Grace's lips from where she stood? I glanced very slowly over my shoulder and could see the tip of her boot in the doorway.

"Yes, Grace," I said to her. "I know you love *us*. I know." Tears began to run down my face.

"Anna," she cried. "I tried to love her too, Kat. I did.

But every time I looked at her, I saw him and what he did to me."

"Who was her father, Grace?" I said.

"I can't speak of that," she choked. "She's marked with my stains. I'm so ashamed. God forgive me. God forgive me."

"Shhhh, Grace," I stopped her. "Speak no more of it." I glanced again to the doorway. Anna was gone. Grace had closed her eyes. She was breathing heavily, and I heard the rattle. The death rattle. God's me. "No, Grace, don't die. Don't die!" I was shouting. I couldn't help it.

She smiled. "That tongue of yours will get you in trouble someday. And you'll suffer more than the duck pond, I warn you."

"Grace," I said more calmly. "Please tell me. Please."

"Your mother was lovely, Kat," she started, her eyes still shut. "Such a good woman. She would have loved you. She didn't deserve what he did to her. A no-good nasty beast, he was. Handsome as the devil, and a devil he was."

I took her hand and held it tightly. She went on. "Your mother died of the childbed fever, not long after you were born. I tried to help her. God help me, I did. But it was too late. And after she was gone, much later, it was dangerous for you. So I saved you."

"Where is my mother buried, Grace?" I asked.

"You . . . staring all the time. They never marked it."

"My father, where is he?"

"He got his just rewards." She laughed. "The bastard." She coughed again, and I heard a growl. The wolf was standing in our doorway. Strangely, I was not scared, even though Grace had taught me my whole life to be afraid of wolves. I clapped my hands wildly at it. It turned and ran, its tail tucked low.

"Grace?" I whispered.

"Go for your uncle. I'm ready," she said softly. "But do not tell him of Jane."

"Grace. You know I heard her. Everything. There's more you are not telling me. Where is the pendant? She said it was worth a queen's fortune. Anna and I could live off it perhaps for the rest of our lives."

"You do not need it. I've given you a trade. And a husband who will adore you."

"I shall not marry," I proclaimed.

"It's buried. Buried where no one will find it."

"I know your hiding places, Grace," I confessed.

"Not all of them, I assure you, Kat." Grace's laugh was

low. "You always were a cunning girl. But I was more cunning. Don't go searching, Kat. Don't. It's dangerous, it is. Marry Christian and be content. You owe me that. The real wolves are there, not here. Mark my word, with that tongue of yours you'd likely get your head chopped off."

My hand went up to my neck.

"I'm ready now, Kat," she said. "Go for Godfrey. Poor sweet Godfrey. He'll take it hard, he will. Agnes and I barely a year apart."

"Is there something I should know of Uncle Godfrey?" I asked her.

"Nothing that is any of your business. It shall go with me to the grave as some things in life should."

"And what of Anna, Grace? Shouldn't you be thinking of Anna?"

"No." She sighed. "I know you'll take care of her. She's part of you, Kat. You do know that, don't you? She's the other side of your heart, as Agnes was to me. Swear you'll marry Christian. Swear to me now. I shall not rest in peace until you do."

I waited a few moments. "I promise," I stuttered. God forgive me. I would not marry him. "Grace, shall we go for Father Bigg? Perhaps he can ease your worries."

"God's death, no," she murmured. "What good would

that do? He can say a few words over my grave. Wrap me in a farm sack if you may; burn the bed and my clothing. Tell everyone I died of the apoplexy." She coughed again violently.

"Will Anna and I fall sick?" I asked her.

"No." She smiled wanly. "I'll make sure of that from the other side. You'll be safe."

I started for the door. "Kat," she called after me. I turned back. "Don't let them."

"Do what, Grace?"

"Don't let them take my hands."

CHAPTER 7

s I ran from the cottage, the sun was rising, setting a defiant amber glint across the dew on the downs. A sob escaped my throat as Christian emerged from the woods, shovel in hand. I could see the telltale clods of dirt and mud stuck to it—grave-digger's gold, it's called around here. Anna followed quickly behind him. I ran and threw my arms around her. I leaned back and tenderly put my hands on her cheeks. "Anna. Grace is fading fast. Go to her." She pushed my hands away and burst into tears before running toward the cottage.

"Grace is worried for her soul, but doesn't want Father Bigg," I said to Christian. "She wants me to fetch your father." Christian stared at me, his shoulders set square and firm.

"Do you want me to get him?" he asked.

I nodded. "Christian," I said. "It's terrible. All of it."

He reached for my cheek, his hand warm. "What happened? Was it the child who brought the sickness?"

"No, not a child." I shook my head. "She was a fool, a little person. She was already deathly ill when we found her."

"Why? Why Blackchurch Cottage?"

I looked him clear in the eyes and, not quite sure why, I lied. "I don't know. She was mad with the sickness. We could hardly understand a word she uttered."

"And Grace couldn't save her?" he asked, looking over my shoulder toward the cottage.

"No," I said. But I was still not sure myself. "Grace says she was too far gone. And now Grace is dying too. Oh God, Christian. What will we do?"

He pulled me close and held me. "I'll take care of you, Kat." His voice was low.

I melted into the warmth of him and whispered into his chest, "You must go for your father, Christian. It may be too late already." He kissed my forehead before running down the lane that led to Nutmeg Farm.

As a child, I once accompanied Grace while she birthed a babe in the middle of the night. It was Farmer Beachum's wife, Lyddie, birthing her last child, another dreaded daughter. I well remember the cries of the mother, animal-like shrieks of terror as Grace desperately tried to pull the turned child from the womb. The mother died not long after. Grace had sobbed as she held the babe in her arms. It was the only mother she'd ever lost, she told me, and she vowed to never midwife again.

But Grace had not told me of my own mother, who died after giving birth to me. Did Grace raise me out of guilt for not saving my mother? Did she let her die, as she did Jane the fool? Did she steal me from my loved ones? *No one wanted you*—she'd said it often enough. But perhaps everything had been a lie all these years. Perhaps she was truly the witch everyone talked about endlessly in the village. The witch with the dirty hands.

Later in the deep, dark morning, for a storm threatened, I stood in the bedroom doorway watching Uncle Godfrey, Christian, and Anna surrounding the bed, weeping with grief. Uncle Godfrey was on his knees, grasping Grace's limp hands. Christian had his arm around Anna. And for a brief moment I thought my heart might rend in two.

But I turned from them and walked out of the cottage into the gloom. I could not share in their grief. If she had truly loved me, she would have told me the truth.

CHAPTER 8

e buried Grace Bab the very next morning in the churchyard next to Agnes. It was imperative we do so, for her body deteriorated quickly, as though she were anxious to join the earth. It was Anna who laid her out, tenderly wrapping her in the fresh white linen I'd purchased from one of the weavers in the village—we burned every remaining scrap that Grace had not burned the night before. I shall never forget it as long as I live, Grace's contorted face. Where is she now? Poor Grace, will you haunt the earth? Will you haunt us?

But in the end Grace's face in death served us well, for when Father Bigg came himself to see her, for there had been tales of mad wickedness that night, he declared her face just the same as his own mama's who died after she spotted a fairy in the hedgerow. And after Father Bigg spread the word, someone remembered that indeed a fairy had been spotted that night on Cahill Road, mad as a poxed hare. And it was proclaimed that indeed, poor Grace Bab did have an unlucky star.

It was raining—a hard, pelting rain. Everyone came, even the old creatures who shun funerals for fear God shall choose them next. But Old Hookey said the morning was fitting since "blessed be the corpse who's laid in the rain." Even an old crippled ancient, who everyone had assumed died twenty years ago, was wheeled around the churchyard in a wheelbarrow to see the spectacle himself.

Father Bigg murmured his sermon over the pelting raindrops as Christian and Uncle Godfrey lowered the coffin into the ground. Anna was a statue, so stiff I pinched her to see if she was still breathing. I glanced at Hannah's Elm and wondered if perhaps Grace should be there instead of here, for I thought her greatest sin of all, beyond lying to me all those years, was not loving Anna as she should, blaming Anna for sins that were her own.

Afterward the old creatures brought Anna and me back to Blackchurch Cottage and sat with us a good long while, staring at us out of the corners of their rheumy eyes until one by one they returned to the village. They'd brought food, a good portion of food, but no one seemed of an appetite, and soon Uncle Godfrey and Christian, who ate only a little, excused themselves, too. Christian had his lambs to tend to, and Uncle Godfrey was not much for sitting around mooning anyway.

I walked them outside, and Uncle Godfrey gave me one of his giant hugs. He looked at me a long time, and regret filled his eyes. I saw him wipe a tear before he turned and walked away.

I turned to Christian. "Thank you" was all I could say. "Thank you."

"Father wants you to come stay with us tonight," he said, reaching for my hand. "He heard the wolves howling last night."

"Did you tell him anything?" I asked, pulling my hand away.

He stared at me hard until I looked away. "No, of course not. He's more worried about Anna than anything."

"Yes, I am too," I said, thinking of how she'd sat in her chair all night after she'd finished tending Grace, how she'd sat unblinking, staring out the window to the woods.

"Come to me later," he said. "At Belas Knap."

I looked away. "I don't know, Christian. I'll try. Anna has not slept. I'm very fearful for her."

He lifted my hand then and kissed it, and a shiver raced down my spine. Then he turned and followed his father into the woods.

We'd nearly lost Anna once, when she was but a child. Her beloved rabbit Satin had taken sick, and although Grace had tried to save it with freshly picked herbs, he wouldn't eat. "It wants to die. There's only so much one can do when something wants to go," Grace had said. And alas, he'd died in Anna's arms. I'd had a rabbit too, Velvet. They'd both been gifts as orphaned babies from Christian, who'd found them abandoned under a pear tree. Only mine had disappeared within a week because I forgot to cover the little basket I kept her in.

"You'd forget your own baby if it was strapped to your head," Grace had proclaimed. And she was right. But I said *fa*, that was one road I'd never travel.

But poor Anna, she took losing Satin very hard. So hard she wouldn't eat or sleep for five days, and Grace had to force a sleeping potion down her throat. She was lost to us for a week after that, stiff as a corpse. But when I peered at her sleeping face, I swore I'd never seen her more at peace. Poor sweet Wren. She's always been attached to this world by a tender thread. Even back then I knew that. Only Grace in her infinitely obtuse way refused to believe that perhaps she was the true cause. "All this trouble," she'd muttered. "Over a silly-brained rabbit. What'll she do when the real world turns on her?"

And it's almost as though Anna knew she wouldn't be able to handle this cruel world, for she stayed tiny and small, never getting a full woman's body, while I seemed to get more "alluring" day by day. Grace had started to slap my hand if I reached for more porridge or a crusty roll—nasty as it was, I was always hungry. Rump-fed, she called me.

I found Anna inside the cottage, sitting in Grace's chair. She was staring out the window, toward the chestnut tree. I followed her gaze, but there was nothing there. The wolves were long gone. I went to her and knelt at her feet. "Anna." She didn't respond, so I grasped her chin and looked at her straight in the eyes. "We are leaving this blasted place for good. We are going to London!"

She blinked. "Both of us?"

"Of course! I could never leave you behind. Grace has

hidden many things from us. And you must help me find her hiding places. I know where she kept the key to the chest. In the yew cross, right?"

She nodded her head.

"Did you know of anything else? Anything?" She nodded her head again, and I could feel my heart beat. "Where, Anna? You must show me."

She rose slowly, like one of the old creatures, and took my hand. She led me outside to the larder. I frowned, for I had spent many a day in here cleaning and scrubbing, penance for my sharp tongue. And I'd never seen anything but the occasional mouse that crossed my path.

She went to the back wall, knelt down, and pulled out a large stone. She stood up and stepped to the side. She kept her head bowed.

In the dark, musty cavity was a beautifully carved wooden box. I sat down and pulled it out of the crevice and onto my lap. I opened the lid, breathing heavily as I did so. On top there was a small golden cushion with the initials MS elaborately embroidered in tiny perfect stitches. I picked it up and held it to my cheek. *Your mother was a very skilled needlewoman*. Was this her work? Next was a baby's quilt in white linen, embroidered with lilies. I inhaled it, and it smelled sweet, like someone had just sprinkled it with lily water. Something underneath caught my eye. A shock of red—a small counterpane of some sort, in crimson silk taffeta. *Your mother loved crimson.* Had this surrounded my little bed so many years ago?

There were several tiny silver goblets and silver spoons, all tarnished. I picked one up and held it to my lips, wondering if I'd ever drunk from it. Then, curiously, a cup, gilded wood, painted with high-sailed ships upon the seas. Next I found a spiraled carved horn, and several small gold rings. I held one up to Anna. She shrugged her shoulders. And finally, a small bound book—a prayer book. The inscription read, "To my most righteous mother." The signature was bold and elaborate—assured and noble. It read "Elizabeth."

I looked at Anna. There were tears in her eyes now. "How long have you known of the box?"

She shook her head back and forth. "I don't know. Years."

"Do you know what all this means?"

"Only that you would leave us, Kat. Forever. I couldn't let that happen. I would have died without you."

"I would have never left you, Anna," I mumbled as I looked carefully through the box one more time. "There is something missing," I murmured. "A pendant." I looked up at her and pointed to my throat.

Anna stepped forward. "It's not there?"

"It was here before?" I asked.

"Yes, beautiful," she croaked. "Rubies and pearls. Royal. I used to play with it while you were with Christian and Grace had gone to town."

"How long has it been gone?" I asked.

"I don't know. It's been a long while since I played with it. A year or two."

"And is there anything else, anything you can remember that was here with the necklace?" I asked her.

She turned her face before answering. "No, no, nothing," she said while peering out the window again, her shoulders slumped.

"We'll leave tonight, Anna," I said. "Our destiny has never been here."

"But aren't you to marry Christian?" she asked, swiftly turning back to me, her eyes hungrily fixed upon my lips for my answer.

"No," I said, and I couldn't help but see a glimmer of something—intense relief, perhaps—slide across her countenance. "We are destined for better things, you and I, and I shall never marry."

* * *

Christian was waiting for me, standing with his arms behind his back, at the top of Belas Knap.

"I knew you'd come," he said softly. He pulled something from his shoe and smiled. "Lad's love," he said as he held it up between us. The moon gilded it. "Perhaps it's true what they say of its powers." His face was so sweet that I couldn't look at him as I handed him a man's long jerkin. It was a fine piece of work, a dove-gray silver silk, leaves and vines stitched all over. It was meant for a gentleman, but I wanted him to have it as a parting gift.

He glanced down at it and smiled. "A wedding gift?" he asked softly.

I couldn't answer him, but I suppose my lack of response was enough.

"I'm sorry for your loss, Kat," he said, his eyes glowing in the moonlight. "But tomorrow we shall marry. We will meet Father Bigg in the abbey in the morn."

"Oh Christian," I said. "I can't marry you. I'm sorry. I can't."

He blinked. "You will marry me, Kat," he said lifting his chin. "You and Anna are unprotected. I've heard Old Man Dar has been asking of you today to Father Bigg.

Is that what you want? An old smelly pig like that?"

"No," I said. "Of course not."

"Then marry me."

"I thought you'd changed your mind," I said, and regretted the words once they were out of my mouth.

He threw the jerkin down and on top of it, the lad's love. He grabbed my arms and pulled me to him. "I love you, Kat," he said before lowering his lips to mine. I struggled to pull away at first, then hungrily kissed him back. But I couldn't marry him. I couldn't. I had to leave and find the truth, no matter the burning in my heart. I leaned back and looked up into his eyes. I shook my head no. His eyes flashed and he pushed me away. "If not you, then Anna," he said stiffly. And I felt a small arrow in my heart at his words. "One of you, by God, will show up tomorrow."

A little while later, I crept to the churchyard to say good-bye to Grace. I knelt down a moment and then fell forward, my arms spread across the newly sown dirt. "I hate you, Grace," I sobbed. "I hate you." I thought back to when I was a child and she had held me tight after I'd seen a ghost in the meadow—long streak of ethereal white hovering in the morning hush. It was the day after Emma Townsend's funeral. Grace, who believed in ghosts, had not said a word, but only rocked me back and forth, and I soaked in her warmth. I lay on Grace's grave a long time, hoping I'd feel her warmth now through the hard earth, but it was only coldness I felt, and it seeped through my bones until I began to shiver. I sobbed for Grace, for Christian, and for what I must do. Finally I sat up, searching for my shawl. Something caught my eye, something not right. Agnes's grave. I peered closer and saw it matched Grace's, as though it had been newly dug. A mound of dirt, heaped like a miniature barrow.

Minutes later, breathing hard, I reached Blackchurch Cottage. I flung the door open. Anna stood there, her arms outstretched, dirtied with the gravedigger's gold. In them she held a shimmering necklace of gold and pearls, its ruby pendant flashing a teasing glint around the room.

CHAPTER 9

had always wanted it—to leave our lovely vale. And now, after sitting on stacks of damp hay in a farm cart laden with potatoes, drawn by two ill-looking mules for hours on end, with a sore bum and a sore heart, I only saw worries ahead of us. What was I thinking, running like this and taking poor Anna? She sat next to me, shaking with silent tears that I suspected were more for Christian than Grace, for every time the six little lambs next to us bleated, she let out a sorrowful sob. I felt bad for her, indeed I did. But Christian could jump in the duck pond for all I cared. I was seizing my only chance, even if the hay bugs had been incessantly nipping at my ankles for hours. London was my destiny, and I knew it even more now, aye, I did.

"You'll ruin the gown, my sweet," I whispered to Anna, holding her chin up and wiping at her face with a handkerchief. I'd decided we stood a better chance of being left alone if we wore our creations—Anna wore a popinjay blue traveling gown, and I a luxurious violet tapestry, embroidered with lilies and crowns of Venice gold, its buttons knotted with a trio of pearls. We wore safeguards over our skirts to protect them from the mud and dust. They were worth more than a small fortune now, especially mine with the necklace sewn in to the hem. "Buck up, Wren," I said. "We'll be in London soon."

The other passengers leaned forward to catch my words. The long wagon to London had broken down on the second day of our journey, the farm cart being the only option for our motley crew of six. After two days together, any conversation was seized upon as fair game. Only one passenger remained aloof, a portly, beaked-nose gentleman, a Mr. Grove, who hadn't opened one eye since we had departed Gloucester. Anna and I had walked there, a five-hour journey in the wee hours of the morning, carrying our heavy bags.

When we'd reached Gloucester, Anna had handed me a time-worn letter. It was from Grace. "*If you've gone against all my wishes, you selfish girl, and indeed gone to London, then I beseech you with all my good heart to find Mrs. Eglionby. And at all costs, stay away from the wolves of the court, especially Elizabeth the queen, for never have I known such a crafty mean-spirited girl.*" It was simply signed "Grace Bab" and dated a year before. *Good heart*. Ha! Like I was going to do anything *she* bade me to do now. Thinking back on that letter now raised my hackles. "Is there anything else, anything you have kept from me?" I asked Anna.

"No," she whispered back forcefully. But I wasn't sure I believed her.

The snoring man's wife, Mrs. Grove, a tiny, crane-like woman, who had more than made up for his lack of conversation with her incessant chatter, said, "What troubles your maid, dear? A lad perhaps? They always seem to be at the bottom of it." She tapped her husband with her fan, but he didn't wince one bit. My eyes were drawn to it, her beautiful fan. The tiny delicate painting reminded me of the hand-painted cup from the wooden chest. I carried it, with the other things, in one of our traveling bags. The other bag contained all our creations, every single one of them, as well as our many-colored threads, my sketchbook, Grace's herbs, the lovely lute finally released from its peg, and lastly, my needles. My fingers ached, thinking of my stitching. I hadn't missed a day in many a year, and now I'd missed three.

"She just lost her mother," I said, no longer feeling in any way that Grace had been mine. *Good heart.* I chuckled and let the reference to Anna being my maid fall by. Perhaps it would be more convenient for everyone to think so. A lady's maid, Grace once explained, must be silent as the wind, and ever watchful—the truth gatherers, she called them.

A queer lady, dressed simply in black silk, a mantilla over her head, crossed herself. She'd introduced herself as Mrs. Salinas. "Was it sudden?" she asked. "It's a blessing when God takes one suddenly." I assume she had been gathering her own truth, for she had not said a word the entire journey, though she'd been watching us with eyes black as coal. Her voice had an odd hardness about it.

"It was long expected," I said, gripping Anna's hand. And now I could see this was the God's truth. Grace had been leaving us for a long time.

"Well then, why isn't the lass wearing her mourning clothes?" asked Mrs. Grove.

"Her death, although expected, came sooner than we thought. We'll purchase something appropriate when we reach London." The lie came easily off my lips. I had no intent whatsoever of donning mourning clothes for Grace.

And then it was quiet a few moments, everyone coming to the same sudden thought, and all our eyes turned to the dark-eyed lady, wondering who *she* was in mourning for. She returned our stares, nodding at each of us, like the wise owl who has no intention of imparting his wisdom.

I peered out of the wagon at the grassy slopes and quilted farmland we were leaving behind. Although Anna had thought our land the most beautiful of all, I couldn't help but think that we'd seen beautiful vale after beautiful vale since we'd left Blackchurch Cottage. There was so much beauty in the world to discover. And London was sure to be the most beautiful of all. I turned around and saw a man running down the road, and my breath caught for a moment thinking it was Christian, but it was only a farmer running after a young calf.

A wide-eared young lad, who sat in the back of the wagon with two crates of leeks and who I presumed by deduction came with the lambs, spoke up. "Me own mother died of the plague," and everyone scooted away at his last word. "Five years ago," he added. Mrs. Grove raised a handkerchief to her mouth and scooted closer to her husband. "It took her away in less than an hour." I thought of Agnes and her quick death. What secrets had they shared, Agnes and Grace? Had Agnes known about me? Had this humble woman agreed to take the necklace to the otherworld? Or had Grace simply wanted to hide it forever and draped it on her cold neck before she was laid in the ground?

The eyes of the occupants who were awake swiveled around looking for the telltale signs of the plague, until I spoke up.

"Has anyone ever seen the good queen?" I rubbed my flea-bitten ankles together. I dared hope that none of them saw our old tattered, muddied shoes, hidden under our fine skirts.

"Good queen. Ha," Mrs. Salinas snorted. "Why, she's burned many a good soul at the stake, that she has."

Mrs. Grove frowned at her. The lad spoke up again, "'Tis treason to speak of the queen as such. I'd give my heart for the good lady. I saw her once near Cheapside. And she smiled at me, she did."

"Why, you are a little liar," Mrs. Salinas said, laughing, "for it's known she's got rotten teeth and never smiles. Some say she's really a man, you know. A man-child was switched with the real baby Elizabeth."

Mrs. Grove leaned forward and hit her on her knee with her fan. "Hush, I'll hear no more talk of this." And then she turned to me with a wide smile. "William and I"—she shouted his name in his ear and he roused a moment but fell asleep again—"have seen her ourselves—"

"Oh, do tell me," I said before I could stop myself. "Is she very beautiful?"

"Oh yes, my dear," she answered. "She's noble, elegant, and of the most regal bearing. Some say she's the most lovely queen in the world. And she did smile at us, she did, and has the most beautiful teeth, white as pearls. And her hair, why, it's as red as yours!" she exclaimed.

"It's a wig," Mrs. Salinas interjected. "The queen's. I've heard she's as bald as a newborn babe."

"She's a full head of hair," Mrs. Grove insisted. "She's still young, you know. Strong constitution, I hear, rides every day, and hunts, and enjoys the pursuits of any king, she does. She may marry yet and bear us a dozen heirs! Bald!" She snorted and then eyed me again. "But your maid there could do well with learning to arrange your lovely hair better." My hand flew up to my unruly hair in embarrassment. "A gentle lady you may be, but if I may say, in London well-to-do ladies wear their hair more smartly. A fine caul so as not to cover all your lovely hair would do. Or perhaps some boxwood combs, or pearls? No hood for you yet, I presume. A hood is for married ladies, you know. A man wants to see what he's getting before the marriage, I daresay," and she laughed, a short loud bark. She tapped her husband's belly again. "Am I right you are in search of a husband?"

I laughed. "Not a husband, I assure you." It was something else I sought.

She watched me for a while with deep interest, her eyes occasionally flitting over to Anna, who had fallen asleep to the rocking of the wagon. "I wonder, though, your bringing such a pretty maid as her."

"Why, whatever do you mean?" I drew my arm around Anna protectively.

"Every woman knows you never have a maid prettier than you, for your man's eyes might be turned. They simply can't help themselves, now can they?" And even my mouth dropped open at that.

"As I said before, I've no interest in a husband, just like Queen Elizabeth," I said, smiling.

"Oh, but you are not a queen, are you?" Mrs. Grove responded with a thin smile.

"Bah," Mrs. Salinas spoke up. "She can always place her love in the Lord, as I have."

"I have no interest in that, either," I said quickly, thinking of Father Bigg's long, monotonous homilies before Grace stopped taking us to church.

"It's a husband you want, my dear," Mrs. Grove said. "You'll come to know it soon enough."

"Don't abandon the Lord," the dark lady said. "For he's your true husband. Men can't help but disappoint you. It's their way, I guess. Even sons."

I changed the subject. "Pray tell me, where can I buy the hair pieces you so wisely suggested?"

The lad spoke up. "The market at Leadenhall, ma'am."

"And what would you know?" Mrs. Grove responded. "You filthy little lad. A nice lady like her at Leadenhall. Ha. Why she'd ruin her lovely shoes, she would," and I pulled my feet farther into the hay at this. "Leadenhall. Full of cows and muck. Fa, hold your tongue." And just as she finished, one of the little lambs leaned over and nipped her. She screamed at the lad, "Get your filthy beasts to behave!"

"It's Cheapside," the dark-eyed lady spoke. "Cheapside you want. They have beautiful things. I can take you if you wish." I could hear a hint in her voice of high seas and foreign lands.

"Fa," Mrs. Grove said. "As if a lovely lady such as our miss would accompany the like of you. Why, I've never heard such a thing. What would you know of fine things, anyway?"

I suddenly became aware of a terrible odor. The lad whistled while Mrs. Salinas sat forward and peered over the mules, who snorted in anticipation. Anna roused awake next to me. "Whatever is that smell?" I finally asked, being the only one to acknowledge it.

"Why, it's London, my dear!" And with that Mrs. Grove finally hit her husband hard enough so that his eyes opened up.

CHAPTER 10

t was not the shining glory that I'd long imagined—London, that is—but I assured myself the nicer elements would be found within its walls. We entered the city by way of Southwark with all the other travelers: men whipping their cattle, shepherds with their flocks of sheep, ladies with over-full vegetable baskets, and even well-dressed dandies. I peered at them, studying their elaborate dress, noticing every fold, stitch, and pattern. But it wasn't long before the odor I'd smelled earlier became even more foul.

"It's the river," Mrs. Grove explained. "The privies, you see." She discreetly covered her nose with her fan, while Mrs. Salinas just sat forward, seemingly determined to endure it. Mr. Grove and the big-eared lad didn't seem to notice.

Anna sat up, peering around, her eyes wide. I took in everything too, my hand over my mouth in surprise and horror. Despite our finery, I'm sure we appeared to all as complete country idiots who'd never left the village. But I didn't care. I was here.

We soon approached a great stone and arched bridge. "London Bridge," one of our travelers murmured. "Keep your eyes down, ladies," Mr. Grove announced. But both Anna and I immediately looked up. There were several decomposed heads piked on the tower. Anna moaned and put her head on my chest.

"Bloody William Wallace was the first traitor piked, and not the last, I assure you," Mr. Grove said. "With all the wild heretics running about."

"Barbarism, pure barbarism," Mrs. Salinas said. "They were only speaking their true faith."

"People have been killed for less," Mrs. Grove said. "It's best to keep one's mouth shut in London, that's for sure. Why, it's only the nobles, I must say, that end up on the pike. Those lower born who find themselves in trouble end up in the Thames with the piss." She aimed her stare straight at Mrs. Salinas.

The wagon lurched as we neared a great gate. "I've lived most of my life in London, thank you very much," Mrs. Salinas responded a moment later. "With all types of people, high and low, and I'd rather be in the river than up there." She threw her head back toward the bridge.

"Me papa once saw himself twelve heads at once," the lad piped in, and the lambs bellowed at his voice. "*Tshh, tshhh*," he cooed to them, and I immediately thought of Christian. My heart lurched a moment, imagining the pain I must have cost him. And poor Uncle Godfrey. I didn't think they'd be able to come after us. They had no one to help on the farm, and now they had our land too. They'd have to let us go. I turned my head back toward the gate and put my arm around Anna.

"Three gates, my dear," Mrs. Grove said. "They look for pox and any sign of the plague. You can hold your heads high, though. I'm sure the two of you have not been near low diseases as such. High! High! Dears, there you go."

I felt Anna tremble next to me, but neither of us as much as blinked. We were both very good, I now knew, at keeping secrets.

* * *

A half hour or so later, after much slow going over cobbled streets, we entered Arnott Street. It was teeming with people, cows, wagons, and carts. Our handler cracked his whip and a path finally cleared. Everywhere street vendors called out their wares. "Apple biscuits, one shilling!" "Come see the bear baiting, scariest of all!" "Mutton pies, two for one!"

The odor of freshly baked bread wafted through the air, as did the smell of slow-cooked meats. My stomach growled. We hadn't eaten a thing all day. I'd been too embarrassed to pull out the crusty pieces of bread we'd hastily packed that morning, and I didn't have the heart to eat Christian's pears, which I'd grabbed at the last second. But more than that, I didn't want to waste one shilling of our money. If Grace had kept a stash of coins, that was another secret she took to her grave. Our future was now in our bags.

The farmer pulled in the reins and called the mules to a stop. "Here we are, ladies and gent." He was an oily-faced fellow, big armed and big bellied. He helped us down. Then the lad got down, gently lifting his lambs one by one. He winked at Anna, touched his cap at me, then walked off down the street herding his flock.

"Well, miss," Mrs. Grove said as her husband worried

about their bags, "it was lovely visiting with the likes of you." She kept her eyes away from Anna. A mere maid wasn't worthy of a good-bye, I suppose. She nodded and then walked off with her husband.

Anna tugged on my sleeve. "The letter," she croaked. "Mrs. Eglionby."

I ignored her and turned to Mrs. Salinas. "And which way is Cheapside, may I inquire?" I had no intention of honoring Grace's request.

"But you won't be buying any tortoise combs or pearled cauls, now will you? No money is my guess."

"Perhaps not right away," I said, wondering what gave us away. "It's food we are more in need of, my dear Anna and I. Can you recommend a respectable establishment?"

"Not for the likes of the two of you," she said, looking us over from head to toe. I was highly offended, but she added, "You'd be quick pickin's anywhere around here, and all of London, I must say. What were you thinking, bringing such a tender thing, your sister, and you yourself, fresh scrubbed from the country?"

"She's my maid," I insisted. "Not my sister," I said, turning my head away from Anna so she wouldn't see my words.

"You can't pull anything over me," she responded. "I've seen everything in my life, and I know when something is not what it is. You two have been raised together, sister or no. And you have some resemblance, I believe. Come with me, before the pickpockets and miscreants get you. I'll give you a hearty meal before you go on." She started to walk away. We stood there, rooted.

A man stumbled up to us, dirty and reeking of sour ale and worse. "Why, look what the country wagon just delivered us. Two sweet gillyflowers!" He lurched for Anna. We picked up our bags and ran after the lady, who had not even looked back.

We followed her down one street after another. She kept her back straight as a tombstone, every now and then glancing at us and tilting her head for us to hurry. I stumbled a few times, my head turned this way and that looking at the spectacle of people and animals, taking in the sounds and smells, good and bad. Anna kept her head down, overwhelmed, it seemed, with her surroundings.

Finally we reached a timber-framed home among a row of like-looking houses. Mrs. Salinas tapped at the heavy wooden door, and not long after, it opened. A mob-capped maid curtsied, and our lady pushed past her breezily. We followed her in.

"A cold meal, please, Maisy," she said, taking her gloves off and handing them to her. The maid peered at us with big eyes, bowed, and left the room.

We were in a keeping room, austere but finely furnished with carved mahogany chairs, a long trestle table, and even a gorgeous handwoven tapestry hung along a long wall. I stared at it, looking at the figures prancing in an orchard grove. I stepped closer to examine it, for I had long heard of tapestries, but had never actually beheld one. I ran my hand over it, feeling the woolen warp and weft and imagined what kind of hands might produce such beauty.

I heard something in the corner of the room. A little dark-headed boy with piercing blue eyes was sitting very quietly on a chair. He couldn't have been more than four or five.

"It represents the harvest season," Mrs. Salinas said, and I startled. "Fall." I looked back at the tapestry, looked at the beautiful dancers beneath the trees, looked for Christian. *Fa!* As if he was there.

"Sit down, girls, you must be exhausted." Mrs. Salinas said.

"No, thank you," I began. "I feel as though I've been sitting forever. My bum is as flat as a potato cake." Maisy, who had returned to the room as quiet as a dormouse, stifled a giggle. And then Anna suddenly lurched forward as though she were about to fall. I ran to her and helped her into a chair at the table. She slumped over, her hands on her ears.

"My word," Mrs. Salinas exclaimed. "Ava!" she screamed. "Bring some ale!"

I stroked Anna's back softly. "It's her ears. They give her much pain." I felt strangely at ease telling the lady one of our secrets. "She needs to lie down, flat. She feels as though the world is turning." Anna moaned, and started to rock. "Can we lay her down somewhere?"

"Of course," the lady said. We each took an arm and helped her up a narrow stair, Maisy and another maid scurrying behind us. "Here." Mrs. Salinas motioned to the doorway of a room and we carried her in. We put her in a small, neatly turned bed, and Anna curled up immediately like a newborn piglet.

"Shall we fetch a doctor?" Mrs. Salinas asked.

"No," I snapped. Then, quieter, "No, I'm sorry. No doctors. Grace gave her a draught. Sometimes she sent me into the woods for some of the plants." I desperately searched my mind for the ingredients. "Willow weed, cider, and pears; we used pears," I said. Those pears, magical they are, Grace used to say of them. Sprinkled with the centurion's gold. Anna moaned.

"Did you hear?" the lady calmly said to the maids. "Run to the market, *apurete*." The girls ran from the room and the lady turned to me. "And Grace is?"

"Our mother." I corrected myself: "*Her* mother." I sat down on the bed next to Anna.

"The one who recently passed to the Lord?" she said as she crossed herself. She sat down on the other side of the bed next to Anna.

She must be one of those Catholics, a heretic. They were the brave ones, those that kept to their faith. And it was indeed not a good time to be brave. Most practiced their faith in private, hiding like rats, but those that were visible and vocal were prosecuted and burned at the stake. I peered at her, this odd woman, and wondered why she had invited us, complete strangers, thieves we could be, into her home. I immediately thought of our bags downstairs, unwatched.

"We must leave her," I explained. "The best medicine is utter quiet. A cool room. Darkness. Time."

"But she's deaf, is she not? A mute deaf?"

I glanced swiftly at her. "No, she hears us in her own way. Vibrations. And other things she cannot speak of. Sometimes terrible things."

I followed Mrs. Salinas down the stairs. To my relief, I saw our two bags were still near the door. Several pears had spilled out. I set them on the table. They would be much needed in Anna's potion. I couldn't help but draw one to my nose as we sat and inhale the aroma. It was sweet, so sweet. The maids had left bread and mulled wine and cold chicken. But I suddenly was not hungry.

I watched her as she ate. "You should never waste God's bounty," she said as she gnawed indelicately on a chicken leg. She pushed a plate toward me. It did smell heavenly, aye, it did. I picked up a piece of warm bread and took a bite. It melted in my mouth, delicious and so unlike the crusty bread we had at home.

"So tell me, dear girl," Mrs. Salinas said. "What are you fleeing from and why are you depriving that poor girl of the peace and comfort of her home? You do know that's why she's curled up like a sickly babe upstairs? London is not for the likes of her." She took a long swallow of the wine.

I laughed. "She wanted to come," I insisted. "We've never been apart." Not even a day. Grace had never let me go to market, and of course Anna had never wanted to go anyway. "I'm not fleeing," I added.

"Sometimes there are no answers for what you are seeking," Mrs. Salinas said, taking another generous sip of wine. "Only more questions. It's the wise one who accepts this, child. Perhaps you should take your sister home."

I could not look her in the eyes. I lifted my glass of wine and took a gulp, although I'd never liked the sour-tasting liquid back home. Grace always said it loosed the lips and everything else and to stay away from it if I knew what was good for me. "And why would you say such a thing?"

"Anyone with one good eye would know you are not what you appear to be. Dressed as grandees." She snorted. "Did you steal your wares, dear one?"

"So you think we are thieves," I said, taking another generous gulp of the wine. Funny how it tasted better and better, like sour berries sprinkled with sugar. "This," I said, holding up my arm, "is my work. No other's."

She leaned over and looked at my bodice, studying my stitching. "You are very talented," she said. "Perhaps worthy of nobles."

"Those of the court?" I asked.

"Yes, the ladies are always looking for something new, particular. Your work stands out."

"That's why we've come to London. To sell our wares. Make a pretty shilling or two." I turned my eyes and took another sip.

"I see." She smiled a little. "Will you tell me your name, dear child?"

"Kat," I started. "Katherine." I did not want to add the Bab, so countryish and common it sounded now. I left it at that.

"And I am Lady Fernanda Ludmore."

"Lady?" I asked. "Not Mrs. Salinas?"

"My husband is dead," she said flatly.

"I'm sorry for your loss," I said. "Did he die in the country?" I wondered why a lady had taken a mule wagon to London and had kept her identity a secret.

"Dear God, no," she coughed, spraying a little of her wine on her stomacher. "The jackass died five years ago. Luddy, he was called amongst his peers, other libertines and whoremongers. But I had better names."

I was astonished. She was indeed an odd duck, so unlike what I pictured a lady of rank to be. "Then why the mourning clothes?" I asked. "If you did not love him and he died so long ago."

"I reason it's safer to affect a disguise while traveling. I think we were of like minds in that category."

I looked away, staring at the little boy who had remained silent while we talked. Lady Ludmore every now and then handed him a grape which he grabbed like a little turtle. "Then why were you in Gloucester?"

"My, you do have a tongue, don't you? A little like me, I suppose. I'll answer you, dear one." She paused. "If you answer me one question."

I nodded my head, telling myself I had no intention of telling her any sort of truth. Not now. It was as though she could see me down to my heart, so piercing her dark little eyes were.

"My son has long been lost to me," she said. "I'd hear of him here, there, all over England. And then not a word for many years. Not long ago he resurfaced, hiding amongst a tatty band of minstrels in Gloucester country. That's why I've invited you into my home."

Minstrels. The Spaniard. I had seen her son. I knew it with a certainty. "Your son. Is he dark, tall, handsome, with a merry twinkle in his eye?" I asked.

"Dear God." Her hand flew up to her cheek. "Did my Rafael seduce you? Is that why you have flown the country?"

"Why no, of course not; he merely looked at me," I shot back, a little too forcefully, remembering his particular stare. I blushed down to my toes again, thinking of his eyes.

"That's more than enough, believe me, child," she responded, taking another long swig of wine. "But you are a strong girl, I can see that," she said. "Full of spirit you are." *Spirit.* I thought I'd never hear that description of me again, as it only came from Grace's lips. Then Lady Ludmore's eyes grew large. "God's faith, he didn't molest your sister, did he? Is that the true reason she's fallen ill?"

"No, no," I assured her. "I only saw him a moment at our revel in Winchcombe and I looked away. Anna never saw him."

"Well, I'm sure he caused some sort of mischief that night, the ruffian that he is. The apple never falls far from the tree, now does it," she said, looking directly at me. I thought of Grace and her fear that I'd take more after my father than my mother. "Bastards," she continued. "My son's sired plenty of them, that I am sure of—no telling how many are strewn across the countryside." She motioned with her head to the little boy. "I found that one in Kent begging for food, his hair full of lice and smelling worse than the Thames. Apparently my son was acting the role of a Hessian five years before, and some blue-eyed beauty couldn't resist."

Christian. What if I had stayed? I would not have been able to resist him and tonight would have been our wedding night.

"And why are you blushing?" Lady Ludmore asked. "Red as a knobby-kneed maiden you are."

"I do not know of what you speak," I lied, but a small smile escaped my lips.

"And now, it's time for my question," Lady Ludmore said just as the maid came running in the door laden with full baskets, red-faced and puffing. "Who is your precious pear farmer?"

I did not answer. But I turned my eyes to the tapestry, once again looking for him.

The Good and Rightful Remembrance of Grace Bab in the Year of Our Lord 1547.

It was with heavy heart that I left my home in the country, for I truly did love the land, and if it weren't for my sad circumstances I'd never have gone. But my own father had sought me after my mother, a gentle-born lady, died, and I could no longer abide it, even if it meant leaving my good brother Godfrey. I stole the few coins Papa had hidden, as I figured they were rightly owed me, bought a proper gown at Stow-on-the-Wold from Charlie Bab, the handsome merchant, who told me I was a comely lass, and headed for London to seek a better life for myself. I was quickly hired as a nurse at a house in Chelsea, to work for a proper lord and lady, the lady being a former queen no less, who were newly married and greatly in love. But I soon came to know there are secrets in houses grand as well as humble, and all was not as it seemed.

CHAPTER 11

nna always had been more comely than me. Elf-skinned she was—her gorgeous, pale white skin clear and soft as an eggshell. But not me. I'd gotten the pimples a few years back and I'd much fretted over them, worrying I'd be as poxed as Old Man Dar. And what man would want a pitted-face girl? Grace insisted it was my emerald eyes and kissable lips that would lure a man, spots or no. And that's why she'd kept me at home most of the time, rarely letting me accompany her to market, so fearful she was of me attracting any man, for they were all no good.

But I knew it was much more than that now—the reasons why she hid me. Indeed I did. I could feel the necklace, the weight of it, brushing against my ankle as I studied Anna sleeping peacefully in her bed. I held a candle over her, watching her slow, even breathing. She was beautiful, so ethereal in the dark. I wondered if perhaps I was the cause of her spell. But Grace had always said there was no rhyme or reason to them, her black spells; they could come at any moment, as every unwanted thing in life does. And this one had lasted two days, longer than most. I'd spent the entire time with her, my meals brought up to me by the maids.

I kissed Anna softly. "Sleep well, my little Wren," I whispered. Then I went to my small chamber next door. We had never slept apart, but Lady Ludmore had insisted, saying it was unseemly for grown girls to share the same bed. It was obvious that she'd never spent much time in the country. Beds were always of a shortage there. Why, the Widower Beachum's daughters were four to a bed, while their papa slept with the cows in the barn.

I put the candlestick on the table next to my bed. I carefully undressed, now realizing why gently born ladies had maids. It was extremely hard to extricate myself from the gown with its separate sleeves, but I somehow managed. I laid everything carefully across a small chair. I found my night shift, then placed our traveling bags under my bed. I'd seen Lady Ludmore's eyes linger on them the day we arrived.

I climbed under the covers and opened up Grace's letter. *And at all costs, stay away from . . . Elizabeth the queen.* Bah, I sighed. Just then, the door opened slightly.

"Who is there?" I whispered. The door opened a little more, and I saw it was the boy. He peeked at me, blinking his large blue eyes, and I wondered if he ever smiled. He started to shut the door.

"Wait a minute," I called to him quietly. "What is your name, little one?"

"Bartolome, miss." And then he was gone.

The next morning Anna had recovered, the spell subsiding like a great wave, leaving a calm pool glowing with sadness in its wake.

We sat at the trestle table, which was laden with wonderful dishes—a round loaf of bread, called a manchet, fetched fresh from the market that morning; a dish of butter; thick pancakes; and scrambled eggs sprinkled with salted bread crumbs. Indeed, we never ate so finely at Blackchurch Cottage; watered-down porridge was the best we ever got.

Lady Ludmore was nowhere to be seen. I took a bite

of the delicious eggs and drank a sip of warm wine, this one spiced with ginger and honey, from a heavily carved silver goblet. There were other signs of wealth in the room—porcelain jars, and heavy plate lining the hearth mantle. My eye caught the tapestry again. One of the maids, carrying a large basket of soiled linen, walked past. I could see her through the doorway.

"Why, where is she going?" I asked Maisy, who continued to bring us dishes. A wonderful aroma of baking bread followed her.

"To the laundress, ma'am," she answered, placing a little plate in front of Anna. We both stared at it. It was one of our pears, carved prettily and sugared. Anna and I exchanged a look before she picked up her spoon and began to eat.

"And where is Mrs. Ludmore this morning?" I asked.

"Lady, miss," she corrected me. "Lady Ludmore, although she doesn't insist on the 'lady,' being the pious soul that she is. And of course feeling the way she do about *him*, Lord Ludmore, and I must tell you she be at her morning prayer, up hours before dawn, and when she joins you at breakfast, you are not to speak to her." She leaned over and picked up my empty plate. "She believes the morning is for God and the evening for the devil."

Another maid, pinch-faced, peeked around the doorway, frowned, and shook her head before disappearing.

"And may I ask whatever that means?"

"Oh, the lady, she does enjoy the drink, she does," she responded. Maisy, chubby cheeked and well-rounded, had the appearance of one who spent a little too much time in the kitchen. But she had a wise gleam in her eyes.

"And can you tell me"—as I guessed she probably would—"how Lady Ludmore came to be married to the lord?"

"Why, don't you know?" She smiled, ever ready to impart more. She plopped down in one of the chairs at the end of the table. "She came over many a year ago with the Princess Katherine of Aragon, King Henry's first poor wife. She was a sweet soul and pretty-faced back then, the queen, before she got fat, but don't let my lady hear me say that, for she thinks it quite the nasty turn he did her, throwing her over for the dark harlot Anne Boleyn. Fernanda Salinas, she was back then, my lady. And me mother came with her as her own maid. And then many years later, Lady Ludmore met old Luddy, but he wasn't called that then, you see, just Lord Ludmore the Handsome, and the next thing you know she married him, so taken in with his charms she was.

But handsome men are never good, are they?

"And then she had Rafael, rascal that he is," and she giggled, a red blush rising up her neck. "And after, three little lass babes who all died in the cradle. But *him*, he grew up into a strapping lad, he did. Why, he got Ava"—she nodded toward the kitchen—"in trouble too, and her mum is raising that one. We didn't tell the lady about the baby. She hid it under her apron, Ava did. She is afraid she'd be dismissed, though the lady is a hard biscuit, she is, she'd never hurt a soul, I tell you. Boys. Always boys Rafael sires, and they are all likely to grow up just as frisky as him." She paused for a second, taking a breath and holding two fingers up to her lip.

"Where is Bartolome? Shouldn't he be taking his breakfast with us?" I asked.

She rose and busied herself wiping down the table. "Oh no, miss," she said. "He's at prayer with the lady. She be determined to save his little soul if it be the last thing she does. Although I wonder at her determination, for I think he has a bit of the devil, I do, the way he looks at me with those eyes. Have you ever seen such strange eyes, I ask Ava? 'Course she don't answer, being so sensitive she is about that one being raised here and hers in rags over in Smithfield. Tried to take her own life she did, 'fore the babe was born, but the lady told us many a time the sin it is. I found her and we nursed her, without the lady even knowing, which was quite a trick, you see, for the lady seems to know all that is about, but she was gone most of this time anyway, in the country searching for her son or another bastard all the while one was being born in her own home. Ha, we did pull one over on her, and I did a hundred Hail Marys, I did, for my deceitfulness. But I am a good girl, I am, never tarry with the grooms. Why, I've only let Harry kiss me twice, without the tongue, of course."

Anna had been intently reading Maisy's lips, her eyes getting wider at the moment. Maisy glanced over at her curiously. "And may I ask, miss, does your maid always accompany you at your meals?" It was simply a question, but one that would be soon followed by more.

"Why yes, she does," I answered, surprised that there existed someone with a bigger mouth than I. "And she always will. I will have more eggs, please. That will be enough." Maisy bowed and left the room. I began to think I could enjoy this way of life very much.

Lady Ludmore finally joined us and, just as Maisy had said, she was silent, grasping her rosary beads. When I asked when she could take us to market, I was roundly hushed. She no longer wore her mourning clothes, but had donned a beautiful azure silk gown with golden embroidery. Although simply stitched, it was very elegant. She wore no jewelry.

I was now on my third plate of food. Anna had finished most of her pear.

Shortly thereafter the boy came and joined us too. Maisy returned with a small plate of the freshly baked bread. He stared at it, and then over at my eggs. "Here," I started. "Take mine, Bartolome." I started to push my plate forward.

Lady Ludmore lifted her hand, and I knew by her stern countenance that I must stop. Bartolome quietly ate his bread.

A long time later, Lady Ludmore stood and walked to the door. "It's time. Fetch the pieces you'd like to sell."

I glanced upstairs, wary of only bringing a few things and leaving our precious bags behind.

Lady Ludmore chuckled. "I trust my maids completely, silly headed though they are." I laughed inwardly at that, considering what Maisy had told me.

Anna and I scurried up the stairs. Anna sat down on my bed as I sorted through the clothing. I didn't want to leave the gown with the necklace behind, so I changed into it. Anna helped me button up the back, then sat down again.

"The letter," she said.

I shook my head. "I have no interest in what that horrid woman has to say. I'll never forgive her. Never."

Anna looked down. I pulled her chin up. "I'm sorry," I mouthed.

She turned away and got up from the bed. She picked up several gowns, sleeves, and a stomacher, and silently handed me the woolen cloak I'd seen her wear the day Christian had asked me to marry him. We locked eyes, and I knew with a certainty that she had seen us and was thinking of Christian's kiss. I reached for her, but she spun and walked from the room. I quickly packed up the pieces and followed her.

Lady Ludmore waited for us. "Why, where do you think you are going? I must see your wares first," she said. "I have no idea if we are for Cheapside or Leadenhall."

I brought the bag to the table. Lady Ludmore gently pulled out a gown, one of carnation satin. Along the matching stomacher was the best of my stitching, daffodils with knotted seed pearls. She ran her fingers over the fabric, her face somber and severe. Perhaps we would be headed for Leadenhall.

Maisy and Ava, who had magically appeared, inched closer, their eyes big. Lady Ludmore pulled another piece from the bag, and the maids sighed. It was a lemon yellow poplin, with bees and vines stitched in black and yellow, and honeycombs stitched along the borders. "This one is not as finely done," she pronounced flatly. Grace had stitched it, not three weeks past, all the while cursing about her weary hands and what used to be. I'd had to finish the work for her.

"I'll take this one," she said, smiling slightly and pointing to the daffodil gown and stomacher, "and this one," she said, fingering the yellow, "for Ava, and if you have another simple one for Maisy." And the maids clasped their hands and squealed. "For church." She nodded to them, and even this did not damper their laughter. "And I'll subtract your room and board for as long as you are here. I'll have no wastrels and waifs hanging about."

"My work?" I asked her. "What do you think of it?"

"Among the best," she said simply. "Now what else do you have?" She pulled the remaining pieces from the bag and examined each one. She nodded in approval. "Don't go getting a swollen head. I've seen better. Come, come, girls," she said, walking to the door. "We are off to Cheapside. I know of a draper who will gladly buy from you. She has the most extraordinary things. I've been buying from her for years."

"Shall I call for the carriage?" Maisy asked as we went to the door. A carriage? My, she was a fine lady, she was, keeping a real carriage. Why hadn't she taken it to Gloucester in search of her son?

"Good God, no," she huffed. "When we could walk ourselves? God rewards those who waste not."

We could hear bells ringing in the distance. I was lost for a moment, for it sounded just as the bells of Winchcombe Abbey that rang before every mass and on joyous occasions, although they be few.

"Why, that's St. Margaret's," Maisy said. "The queen must be traveling to one of her palaces."

And then there seemed to be a commotion outside our very door, and Maisy and Ava ran to the window.

"It's a fancy litter, Lady Ludmore," Maisy said over her shoulder.

Lady Ludmore opened the door, and Anna and I followed her out to the street. Maisy and Ava peeked through the window, their noses pressed up to the glass.

The crowds on the street had parted and people were

squashed up against the walls of the buildings, hushed and expectant.

I couldn't bear to look. Finally Anna nudged me and I had the courage to lift my head. Ah, God's me. The most beautiful contraption I'd ever seen was coming our way. It was covered in a golden and cream-colored brocade, quilted diamond-wise and set with glittering jewels at the points. A large, waving white feather steepled at the top. The base of the carriage seemed to be entirely gilded in gold. Six men, three at each side, walked in unison, their legs pumping like a millipede. Somewhere inside was the woman I'd waited my whole life to see.

I held Anna's hand. Would I have a glimpse of the queen? Would I? Yes. Now, I could see—ruffles, and finery and red curls—then God help me—dark eyes bearing upon me. Or had I imagined it all? I truly did think I should faint, even though Grace always said I wasn't the fainting sort. It was Anna who braced my back up.

The litter stopped. And suddenly the queen herself looked out. And it was me she was looking at, there was no doubt. She stared at my gown, starting at my elaborate stomacher, then very slowly, scanning the violet silk down to my feet. My shoes. My muddied, tatty shoes. Oh, Lord. Her eyes narrowed and quickly rose to my face. Oh, she was beautiful! I managed a wobbly curtsy. She turned her head and leaned back into the cushions, and the litter lurched forward.

The smell of juniper is always about, for my good lady much loves it. She even sends me out in the fields to fetch it and prepare bouquets for her private rooms. It was here in a field of gillyflowers her handsome lord of a husband found me first. He gave me a lute and told me its beauty could not match mine. I've never received such a gift—it was only blows I received from my father, you see, and much more. He's a very courtly fellow, my lord, high-spirited and merry, and sweet with his words, and so kind to me. So very kind. Agnes warns me of his intentions—seems he has a reputation for the ladies, high and low—but I say fa, for everyone can well see his great love for his beautiful wife. And what wrong can there be if I seize a little happiness for myself?

CHAPTER 12

hat did she see in me? I stood there frozen, completely mystified, while everyone around me stepped back into motion.

Lady Ludmore, our bag in tow, grabbed my elbow and pulled me along the street, Anna following quickly behind. The early morning sun had hidden itself behind gray clouds, and it was cold. My whole body tingled. We swept by a hog-faced young lady selling cherries, while other maids, carrying large baskets of linen to be laid out upon the fields, chattered about the queen. Two ruff-necked men, standing before a great barrel of rotting fish, argued the price of pike. Horses grunted and a dog barked. I had not realized until now how quiet the country was, and pretty smelling, too. God's me, but terrible odors seemed to emanate from everywhere: malted liquor, sweet cakes, and quince pies mixed with the dung of work beasts. And every now and then a breeze brought us the foul stink of the Thames. Lady Ludmore was silent, but when I looked back, hoping for one last glimpse of the litter, she asked calmly, "What is the connection between you and the queen?"

"I have no idea." At least that was the truth. There was no connection between me and the queen, only Grace's cryptic demand that I stay away from her.

"You are lying to me, Katherine, and I don't like liars in my house."

I had just come from a house of lies, aye, I had. I glanced at Anna, and she cocked her head. Then I said to Lady Ludmore, "There is no connection, none that I know of."

"Was selling your wares a ruse to get to London?"

"No. We are penniless," I said. I felt the heavy necklace brush against my ankle. It was only a half lie, and Grace always said a half lie was halfway to the truth.

"And your name. Have you given me your true name?"

I sighed. "It is indeed Katherine, although I was known as Kat back home," I said, thinking of how Grace first started to call me Kat because I was sly as a barnyard cat, always creeping about with my nose where it shouldn't be. "But I did keep our last name from you. It's Bab, and I was embarrassed by it." And that was the truth.

"Never be embarrassed by your beginnings, my dear," she said, softening somewhat. "It's where you end before the eyes of God that's most important." Just then an older gentleman in a chestnut-colored silk suit caught my eye, and I blushed as we walked on.

"You must learn, my dear, to lower those dangerous eyes. You are not in the country anymore." She didn't elaborate on this, but continued, "There is more you are not telling me."

I took a deep breath. "I was not born of the woman who raised me."

"Why, you could be anyone," she snorted. "You could be the daughter of the butcher's wife born in Tilde's barn. Or born of a barmaid in Moore's field. A babe was found there, not a fortnight ago, left for dead in the cold of night. The poor soul who left her will hang if she is caught. Or did you think perhaps you are the long-lost daughter of good Bess?" She laughed. "Because of that wild hair?" She laughed again. "Red hair is said to come from the Vikings, and they left many a fool scattered about, I have to tell you."

"No, of course not," I responded heatedly. "It's just that I have indeed always admired her. Since I was a girl, for her dress and her style and her jewels." I added quickly, "How old is she, the queen?"

"Thirty or so, I believe, child," she responded. "And you?"

"Sixteen."

"Hmm. The queen would have been fifteen when you were born. Not too young, after all. My own grandmother birthed my mother at that age. But it's extremely outlandish to even think such a thing, Katherine. Stay away from her. Stay away from the court, I warn you. What little time I have spent there showed me it's an evil, evil world unto itself, even if they are dressed finely. Only the very strong and the very lucky survive. Stick to your sewing, my dear."

"So you've been to Elizabeth's court?" I asked as we continued to walk along. The hustle and bustle of the crowd had begun to grate on my nerves. I turned and saw that Anna felt the same. She held her hands over her ears.

"Only but a few times. I had my fill long ago, and of course I have had other matters to occupy my time. I knew her mother, I did, and there never was a more determined and cunning woman, and Elizabeth inherited the worst of her. And she got the worst of her father, too—his temper. God has a sense of humor, he does." She laughed.

A long, cold shiver went down my back. It was as though Grace was walking next to me, her words echoing in my mind—*You've inherited the worst of your parents, God save you.*

We walked in silence, Anna humming to herself like a little bee. All sorts of people—young and old, wide and thin—bustled about: a lady carrying a tiny dog that yapped at us as we passed, little children dressed in finery, a dirty maid sobbing into her apron, a red-faced gentleman with a hawk upon his arm, singing to himself. I started playing a game—searching the crowds, looking for a glimpse of the dozens, if not hundreds of pieces of clothing I'd stitched through the years. They'd been taken from me, sold, and sent off into the world. And now, perhaps I'd see them again, touch them again, and know they were loved.

Finally Lady Ludmore entered a timber-framed shop. I glanced at the shop sign: MINIVER's. And underneath a small royal crest that read, "By honor of the Good

Queen Elizabeth." Anna and I followed Lady Ludmore.

The shop was dark and low-ceilinged. There was a wooden counter in the middle of the room. In one corner a maid sat on a stool stitching, and in another corner I could see a dress form fitted with a lovely gosling yellow frock. Two other gowns, not very well made—why, I could see missed stitches even from where I stood—were displayed near the entrance.

"Where is your mistress today, Lily?" Lady Ludmore asked the maid.

"In the back, ma'am, wrapping a package. We've another order from the queen! Nicholas . . ." She blushed. "I mean, Mr. Pigeon, Clerk of the Wardrobe of Robes, is expected to come for it!"

"Go along and fetch her anyway!" said Lady Ludmore. "Tell her whatever she's packing pales to what we have for her here." Lily looked us over curiously, frowning at Anna, who was examining the yellow gown in the corner, and went to fetch her mistress.

Lady Ludmore removed her gloves and placed them on the counter. Anna, hand on the gown, turned to me, her eyes big. I went to her. It was of yellow sarcenet, a day dress. My heart began to beat. Yes. Strawberries, snails, and leaves in elaborate couch stitching, double backed across the stomacher. One of my signature stitches. I'd finished it several months ago. I'd accidentally spilled cider on the back hem. Grace was always chiding me, so careless I was. I'd scrubbed the stain out best I could and never showed it to her, of course. I carefully lifted the bottom hem. It was there—the pale faded area where I'd scrubbed the cider out.

A woman came through a curtained doorway. She was beautifully dressed, but she was snout-faced and poxed like old Mr. Dar. I stepped away from the yellow gown.

"Well, well. I can give you a good price for that, I can. Stained, it is. Only time I've ever been cheated from that old goat of a man and now he's disappeared and I can't get my good money back. Used to bring me gorgeous things, he did, from orders I had from Edmund Pigeon, of the queen's wardrobe, who bought them from me, paid a pretty piece of gold for them, he did. We go back years, we do, and now what do I have to show for it? He's sending me his son in his place."

"I have to say I have things much more beautiful than this." I pointed to the gown, my fingers shaking slightly. Lady Ludmore's mouth dropped open. I could feel her eyes silencing me.

"This is my ward, Katherine Ludmore," she said. "Her

mother, my husband's youngest sister, has recently died of the ague. She's been gently raised as best as one can in the country, but she has a few manners to learn." Why, it was a bold-faced lie, it was! Her ward. And how she'd said she'd stand no lies! "And her maid," Lady Ludmore added, nodding toward Anna. Anna nodded back. "Her mother taught her the most beautiful, gorgeous stitching, I assure you." She motioned for Anna to bring our things to the counter.

Lady Ludmore pulled out the fanciest piece, a luscious seawater green velvet, a damask pattern of cowslips and fall leaves gently sewn on the surface, pale gold bugles shaped like flowers set within. I'd had the good sense not to spill anything on that one; the velvet alone was worth a tiny fortune.

Mrs. Miniver's eyes got large. "Aaaah," she sighed. She grasped my work in her hands, examining it. Would she know the embroiderer was one and the same? She looked up at me a moment and then at Anna, but she didn't say anything. She only smiled like a cat whose long-lost kittens have come home. "Yes, yes. What else do you have?"

Lady Ludmore displayed the other pieces and Mrs. Miniver examined them, glancing back at me again.

"Well, I'm sure," she said. "Perhaps. Not the quality that I was hoping." My face fell.

Lady Ludmore laughed. "Now Minerva," she said. "How many years have we known each other? And you think I'm an imbecile half-wit, do you?"

Mrs. Miniver frowned, stroking the green velvet.

Just then the door opened and a young man entered the shop, dressed finely, in a golden doublet with a matching cloak.

"Why, Mr. Pigeon!" Mrs. Miniver called to him. She quickly folded my garments and put them back in the bag, with a wide, stiff smile.

He approached us, his eyes on my face. No matter what Lady Ludmore had said about lowering my eyes, I could not do it. I couldn't pull mine away from his. He was smiling. He was young, perhaps five or six years older than me. And devastatingly handsome.

He turned to Mrs. Miniver and bowed to Lady Ludmore. "Lady Ludmore," he murmured.

She nodded back. "Mr. Pigeon."

"And who is this, may I ask?" he said, looking straight at me as Anna shrunk back in the shadows.

"Miss Ludmore, my niece, new from the country," Lady Ludmore responded, frowning at me disapprovingly, for I still had not lowered my eyes.

He nodded to me. "Nicholas Pigeon," he said. We stood smiling at each other until Lady Ludmore grabbed the bag and pulled my arm.

"We must hurry home. I trust we will hear from you," she said to Mrs. Miniver as I stumbled after her, looking back over my shoulder at Nicholas Pigeon.

Grace always said thrice a surprise in one day and you might as well dig yourself a grave in hallowed ground and pop yourself in before the devil finds you. For when we walked back into Lady Ludmore's home her son, the minstrel Spaniard, was sitting there, Maisy on his lap.

Lady Ludmore screamed. Maisy jumped up with a squeal, like she'd been bucked off a horse and ran just out of Lady Ludmore's reach into the kitchen, wailing all the way.

We all turned our attention back to Rafael, who sat at the table with the wide grin of a wolf on his face. There was no sign of the minstrel he last was, for he was dressed now for all the world to see as the son of a lord, his clothes rich and fine, with a bit of a foreign look to them. He pushed away his elaborate breakfast and put one booted leg up on the table.

"Well, Mamá?"

"*Fa*, you bad son, you." Lady Ludmore slapped him on the top of his head.

"Ouch," he yelped.

And she slapped him again. "Do you know how much misery you've caused me?"

"Yes, yes." He was half yelping, half laughing. She continued to slap at him. Maisy and Ava peered from the kitchen, their hands over their mouths.

"Why, I've almost died, I have, looking for you. Kicked by a cow in Wiltshire. Brought down sick in Oxford by a ghastly blackbird pie. And do you know what trouble you've sown with your wicked ways? Do you?" Ava's face disappeared from the doorway, then Maisy's.

"Mamá, is this the greeting I'm to get?"

She finally stopped slapping him and stood back, breathing hard. "Get your nasty feet off my table. Have you not ever learned your manners?" He moved his feet down, still smiling at her.

"You must be hungry. You are thin as a bog reed, you are." She clapped her hands. "Maisy," she bellowed. "More food for my boy!"

But her boy had turned his attention on Anna. Anna did not return his stare.

Lady Ludmore narrowed her eyes. "You won't be staying here tonight. I have guests. And they are good girls, the both of them."

He turned his eyes to me. And I held them fast. "You, I've seen before," he said. He smiled and laughed. "Why, it's the little country heartbreaker."

Lady Ludmore narrowed her eyes at me, then looked back at her son. "As though *your* heart could be broken," she said. "That will be the day I can rest in peace—when I know you truly possess a heart."

"Oh Mamá," he said, taking a swig of ale. "Always hysterics and tears. She didn't tarry with *my* heart. She tarried with some poor, spineless pear farmer. I heard all about it in an alehouse in Gloucester. Seems she left him standing in the abbey, and when he set out to search for her, the idiot stepped in a rabbit's hole and broke his foot." He laughed.

Anna had moved behind me. She was gripping my arm, trying to get the best view of his lips she could. "Your mother is right," I said loud and clear. "You have no manners or heart."

"Oh, don't look so stricken maids, the *both* of you. Your love will be fine. Some old hooked-nose woman set the bone." But this knowledge did not in any way ease my worry—Old Hookey, for this is who he spoke of, for sure—used the ancient ways in setting bones. The last one she set belonged to her own husband, and he hobbled for years afterward. "And all those old women are bringing him food. And of course he has the marked attention of the alehouse's daughter." God's me. Piper. He was talking of Piper.

Maisy entered with another tray and set it in front of Rafael. He pinched her rear and then started to eat, like a big hungry bear. Lady Ludmore collapsed in the chair next to him.

"If you will excuse me." I nodded to Lady Ludmore, curtsied, and backed up, ready to make my escape. I started for the stairs, feeling Lord Ludmore's gaze upon me as I did so. Anna, relieved, followed. I'd immediately pack our bags. We'd go home to Christian. He needed us. Those old women would not know how to take care of him. Nor his lambs. And Piper. My face started to burn. But there at the top of the stairs was Bartolome, wide-eyed and agitated. When I reached the top of the stairs, he clung to my legs so long I thought I'd fall over. Finally he whispered, "Don't leave."

The next morning Anna had another one of her spells, not as bad as before, but she could not sit up. The night before we'd all stayed late at the table, Lady Ludmore full in her cups with joy that her son was home, Lord Ludmore flirting with the maids. He never addressed me, but ah, I could feel his eye on me, aye, I could. Anna pinched me under the table if I even lifted my head in Rafael's direction. I was just walking back up the stairs with a potion for her when there was a knock at the front door.

"Why, it's a man dressed in livery, Lady Ludmore!" I heard Maisy exclaim. I turned and listened as the front door was opened. I walked down three steps and peeked. An elegant man in black livery had entered, his extended hand holding a note.

"I've been sent by the queen," he announced, "for the young lady with the flame-red hair."

My lord often talks to me of his days on the high seas fighting the Turks and pirates. We meet in secret in the orchards full of cherry, peach, and filbert trees. There is a frost in the air, but I do not feel the cold. He sings to me, his voice light and airy, and sometimes he even calls me "Fair Nymph." And he shows me how to play a merry tune on my lute. Oh, but he is a man full of worry and heavy of heart, I can see. His evil brother, the Lord Protector to the young boy king, is not pleased with my lord's new marriage to the former queen. He has taken much from them—the queen's rightful jewels and lands—and plagues their lives with misery. I long to reach out to him and touch him but know it would be a mortal sin against the former queen who has been so good to me—like the mother I never had. She's taught me to embroider beautiful cloths, and I in turn have taught her the leechcraft of the woods and fields. But the queen's ladies, Mary Odell and Elizabeth Tyrwhit, her stepdaughter, give me much evil looks. Agnes says they are full of the gossip and jealous of anyone who nears their lady, but I wonder if they know of my visits to the orchards. Only Jane, the queen's little fool, likes me and seeks me out for my knowledge of potions and the like. Be wary, Grace, Agnes warns me. Those who near the fire must get burned.

CHAPTER 13

hen I was a little girl I dreamed I stitched wings of gossamer, with tiny moons and suns embroidered in gold along the edge. I wanted to fly away forever, you see. But I wasn't able to fly; I could only float above Blackchurch Cottage until finally I was pulled closer and closer to the ground. Grace found me sitting in my night shift on the roof with no clue of how I had got up there nor how long I had been staring at the stars.

And now I found myself standing directly behind Lady Ludmore with no memory of walking down the stairs and across the great room. The door was shut, the liveried man gone. Lady Ludmore turned and held out the note. Anna, I suppose, had stayed upstairs with Bartolome.

I turned the letter over in my hands. There was a beautiful wax seal on the back. An elaborate *E* had been pressed into the purple wax. I opened it carefully and read.

"And what does it say?" Lady Ludmore asked as she poured another goblet of ale for her son.

"I am to attend a masque tonight by orders of the Queen Elizabeth."

"Well, there's nothing to be done now." She sighed. "One doesn't refuse the queen. I suppose we'll have to find you a mask. I may have one moldering somewhere. *My* queen was quite fond of a masque when she was young."

"Am I to dance?" I asked, plopping down in a chair, dizzy. "I don't know how to dance properly."

Rafael snorted. "I can teach you to dance."

"You shall do no such thing," Lady Ludmore said to him. She turned back to me. "That woman who raised you had to have taught you the simplest of country dances, did she not? You were not complete country rustics, were you? Clearly you can read."

I held the note up to my chest, near my racing heart. I was to meet the queen! "Grace believed dancing led to dangerous things," I said.

Rafael snorted again. "Hush," Lady Ludmore admonished him. "Full of crazy notions, your Grace was, indeed. I'll have to teach you myself. What shall you wear?"

"The sea green," I murmured. "It's the best."

"The velvet?" she asked. "Yes, perfect." She stared down upon me. "But that hair of yours! Ava will do it. You will be gorgeous." She frowned. "Perhaps it's best it is a masque."

"I'll accompany her," Rafael said as he casually bit into a roasted chicken leg.

I glanced over at Rafael as a shiver went up my back.

"You stink!" Lady Ludmore said, slapping him on the top of his head. "You'd be better off out back with the pigs than near Queen Elizabeth. And stink or not, you'd only do much mischief around the likes of her. She's always been partial to a pretty boy with a twinkle in his eye."

"That I've heard while I've been away," he started.

"Been away," Lady Ludmore interrupted. "Is that what you call it? Missing for ten years? Breaking your mother's heart? 'Been away'?"

He waved his hand as if to say he was ceding the point. "I was only going to say I've heard she enjoys her men."

"And the men enjoy her," Lady Ludmore enjoined. "She has them dancing at her feet."

I blushed. I still had not moved. The queen! I was to meet the queen! "Up the stairs with you," Lady Ludmore said. "Ava!" she bellowed. For a woman so small, she carried a very large voice. Ava appeared, her face ashen, her eyes averted from Rafael.

"Prepare two baths, please." She pointed to Rafael. "His in the courtyard and Katherine's upstairs. And do her hair properly. Use whatever ornaments of mine I have left, if you please, perhaps the pearl and gold combs."

Ava nodded and sneaked a peek from under her lashes at Rafael. He smiled back. She retreated, tripping through the door.

"Off with you, Katherine!" I rose to my feet and started to climb the stairs. I lingered on the landing, though, when I heard their voices start up again.

"Do you know how much trouble you've caused me?"

"I couldn't stand him any longer, Mamá."

"He died five years ago," Lady Ludmore said quietly.

"Yes, I just heard of it," he said. "I've been overseas the last few years. I made a coin or two of my own and decided to return."

"But ten years, Rafael?" Lady Ludmore replied.

"I found that I rather enjoyed the life of an adventurer. And I did not want to leave it."

"You did it to spite me?"

"No, Mamá," he murmured. "I did love you, I did. But life under Father, as you know, was unbearable."

"I bore it," she responded. I heard a chair scoot away from the table and the sound of boots receding down the hall.

Lady Ludmore had changed her mind. Apparently Rafael was to accompany me to court. It wasn't proper for a young lady to go alone, she said, and that was that. So while Rafael bathed, Lady Ludmore showed me some of the courtly dances. "Smile, and perhaps your partner won't notice your lack of gracefulness," she snapped after I'd stepped on her feet more than once.

And later, after I'd been bathed, I was plucked like a farmyard chicken. Thin-as-reed eyebrows, I was told, were the style, not the hairy caterpillars I had above my eyes. Ava even held my head and plucked along my hairline, for it seems a high forehead signifies intelligence. Then I was carefully dressed, horse tied I felt, so uncomfortable the undergarments were. Why, I had no idea a gentle lady wore so many things! A chemise to protect from sweat, a petticoat (my crimson taffeta), a farthingale—a contraption of bands that widened the dress—stockings, a kirtle, the heavy green velvet gown over a forepart, and finally the sleeves. I could barely breathe! My chest nearly spilled over the bodice, and when I tried to drape a handkerchief across the top, like a partlet, Ava pulled it away with a naughty giggle. "If you are to be masked, you oughta show 'em your other assets." Next she worked on my hair, laying a combing cloth upon my shoulders and gently stroking my curls with ivory combs.

Anna watched sad-eyed and wordless all the while Ava gave her bossy instructions on the care of a lady's hair. Bartolome sat by Anna's side until Maisy came and got him for his afternoon prayers.

"Glorious. Your hair is glorious, miss. No rats for you, that is sure."

"Rats?"

Ava laughed. "Yes, miss. That's what the queen uses to fluff up her hair. Small bits of real hair, from God knows where, ratted and stuffed in her hair to make it more grand. Named for its shape and the company she keeps."

"And how would you know of the queen's hair?" I asked her.

"Maids prattle, high and low," she responded. It was quiet while she pinned my hair up, working from the back, toward the crown of my head. "Oh my, miss," she exclaimed, standing back a little from me. "Why, miss, you have a mark, a perfect half-moon." She pointed behind my ear.

My hand flew to my ear. Anna stood and silently looked, then walked over to the window and peered out, never saying a word. *A devil's mark is hard to cover,* Piper had said long ago. Her words pierced me now as though she stood next to me.

"Does she ever talk?" Ava asked, looking at Anna.

"When she's a mind to it," I answered, distracted by yet another secret Grace had kept from me. A birthmark. A sign of the unlucky—of devils and things unwanted.

Ava laughed. "Lady Ludmore says that's all we've a mind to, us maids. Gossiping and flapping our mouths. There, you do look lovely. Just lovely." She held up a small mirror.

Clear green eyes peered back at me—seawater green, like the gown I wore. I touched my full lips and thought to myself, Is this alluring? Is this the face that Grace had so many times spoken of? I'd never felt so beautiful, despite the fact that I couldn't breathe. Anna came away from the window. She smiled at me, the way one does when it's the least thing one wants to do.

"Too bad you don't have any jewelry," said Ava. "All the ladies at court are heavily adorned. You'll look as bare as a hedge pig amongst them. Lady Ludmore would likely lend you hers, but she sold many of her pieces when her husband was alive. Gambling being one of his many vices."

I thought of the necklace still sewn in my traveling dress. Perhaps I should wear it? Nay. It would stay there for now. Thank goodness Lady Ludmore had been able to find a mask. It was quite pretty, with green and golden feathers fanning out around the bejeweled lined eyes. The handle was wrapped in gilded cording.

I held it up to my face. "Why did Rafael leave?"

Ava laughed. "My, you are bold, aren't you? You just rightly asked what we've wondered ourselves for ten long years. And I'll give you some kindly words, if I may?"

"Of course," I answered.

"As soon as you get to the masque, excuse yourself on some female errand—at this a man will never question you, mark my words—and lose him for the rest of the night."

* * *

As we pulled away in the carriage, I looked up to see Anna in the window, her hand on Bartolome's shoulder, staring down at us. She lifted her hand slowly to wave good-bye and, for the first time, I truly did feel that I was leaving her. "You love her, but mark my words, someday you will betray her. You have it in you, a streak of meanness from your father," Grace had told me once. I waved back, wearing the fancy pearled gloves I'd made at Blackchurch Cottage.

Across the seat, Rafael was watching me intently. He wore a lush black silk doublet, flourished all over with trails of gold twist. It fit his dark looks perfectly. I settled myself as far away from him as I could, catching my hand in the cushion. I glanced down. It was torn. I looked around more closely and I saw that the whole interior of the carriage was shabby, despite its shiny and polished exterior. I would offer later, I told myself, to mend the holes and tears. For now I needed to steady my beating heart. I took a deep breath.

"My mother has always been a strange creature," Rafael remarked as he looked out the window. "I suppose she's given my inheritance to the church. Father, curse his soul, would never have allowed things to fall as they have."

"I hear your father gambled heavily. And you rightly forfeited any inheritance when you left your mother so cruelly," I remarked. I took another deep breath.

"May I say, Miss Heartbreaker, you do not know from which you speak. And a lady who is silent is much preferred to a lady who speaks too much." He was smiling, but there was a deep sadness in his dark blue eyes.

"Well, I suppose that's how you would prefer a lady. Silent."

"I'm only warning you out of a tender care, I assure you," he said quietly, looking out the window again at the bustling streets. "Unheeded words have strong consequences."

I rolled my eyes. As if he had any right to scold me, the scoundrel that he was. I was not going to let him goad me like the wily fox in the henhouse. I had waited for a night like this all my life. Dressed grandly and meeting the queen! Why, I had never even been in a carriage before, much less one led by a uniformed groom. I leaned back against the cushions, closed my eyes, and listened to the steady clip-clop of the horses.

"And what secrets lie behind those lips?" Rafael asked.

"You've just told me to stop babbling," I said, smiling.

I could hear music coming from down the street. Perhaps we were there. "And I shall do as you say." I gripped my stomach, hoping to calm the wild butterflies.

"I have a feeling you will never do the bidding of any man."

"And why should I? When the queen does not."

I stuck my head out the window. Lady Ludmore had told me we would be going to St. James's Palace, one of the queen's residences, and indeed a grand red-bricked structure loomed into view. Why, there were even liveried men playing trumpets and drums! And magnificent soldiers standing shoulder to shoulder. And flags and banners! And lots of regular folks jostling and craning to get a better look at the proceedings.

I laughed and leaned farther out the window to watch as many young knights on horses in rich array and gentlemen in grand coats with gold chains about their necks gathered and talked at the palace entrance. Their ladies, shimmering in their gowns, greeted one another.

He pulled me roughly inside. "You are acting the fool," he hissed. "Sit down, or everyone will know you for the country simpleton that you are."

My heart burned. I brushed his hands from my waist.

He continued, "And as to your good queen, I must now warn you. She is not the woman her people think she is."

The carriage came to a sudden stop. A groom opened the door. Rafael brushed past me and stepped out of the carriage first. But then he turned and reached out his hand, and I saw distinctly, as his sleeve went up, a long, vicious scar. A burn scar I was sure it was, for Alice Ogilvey once poured a pot of scalding porridge upon herself and the scar looked the same—like swirled melted wax with the devil himself imprinted there.

I took his hand and as he helped me down I looked into his eyes. "That," he said, answering my silent question, "was a gift from your *good* queen."

We walked through the magnificent arched front doors of St. James's Palace. It was a good thing Rafael had my arm, for I truly thought my heart would beat out of my chest and across the floor. "Your blood beats too hard," Grace used to say. "That's why it never reaches your brain." I swallowed. Why were her words haunting me so now? "Think, child. Think before you use your tongue. It's the wise woman who does."

We were led down a long hallway and into a great

room. I clutched the mask to my face, fearful of the wolves of the court whom Grace had long warned me of. But as I looked around, all that I saw was beautiful. Oh, the most sumptuous fabrics, lace ruffs, rich velvets, gold trims, feathers, and plumes! I could barely focus on one lovely gown before another caught my eye. One, pale blue velvet like the morning sky, with tufts of gilt taffeta pulled through the slashed sleeves—a partlet of white passamaine lace edged in gold. And another, a pearled and spangled French gown of tawny orange satin with raised embroidered unicorns and feathers. And the jewels, so fine and noble—simmering strands of pearls, and large sparkling stones, as large as sparrows' eggs. And I'd never seen men so finely dressed—the workmanship and embroidery were as rich as the women's. In the country a man might not change his dusty clothes for a fortnight! A new gown caught my eye—a maiden's blush-colored satin patterned with moons and suns, stitched with spangled rays on the silk sleeves. I glanced up to find the woman, no maiden she was, making eyes at Rafael, who refused to wear his mask. He winked back at her.

I turned my attention to the walls, which were dark-paneled with heavy carved rosettes. And fine tapestries ten times as glorious as the one in Lady Ludmore's home, and heavy chests with hunting scenes, and gold plate everywhere.

"Where is she?" I whispered to Rafael.

"She'll show herself soon enough," he remarked. "She likes to make a grand appearance." He downed the goblet of wine a servant had handed him. My eyes grew large—the goblet had a ruby set within it.

At the front of the large hall was a stage with grand scaffolding. Roses and vines and shimmering iridescent fabrics were intertwined over a great woodland arbor.

"What is that?" I asked Rafael, my fingers clutching his sleeve.

"There will be some sort of theatrical after dinner," he answered. "A garden allegory, my guess, in honor of the queen, the maker of our garden of paradise." His voice dripped with sarcasm. "Dancing, even later, into the night."

"Perhaps you should be up there." I smiled, tilting my head to the arbor. "As I recall, you are quite the actor."

He laughed. "My minstrel days are over."

I could hear loud music—trumpets, perhaps. "Yes, just why have you come home?" I asked, tipping up on my toes for a better look. He didn't answer me, but was as much interested as I as a parade of ladies, young and old, walked in.

"Her maids of honor," Rafael murmured. The crowd grew silent. My heart thumped in my chest. Five whole seconds passed by, or was it forever?

And then she came.

I've learned to play the lute beautifully, but my lord hasn't come to me of late to hear it, for you see he is much busy with the Princess Elizabeth, who's been put in my lady and lord's charge. There is much love between my lady and the princess, her former stepdaughter, but I don't like this girl, even if she be a princess, for she has many demons inside her and eager eyes for my lord. Her governess, Mrs. Ashley, teases her about her crush and says perhaps they shall marry someday, for it is not a sure thing ever, that a wife will outlive her husband. And there indeed is much to fear, you see, for the queen, after three old husbands, has conceived, and by St. George's Day shall deliver my lord a son, something the whole household prays for, but more importantly a healthy delivery she shall have. The queen is much ill in the mornings, so I've made her three cramp rings for the stomachache, and Jane the fool gifted her with a real unicorn's horn to ward off the evil spirits that plague an expectant mother. Ah, he has come to me here under the trees. I must put down my pen.

CHAPTER 14

Magnificence. Pure magnificence. My heart soared as she entered on the arm of a distinguished-looking man. "Robert Dudley," I heard whispered around me. And indeed he was handsome, almost as handsome and dark as Rafael. Elizabeth nodded regally as she walked down the room, people bowing to her.

"You look as though you could eat her," Rafael whispered to me.

"Hush!" I said, pulling my arm from his. I remembered Ava's suggestion that I lose him, and she was right. "That lady over there," I said, nodding my head to the first woman I saw. "She's been waving her mask at you since we arrived."

He grinned, and for the first time I saw it reached his eyes. "Not so easy, my love. I have strict instructions to stick to you like honey." Still, though, he nodded at the lady with a generous smile. She tipped her mask in return.

Queen Elizabeth was making her way down the room. She wore the most elaborate creation I'd ever seen, the black silk gown richly embroidered and tufted with glimmering jewels, the large white satin harlequined sleeves and forepart decorated with ribboned bows at the points. Among the interlacing designs were images of clasped hands, hearts with crossed arrows and flames, daffodils and gillyflowers. And even a grotesque sea creature. Her red hair was crimped and intertwined. And at her waist hung a tiny prayer book, attached by a beautiful rope of pearls.

My heart fluttered as she neared. And then she stopped directly in front of me. I curtsied deeply, then rose. Her face was pale white, the whitest I'd ever seen on any human being except Anna. Her dark eyes were piercing yet fine, and her nose, a little hooked, was regal. Robert Dudley, at her side, held his nose so high in the air that all I could see was his swarthy chin atop his large ruffle. He wore a gorgeous cloak, embroidered with peacock feathers, over his silk doublet.

Elizabeth inspected me just as she had earlier in the

day. "Lovely gown, my dear," she finally said. "Seawater green. Velvet. Any finer, and perhaps I'd send you home. One must never upstage a queen, you know." She laughed. There was a murmur of laughter, although I had the feeling the queen was not jesting. "And I see, darling, you have forgotten your jewelry. Poor dear."

My hand flew up to my bare neck.

"Sometimes beauty needs no adornment," I said, before I even knew it. It was something Grace had said to me often when I had begged to wear our creations. The queen arched an eyebrow as several of her ladies gasped. I could hear Rafael chuckling in the hushed silence around us.

Elizabeth now turned her sharp eyes on Rafael.

"And who are you?" she said haughtily, but I could see her desire and curiosity. She looked at him as one might admire a beautifully colored snake. Robert Dudley's chin came down as Rafael bowed. "Lord Ludmore, Your Majesty." Lord Dudley lowered his mark at Rafael, his look pure indifference.

"*You* have forgotten your mask," said the queen. She smiled at him before turning back to me. Lifting her hand dramatically, she pulled off a small gold ring and stepped forward.

"Your glove," Rafael whispered. I fumbled and pulled it off. She slipped the ring on my finger. It was two hands clasped with a small ruby in the middle. It was lovely.

"Appreciating beauty is a way to acknowledge God's gifts," she said, looking at me, and Rafael chuckled again. "The ring was from an old friend. It signifies lasting friendship."

"But I must not accept it," I said, tears stinging my eyes, "if it has meaning to you."

"Friendship can be a folly." She smiled. "Sometimes it does not last."

"Well, then I must give you a gift," I responded, my voice shaking. I pulled off my other glove and held the pair out to her. It seemed an eternity before she took them from me. She looked at the gloves carefully, with hardly a change in her expression.

"Nicely done," she said, and I bowed my head. A page stepped forward and took the gloves. When I looked up, the queen had walked on. But it seemed that everyone else stared upon me with onion-eyed curiosity.

"Bravo," Rafael said as the crowd began to talk amongst themselves, the queen's ladies following her like ducklings behind their mother.

"I thought you said it was best to curb my tongue," I responded, not sure if I had impressed the queen or utterly insulted her.

"Yes, it is in most cases, but I think she did enjoy it. I certainly did." He took my arm again and we walked a few lengths behind the queen's ladies. I studied their beautiful gowns.

"She didn't seem to know you," I said, nodding to some of the people who continued to stare at me.

"Keep your eyes down," he whispered. "You have not been introduced to any of these people." Then, "She doesn't. Never met me a day of her life. Why, I could be the king of Spain come to look her over for all she knows."

"You weren't at court before you left?"

"No." He frowned. "My father kept me at home, in case anyone should see the many bruises from his beatings. And Elizabeth was kept in the country and even in the Tower should she try to wrest the crown from her sister. I guess we have that in common, the two of us." He laughed. "We were treated terribly by the ones who should have loved us."

"Your mother, she was not good to you?" I asked. Another beautiful gown went by, a peach-colored silk with a diamond pattern of Venice gold embroidered on the sleeves and forepart, little birds and grasshoppers stitched within. The lady blinked at me curiously from behind her mask, before I remembered and lowered my eyes.

"No, my mother looked the other way," he said. "And in so doing damned me."

"I believe she suffered much," I began, "while you were gone." He didn't respond, so I added, "May I ask, sir, if you have never met the queen, how in the world she could be the cause of the scar on your arm?"

He was quiet a moment before answering. "She caused it simply by her words." And then, despite his pledge to stick to me like honey, he walked away.

Before I even had a moment to worry, someone was at my side. "My, you look ravishing, you do."

I turned and looked into the most beautiful blue-gray eyes. Nicholas Pigeon. And dressed sumptuously, with a stiff ruff, gold leggings, a celestial blue jerkin with embroidered gold guards.

I tried to lower my gaze but I couldn't. But then his eyes dipped to my chest and then my waist. I blushed.

"That is the most gorgeous stitching I've ever seen," he finally said. "What kind is it? Double thread? Couched?

How long does it take to make such a thing?"

I was taken aback. "Weeks," I responded. "Maybe more. Grace did the sewing. My talent is with the needle."

"Grace?" he asked. Over his shoulder I could see Rafael heading back our way with the look of a giant bear who's left his mate.

"She was my maid . . . my maid in the country."

"I see." He smiled, and I noticed he had fine teeth, too. "We'll have to send for her as well."

"Send for her?" I choked. "Why ever would you do that?"

"You've not been told?" he asked.

"Told what?"

"I've misspoken," he said. "So where is this Grace? She did the sewing, you said? The cut is beautiful. My tailors could learn a thing or two from her."

"But she is dead," I responded, too quickly. "Buried not a week ago." I suddenly felt sick.

He stared at my breasts again. "God but your designs are beautiful. Where did you get them?"

"Why, right outside my door!" I laughed. "They are my own designs, drawn from the beauty of nature. I keep them in a notebook."

Then Rafael was at my side, taking my elbow. He

bowed to Nicholas, who did not nod back.

"Lord Ludmore," Rafael said. "And you are?"

"Nicholas Pigeon, Clerk of the Wardrobe of Robes."

"You mean you carry Elizabeth's train."

"And I would wipe her feet if she bade me," Nicholas quickly responded. He blinked. "As any true gentleman would."

"Many things make a man," Rafael said with a tiredness in his voice that sounded ingrained forever. "Many things make a *good* man. You are a mere boy who's done nothing more than sew the queen's buttons."

"She has men for that. Dozens of them. I'm in charge of her entire wardrobe, including the robes of state that kings upon kings have worn through centuries. And what have you done, Lord Ludmore? More than roam the countryside?"

"More than any of you here would know." Rafael looked at me, his entire expression demanding I behave, and then he stalked off to join a pretty lady in blue motioning to him with her fan. He quickly took her arm and whispered in her ear.

Nicholas turned to me. "So where has he been all these years? The court is all atwitter of his return."

I watched Rafael. "I don't know." And it wasn't really

a lie. "I think perhaps he was lost." This was more the truth.

The queen and her ladies continued to walk the room in procession and I stood quietly next to Nicholas Pigeon, watching with wonder.

"Who is the child?" I asked, for there was a little girl in the procession, dressed as sumptuously as the other ladies.

"The queen's current pet," Nicholas answered. "Ipollyta the Tarletan she's called. A dwarf. The queen is quite besotted, although fearful of her."

A dwarf, like Jane the fool. "Where did she come from?"

"She appeared at court a couple of years ago," he said, "drunk as a skybird. The queen herself nursed her, forming an ill attachment to her, and when she recovered she ordered a small fortune in clothes for her. It is said she's the child Elizabeth will never have."

"But the queen is young," I proclaimed. "Is she not very much in love with him?" I asked, nodding to Robert Dudley.

"My, you are forward, aren't you?" he said, but with a smile. "Eyes. That's her nickname for him. She's even had her embroiderers stitch an eye secretly on her gowns. Usually underneath the hem. I have no reason why; it's not exactly a romantic symbol. Pray me, now I'll have to kill you." He laughed. "I've divulged a secret of the Wardrobe."

"I shall not tell a soul." I smiled, looking away from his own commanding eyes, perhaps guessing why the queen had chosen such a nickname. "But tell me, does she truly love him?"

"I do not know." He frowned suddenly. "But one cannot always marry for love. Especially a queen." He turned from me as he talked. "He's not good enough for her; he will always be her horseman. But some say she will have her way anyway and make him royal, and the whole world will come down around her. Even now her council seeks a suitable husband for her overseas, but everyone they parade before her she dislikes for some reason or another." A masked lady in russet walked by, nodding her head to Nicholas.

"Now *she* has an admirer, a merchant too low," Nicholas said of the lady in russet. "He who sends her a rose every single day. She will never marry him, but still she has us embroider roses in her gowns. It seems we all suffer as the queen does."

I frowned. "Do you speak for yourself, Mr. Pigeon?" I asked him.

"It's Nicholas," he said. "Please call me Nicholas."

"Now who is being too forward?" I said as I realized I'd again been looking at him too long. I turned my attention back to the rose lady, as did Nicholas.

"What do you say of our work?" he said.

I looked at the gown, an orange tawny satin lined with a blue sarcenet, done all over with spangles of gold. The pomegranate and butterflies were couch stitched and knotted. "Nicely done," I said.

"Nicely done," he repeated, impressed.

"There was no need for the extra knotting," I added, and his smile dropped. "The stitching was lovely; it would have been enough."

"Trueloves," he murmured.

"Excuse me?" I asked.

"The knots are named trueloves, for they are overly complicated, as most love is. I think perhaps your escort has abandoned you." He smiled broadly, and I realized he had dimples—Satan seducers, Grace used to call them. I blushed, but his smile quickly faded as one of the queen's ladies approached us.

She took a breath, as one does who is about to make a speech and is nervous about it. "The queen has taken a liking to your work," she said to me, averting her eyes from Nicholas. She was young, perhaps my age, with large blue eyes and blond hair. "You are to be a lady of her chamber. You are to teach us ladies your stitching. And make things for the queen, too, of course. You will report tomorrow and you will have your own room at court. Your maid may accompany you for your comfort." She looked me over then, a little puzzled. And then she added, "I think I shall like you." She turned and quickly walked away, stifling a giggle.

I was stunned. I looked up at Nicholas. "I was dying to tell you," he said. He lifted his arm and I took it. "But stay away from her; that one will pull you deep into mischief."

"I see. And the reason she wouldn't look upon you? Perhaps she's your true love?"

He laughed. "Ahh, indeed. You have much to learn. Come, the masque is about to begin. And I shall have your first dance."

On the way home in the carriage, I couldn't stop thinking of Anna. Once when we were children, I'd eaten a whole pie on the way home from the village, knowing quite well that Anna loved sweets. But I wasn't able to clean the stain of the dewberries off my lips, as sinful stains never leave. Grace had smiled and said, "You have a cruel streak, Spirit. And someday you will break her heart." Anna had only smiles, but she knew. Somehow I felt I'd betrayed her again at the queen's masque.

Rafael was silent until we pulled up to his mother's house. But I knew he watched me from the shadows of the dark carriage. "Consider yourself warned," he said as he handed me down. He lifted my hand and peered at the ring. "You are playing with fire."

He bowed to me low, smiling and turning my hand in his. He placed a kiss on the inside of my wrist. My stomach dropped. But then his face turned somber, and he backed away and stalked into the house. I followed, but he was already gone. I went upstairs. The house was quiet. Anna was in my room waiting for me. A small lit candle was next to the bed.

Silently she helped me undress, but I could feel her mood, as I always could. Anna was gently tethered to this world. And here in London, her tether was unraveling.

I could barely meet her eyes, with what I had to tell her. I was standing in my chemise when our eyes finally met. Then she reached down and lifted my hand. She looked at the ring and let my hand go.

Our eyes met again. "Christian," she whispered.

"We can't go back, Anna," I said to her. "Not yet."

"How can you be so heartless? He's hurt."

"Rafael, for all we know, was only jesting. His words are neither here nor there, full of riddles and false talk." I knew, though, deep in my heart that Christian needed us, needed me, but I couldn't go back. I wouldn't.

Anna just stood looking at me, her eyes empty, her chest slowly rising and falling.

"The queen has asked us to become part of her chamber. It's quite an honor. Beyond my dreams."

One pale eyebrow lifted. "Both of us? Or just you?"

"Yes, both of us are expected."

"And am I to be your maid?" She frowned.

"Only for a little while, Anna, I promise. I'm sorry. Truly I am. People just assumed you were my maid and I let it be. But once I find out the truth, I'll take you home."

"Grace warned you to stay away from the queen."

"And in doing so I believe she gave me the clue I've waited for my whole life. Perhaps the only true thing she ever gave me. And what would Grace know of the queen and court life anyway? Nothing. She was always full of false predictions and omens. Loose of her senses. Everyone said so."

"She gave *you* everything, Kat. Everything. And what did you give her? My mother, hard as she was, was right about you." She didn't have to say it. She had heard those words all those years ago, just as I had. *You have a cruel streak, Spirit. And someday you will break her heart.*

I now know he is the devil. For he talked to me of sweet things and kissed me ardently that day in the orchard, and before I knew it we had sinned. And afterward, when he had finally had me, he turned from me and has never looked upon me again. And now he's set his eyes on the young princess, who is by no means an innocent herself. They deserve each other, I say. She laughs and giggles when he visits her in her room in the morn even before she has arisen. And he tickles and teases her and slaps her on her backside, Agnes has informed me, for she saw it herself. I stood listening at the door one day and I heard him call her "Spirit" and "Fair Nymph," his name for me, and I thought perhaps I would kill him right there if I had had a dagger in my hands. And she, the little strumpet, calls him "Moon," for he has a perfectly shaped crescent on the back of his ear, I'd seen it myself. The devil's mark.

CHAPTER 15

he next morning I was awakened to Ava's excited babbling as she lit a meager fire in the fireplace. "And Maribel just saw her yesterday at market, happy as a canary, buying her mistress fish pies for dinner, she was. And then today dead as a dormouse, and blood everywhere all over the linen sheets and floor. It was the groom's son who found her, poor thing. The mistress had to call for the doctor, not for Millie. She'd been gone for hours, the doctor said. But for the poor boy, he was given quite a fright by what he saw. Gave him a sleeping potion, he did, and he still hasn't awoken."

There was a sudden commotion on the street. I sat up. Anna was gone. She'd slept with me most of the night, but must have slipped away in the wee hours.

"Come look, miss." Ava motioned for me. "Aah, it's an awful sight. Indeed it is."

I joined her at the window. It was strangely quiet. A man pushing a cart, its wheels eerily squeaking, was coming up the street. I could see a body completely wrapped in linen.

"What happened to her?" I asked.

"Why, she took the shears to her own neck, she did," Ava said, crossing herself as the cart went by. "And will be buried with the other unfortunates at Bedlam Court. Poor thing. She was such a sweet girl. But too pretty for her own good, she was. Just like your Anna. A pretty maid is always trouble. I hear she tarried with a groom of the court and got herself in trouble, but who knows."

I frowned at her. "Oh, I do apologize. The lady is always saying how I run my mouth so," Ava said.

I started to turn away from the window, but a movement on the street below caught my eye. A woman was peering up at me intently. It was Mrs. Miniver, the draper. Ava stopped to look too. "She came for you last evening, she did. But you were at the masque. She was insistent that she speak with you. The lady says you can trust her as far as you can heave her."

"Can you bring her to me? Up here?"

"I suppose so," Ava said, looking at me with one half-closed eye full of suspicion. "The Lady and Lord Ludmore are off on some important business. But you aren't dressed, miss."

"That's all right. I'll dress now. Hurry. Go get her."

I threw on a simple poplin frock, and not a moment later Mrs. Miniver appeared. Ava stood in the doorway till I motioned her to leave. She shut the door behind her.

"Who are you? I need to know," Mrs. Miniver said, wringing her hands.

"I'm Katherine Ludmore." I began to put my shoes on.

"Daughter of that whore from Winchcombe," she hissed through her teeth.

I dropped my shoe and I looked up at her. "What do you mean?"

"Me Charlie's run off with her, I know it," she said, a distinctly common accent revealed in her distress. "I haven't seen him in weeks. Once a month he'd come see me, and I'd give him specifications, and he'd return with the most gorgeous garments—yours, I was sure of it when I saw your things yesterday—that he'd brought from Stow-on-the-Wold. All these years I've shared him with her, you see, but he always comes back to me. And this month he doesn't come, so I figure he's run off with the Winchcombe witch."

"She's dead," I said flatly. "Less than a fortnight ago. He's not with her, I can assure you."

"Dead," she repeated. "Are ye sure?"

"Yes," I said as I leaned back down to put my shoe on. "She's dead and buried."

She crossed herself. "God's faith, I've dreamed of this day. My Charlie Bab will come back for me."

"Bab?" I asked.

"Charlie Bab, that's his name," she responded, looking at me carefully. "Did you know him?"

"No, not at all," I answered, astounded that perhaps there was indeed a real Mr. Bab. Had Grace married him? Was he Anna's father? Was he my father? "Can you tell me please," I asked, fighting a sinking feeling in my chest, "why you felt she was a rival for your Charlie's affections?"

"He talked of her, said she had the hands of a witch." She started for the door. And then turned back, "But she was also the dumbest half-wit he ever knew, for he cheated her, you see, all these years, he cheated her. And I got my revenge too, making my own pretty shilling off the court."

"Well, that's all come to an end." Grace was no half-wit, that's for sure. She must have known. Or perhaps she had no choice. She'd said that many times. She couldn't come to London on her own and sell our things. "You'll have no more things from me," I hissed. "I'm to go to the queen. As a lady in her chamber, no less."

"You'll be a servant. A chamberer," she said. "Meaning you'll be flopping the chamber pots out the window into the Thames, you will," And then as she left, "Those are the ugliest shoes I've ever seen."

I couldn't stop my tongue. "Yes, and I'll have new shoes tomorrow, and where will you be?"

Ava came back, combed my hair, and began to curl it in tight rings around my face. She was quiet, but I knew she wondered what had happened.

After carefully packing our things, I went downstairs. There was a lovely breakfast spread, almost a feast really, with a large ham, freshly baked breads, and fat sausages. Around the table sat Anna, Lady Ludmore, Rafael, and Bartolome. He sat next to Rafael, and they were like mirror images, they were, so similar were their dark countenances. But Bartolome had a light in his eyes that I hadn't seen before as he looked up at his father. Rafael mussed his hair affectionately. I sat down next to Anna, who didn't look at me. Her full plate was untouched.

"Mamá, you haven't changed a bit. It's just like you to bring in waifs and strays. Shall I go fetch another from off the street?" Rafael laughed.

We all passed loaded looks across the table, including Maisy, who crossed herself as she walked by with a serving tray.

"Pour her a glass," Lady Ludmore said to Ava. Ava poured me a full glass of mulled wine. "We are celebrating, my dear."

I glanced at Anna, who was still as a statue. Had she told them my news? I doubted it. Her eyes were on my ring, the gift from the queen.

"Isn't it quite early to be partaking of wine?" I asked as I took a generous gulp. It would help my resolve, and God's me, it did run down my throat easily.

"It's never too early for news such as this," Lady Ludmore said, taking her own generous gulp. "We have had our fortune restored, you see. Luddy's will—God rest his blasted ratty soul—was contingent on Rafael assuming the role of Lord Ludmore and taking on his rightful inheritance before the age of thirty. Something Luddy rightly guessed his long-suffering son had no intention of doing. But now Rafael's back, and he has agreed to become the man he was born to be." She took another gulp of wine, then tapped her glass for Maisy to pour more. Maisy frowned as she poured a tiny splash. Lady Ludmore tapped her glass again and Maisy poured another drop.

I glanced at Rafael. He returned my gaze with a mysterious calm. He raised his glass to me.

"Perhaps you have heard I have good news myself," I said, looking away from Rafael, fixing my eyes firmly on his mother. "The queen has asked Anna and me to come to court." And here Maisy and Ava suddenly appeared, fussing at the table. "To embroider," I added.

All eyes shifted to Lady Ludmore. "Well, well," she finally said. "I guess you made quite the impression."

"Yes, she was the beauty of the night," Rafael said darkly. "The queen even gave her a gift."

"Let's see, let's see," said Lady Ludmore.

I sighed and held my hand up.

"Lovely. A ruby. Desire. Hands clasped. Friendship. An interesting combination, coming from the queen. I suppose you are to go right away."

"Yes." I was surprised at her response. There must be something coming. As I learned well with Grace, a wise woman bides her time. "We are to leave today."

"Oh, but you do not intend on taking Anna, do you?"

Ah. Here we go. "Of course," I said, taking Anna's cold hand. "We are never apart. Never."

"Why, she'd be eaten alive at court," said Lady Ludmore. "And it would not be good for her health. See, she's already peaked this morning, the time of day when a lady should shine the most."

"I beg to differ, Mamá. A lady looks most beautiful in the hues of the night."

I snuck a glance at Rafael and then took another gulp of wine. "We'll leave this morning, if you please. Both of us."

Anna pulled her hand out of mine.

Later in my room I checked our belongings one last time. I pulled out the lute and held it to my chest. I strummed it softly, and Anna, who was folding her own few things, turned and smiled. I kept on, running my fingers across the delicate strings.

"Do you like it?" I asked as she continued to smile.

"Yes. Beautiful."

Suddenly, behind me, the door opened. It was Rafael.

He came in, closing the door behind him.

"Lord Ludmore," I said, tucking the lute behind my back. "What do you want?"

"I have something to ask, if I may," he said, looking at Anna.

"She can't hear you," I said.

"My mother wants me to call upon you at court from time to time," he said. He leaned against the door.

"Is that why she is not trying harder to keep us here?"

"She's still not happy about Anna going, and you are welcome here anytime." He looked at Anna and she nodded back. He smiled at me, letting me know he was slyer than me. "But, yes, that's part of the reason. My mother wants me to be accepted back into society."

"You don't seem the sort who would have a care for society," I said before I could stop myself.

He laughed. "Well, at some time one must grow up, seek a wife. Produce heirs."

I hid a smile beneath my hand.

"May I call upon you sometime at court?" he asked. God's me, but he was handsome.

"I suppose you may," I answered. But I wondered what he was up to.

It continues, this madness between the two. There is much talk among the servants of it—that it can't last much longer before word of their unseemly romping reaches the admiral's brother, the Lord Protector. It's treason it is. But her governess boasts, like an idle-headed nincompoop, that someday they might make a merry match and it will be all her doing. I think she too has come under his spell. He seems to have every female at Chelsea dancing a merry tune at his feet. My lady the queen still very much loves the both of them and puts on a brave face and is much pleased for the babe to come. If I could only feel the same for mine—although Jane the fool gave me a foul weed to rid myself of it, when it came time I knew I could not double my sin. Agnes, my only true friend, consoles me at night, for I am most fearful for my soul. But I cannot sleep, for many demons plague me in my dreams. So one night a week past, I came upon the man himself in the hall, hovering outside the princess's door, and I hid myself and watched. And just as he was about to turn the knob, I wailed like a ghost, and he was much startled and ran down the hall like a fool.

CHAPTER 16

hen she shines, we all bask in her happiness, but when the thunderstorms come in, let me warn you, find a faraway hiding hole," said Dorothy Broadbelt, the maid of honor who'd informed me at the masque of my new position. She'd been charged with settling Anna and me in. We'd been given a tiny room, spare but livable, with two comfortable feather beds. "Kat Ashley and Blanche Parry," Dorothy continued, "senior ladies of the bedchamber, always stay with her and weather it out, poor things, both of them being with her through many tough times since the queen was but a child, you see. Blanche even rocked her as a babe, I hear. Stay clear of Kat Ashley; no one likes her. Blanche is divine, oldest of us all and wisest of the wise. And she'll read your palms if you like, tell you if you've fated a good life. Her cousin, Lord Burghly, is one of the queen's high councilors. Be wary what Blanche tells you, though, for she says I'm to marry some handsome low-born. My father would have the fits if he heard her talk so, for he paid a pretty penny and bowed deep to get me here." She finally paused as Anna put our bags down.

"And *she's* to stay in hidden, not underfoot, I tell you, batting her eyes, trying to raise herself up, as many of the lower chamberers do. Why, Elizabeth Marbery, the little nit, managed to get a gift of a petticoat from the queen before she figured what she was about. The queen is very careful now on who attends her." Dorothy, pretty and blond herself, looked Anna over.

"I assure you," I said quickly, before she could go on, "you will not see her."

Dorothy eyed our bags. "We maids of honor, you see, are very beholden to the queen. Why, every girl in all of England would die to take our place." She looked wistfully out a small window that faced a garden of peach trees. "She'll find us a husband, you see, a suitable one of rank. Hopefully it will be one to our liking." She sighed.

"What if you detest the man, what if he smells and is old and has fish breath?" I asked.

Dorothy laughed, a hearty, horsey laugh. "Why, you are a funny girl aren't you?" she said. "Anyone knows it's a rich girl's lot that she may not choose her husband. We'll be lucky if we land a fifty-year-old baronet, no less. Even if he has hair on his back and between his toes, we must fall at the queen's feet and bless her."

And I thought to myself, It is a poor girl's lot too. Could any girl ever choose her destiny? Rich or poor?

"Laundry day is Wednesday, Anne Twiste is our laundress. Stay away from her son Oliver, and George the sweeper, too, although a half-wit—knaves the both of them," Dorothy said, aiming her words at Anna. "They've both tried for my maid Beatrice," she continued. "It's so hard to find good maids these days, don't you think? They are forever running off, or getting into some mess or another.

"You must change out of your traveling shoes now," she said, looking down at my feet. "My goodness, did you swim in the Thames?"

"Ohh," I said trying not to blink, trying to think of a valuable half truth.

"I understand," Dorothy said, suddenly serious.

"Completely. My own mother at home is practically in rags, so I'd be presentable at court. Illusions, Katherine. It's all about illusions."

A little while later, she escorted me, her pinked, peach-colored shoes upon my feet, into the queen's privy chamber. The floors were covered in woven rush matting, the walls in tapestries. There were three windows, and in each birdcages with little golden birds. A young lady sat at a harpsichord and played soft music as other ladies perched on large cushions, some watching, others stitching. Dorothy led me to a cushion and we both sat down. "Ouch!" I squealed, and a few of the younger maids giggled. I reached under my bottom and pulled out a hoop of embroidery, the knife-sharp needle sticking straight up. The half-finished needlework, a panel of stitched strawberries, was pitifully done; no wonder it had been abandoned.

I looked around for the queen, but she was not there. "She's with her privy council," Dorothy whispered to me, seeming to read my mind. "Mary Howard." Dorothy nodded to the lady at the harpsichord. "The queen's cousin." Dorothy ran her finger across her neck and made a ghastly face. "Mary's relative," she whispered.

Then around the room: "Anne Windsour—thinks she's better than us. Katherine Bridge—duck face, talks of ghosts in her sleep. Anne Russell—a bit of a pea goose, but as sweet as can be—will marry next year, it is predicted. And Mary Ratcliff—shall never marry, claims Blanche Parry, and it's a good thing, for who shall abide that breath? And Katherine Knevit—flap-mouthed, mischief-maker, pray me never confide a thing in her. And Mary Shelton, dumb as a flea." They were all taking their turns looking at me, gracefully but intently from under their lashes.

A moment later the queen walked in. She was beautiful. She was dressed in a simple yet gorgeous gown of black velvet, quilted chevron-wise, her hair captured in a caul spangled in gold, with pearls and stones set upon it. She was followed by several ladies, all dressed in black satin and velvet. "Blanche Parry, Catherine Carey, and Katherine Ashley, senior ladies of the privy chamber," whispered Dorothy. "Only they among us are allowed her black livery." Blanche held some sort of small black-furred creature, a ruby and diamond collar around its neck. And then finally, behind them, the dwarf I'd seen the night before, dressed like a miniature version of the queen, her head held high. "Ipollyta, the little witch," Dorothy breathed in my ear.

"Continue playing, Mary," the queen said as she sat. She patted the edge of her cushion and the little witch sat down next to her. Mary continued to play, and I found the music beautiful and soothing.

I watched the queen from the corner of my eye. She wore my gloves. I was pleased to see that she continually pulled one off and put it back on, holding a hand out every now and then to admire my workmanship. When the music stopped, the queen politely clapped, and everyone followed suit. Mary Howard got up from the harpsichord and joined Anne Windsour on a cushion. Next to the queen, Ipollyta worked on something carefully with tiny tools.

"What is she about?" I whispered to Dorothy.

"Sharpening our needles and pins. That was one of hers you sat on." Dorothy snorted. I winced, still aching from the prick. "Stay away from her; she is sharp in more ways than one."

"Ladies, this is Katherine Ludmore," the queen suddenly announced. "She will be instructing us on the finer points of embroidery. Hers is amongst the finest ever seen. Some of you need her guidance more than others."

Several of the maids of honor narrowed their eyes upon me, some with simple interest, others with jealousy. But the dwarf, Ipollyta—her stare sent shivers down my spine, as if a fairy demon had set a spell upon me. A door opened. A servant brought in a silvered tray of sugared fruit and a small ewer and laid it at the queen's feet. Katherine Ashley leaned over and poured from the ewer into a small gilt goblet.

"A posset," Dorothy whispered to me. "Hot sugared milk. The queen has little appetite. It is her senior ladies' duty to tempt her."

"What is the creature in Blanche Parry's lap?" I asked as I watched the thing nibble at the tufts in the queen's dress.

"A musk cat," Dorothy whispered. "A ferret. It was a gift to the queen. Day, she calls it, for it never seems to sleep, day or night. Poor Blanche must keep charge of it."

The queen spoke. "My cousin and kinswoman, I think, will reject a marriage for my Robert." She sighed as she pulled off a glove once again. She took a grape and rolled it between her fingers. "What am I to do with the poor man? Perhaps I'll have to marry him." She laughed, and everyone laughed with her. "Blanche, what say you, shall I ever marry?"

Blanche Parry smiled as she petted the little creature in her lap. Its fur shone like velvet. "Your Majesty, I've told you many a time that's the one thing I shall never predict."

"Oh, how you tease me," the queen said as she turned her eyes on me. "But I do think perhaps I'd rather be a beggar woman and poor than a queen and married." She clapped her hands and Blanche handed the queen the musk cat, who immediately nipped at her gloved hand. "Tell me, Katherine . . . oh, I shall have to think of a nickname for you. I'm very fond of a nickname. We've too many Katherines now, don't we? Most named for queens, some good, some bad. So pray tell, what do you think makes a man handsome?"

I looked around the room, for indeed there were many Katherines, but the queen was looking at me. I blushed. "Handsome. Hmmmm. Why, I think perhaps his eyes, and a goodly head of hair, for a man without any, well, you know . . ." It was something Grace had said, although I didn't have a whit of what it meant. It was quiet a good moment and my heart dropped. Then Elizabeth burst out laughing, followed by her senior ladies.

"My, you are a fresh thing, aren't you? You are delightful! And you are right, my dear. There is nothing more important than the eyes." Holding tight to Day, she patted the other corner of her cushion. I sat frozen where I was until Dorothy nudged me.

I rose and joined the queen. She was so close. Aah. So close I could almost feel her warmth, and her musk cat stared at me with eyes like little black beads. "Tell me, my sweet," she began. "What kind of eyes attract you?" I thought of Rafael's sky blue eyes and then Christian's honey eyes. "Why, look at her, her cheeks shall match her hair in a moment. We'll not get another word from her, will we now?" The queen laughed and Day reached to nip at me before she pulled him back. "She's keeping a secret from us. Blanche, come read her hand and tell us what it is, or who it is." And although she said it with great merriment, her eyes were on me sharply like the little beast upon her lap.

I pulled my hands from my lap slowly, ever so slowly, and hid them down at my sides. Blanche, laughing, got up from her cushion and came over to me. She was much older than the other ladies, although her face was unlined and kindly. And she had the largest eyes I had ever seen. Everyone laughed again when she had to tug to retrieve one of my hands.

"My, oh my, dear one, I am not Day; I shall not bite

you," she said, her voice low and soft. Finally I relaxed my arm and Blanche lifted my hand up, close to her face. She stared at it a good long time. Then she looked at me, and her smile vanished.

"Tell us," the queen said, laughing. "Break the suspense!"

"She does not know her own heart," Blanche proclaimed. "But she may have happiness one day if she is wise." She forced a smile upon her face, stood up, and walked away.

"Fa!" The queen frowned. "That could be any of us now, couldn't it? But it is only the lucky who are wise." She took my hand in hers and turned it over, running her gloved finger over the lines of my palm. "I see you shall have twelve babies like my good Catherine Carey." Everyone laughed, and I saw the queen was just jesting with me, so I smiled too. Ha. Twelve children. I had no plans for having any.

"I shall have none," I found myself proclaiming.

"Why, whoever has put such silly notions in your head." She smiled and Day seemed to smile with her, its little teeth sharp and white.

"I think one has to have had a good mother to be a good mother." It was something Grace had said often, since her own sweet mother had died young and she had been raised motherless. The queen dropped my hand. The room was silent. And then I realized. The queen's own mother, Anne Boleyn, had been beheaded.

"Well now, I was very lucky," the queen said finally, after an endless silence. "For I had my good Katherines, I did. Kat Ashley," she said, nodding to her across the room, "and the most loving of mothers, my good mother Katherine Parr. The only one of my ghastly stepmothers to befriend me."

Katherine Parr. The queen who died at Sudeley. "I carry her words with me at all times," the queen continued. She let Day loose and the ferret ran across the room and curled itself on Blanche Parry's lap. "No one else have I ever held in higher esteem." She lifted the prayer book that was chained to her kirtle and kissed it. "Except for perhaps my father." Her face seemed to fall. "But no more talk of the dreary past. Tell me a story of the country," she said, looking at me. "A tale of fairies and beasties." Everyone laughed. "I can't get anything out of my sweet Ipollyta. Her past is still quite a mystery. And everyone knows a fool's greatest talent is the telling of tales."

"Oh, but I am saving my voice, my fair queen," Ipollyta said, her voice high and melodious, like a songbird. "For when I sing to you."

"How I do treasure your voice," the queen said to her. "You are right, dear one. You must give me a song tonight. Something new."

Then she turned to me. "A story. From you I have asked for a story."

I closed my eyes a moment. "A fairy . . ." I stuttered. "A fairy came upon a village on a cold revel night not a fortnight ago, and scared a band of minstrels and then thiefed her way into a cottage, stole a child's golden dress spun of gold, and then climbed into bed."

Ipollyta leaned back and looked at me, her eyes barely blinking, like a rat discovered in the rum roll.

"Whose bed?" The queen laughed. "Was it a man's?" And all the ladies, even the young maids, tittered.

"Why, yes," I exclaimed. "And the next morning the man woke up with the tail of a pig and the ears of a jackass."

"Why, I guess the fairy was not well-served," the queen responded, and everyone burst into laughter. "Wondrous," she said suddenly as she pulled a glove off and examined the stitching. "I want you to stitch me wondrous things—beautiful beasts and exotic flowers. Things that no other queen or noble has, prettier than anything my sweet cousin, Mary of the Scots, shall ever own. And you shall attend Dorothy in the wardrobe store, where you'll quickly learn my taste. I should have you installed in my Wardrobe of Robes, but I think your allure would cause great havoc and I'd have a riot on my hands." The ladies nodded to me. All but Blanche Parry, the reader of palms, who watched me with a firm, closed mouth, and puzzled eyes, like a child who's seen her reflection in the mill pond for the first time.

Later, as Dorothy and I walked down a great hall back to my room, Blanche Parry appeared from around a corner. In her arms she held several leather-bound books, their bindings the likes of which I've never seen before, nothing like the simple books Grace had taught us from. "I shall have a word with her, please," she said, her thin lips pursed. Dorothy looked between the two of us and walked away, glancing back over her shoulder suspiciously.

Blanche handed me the great books and I nearly dropped them, they were so heavy. "Have a care, love." And I realized she had the lilt of the Welsh. "These are from the queen's own library. You will find in them wondrous things she speaks of. The things she wants you to embroider. There's *Cosmographia*—Munster's maps of the world with great sea monsters. And Gesner's *Historia*

Animalium—every animal known, and a book of every known herb and plant—although I suspect you'd find excellent examples in the queen's garden. And there's the last—a book of emblems. The queen is very fond of her emblems. Do you think you are up to the task?"

I quickly nodded.

"You know, some think Katherine Ashley has been with Elizabeth the longest," Blanche began as I ran my finger over the beautiful raised lettering of *Cosmographia*. I looked at her when she paused. "But it's me who was there from the beginning, and it's me who will outlast them all. I remember seeing that sweet, redheaded babe in the arms of her mother. Her mother did love her so, she did, in the few short years they had together. It's been a difficult life, no matter the brave, merry face the queen gives us all. And for now, my queen is happy, and I'll not see anyone ruin her happiness. Am I being clear?"

"As though I, a mere girl from the country, could. I love the queen. I always have," I responded as I held the books to my chest. God's me, they were treasures, treasures I had wished my whole life for.

"It's taken less to bring a monarch down," Blanche responded icily. I stood staring at her, her large eyes unreadable. "Why have you come here?" she continued. "What do you want from the queen?"

"Why, as you said," I told her, my head held high, "I do not know my own heart."

She blinked several times, and I saw, despite her forthrightness, that she was kind. "I believe you," she said. "But that is why I worry for my queen. For you possess the ability to love and hate with equal passion, just as the queen does. And who knows what ill winds may turn your heart."

She gave me one final inspection and said, "I don't suppose a girl from the country can read, can she?"

"I can a little," I told her, in half truth.

"Just as I thought. I'm in charge of the queen's jewels, her papers, and most importantly, her library. You may visit me sometime if you wish." She started to walk away. "And one last thing. Do not cross Mrs. Ashley in any way."

I nodded and called after her, "I hold the queen in great admiration. I do not seek anything of her." Once again, a half truth, but it did not matter, for she had already seen the full truth in my palm.

The gravity of the situation has finally settled on my poor queen. Just yesterday she found the two, the admiral and the princess, embracing in the garden under the same peach tree where I was seduced, and the princess tickling his neck, no less, as they kissed. The queen won't come out of her room, even though my lord pounds on her door and the sound reverberates through the entire house. Everyone is on edge; even Jane the fool does not seem my friend anymore. Yesterday as I came down a hall, I perchanced to see the admiral standing outside his wife's door yet again. The door opened and a young groom, Porfirio (the Handsome, we maids call him), walked out innocently enough with a bucket and broom, but the admiral noticed his shirt in disarray, and there ensued quite a commotion with much yelling and screaming between husband and wife, with him proclaiming he shall have them both, Katherine and

Elizabeth, meaning the queen and the young princess, and that he was the master, no matter if she be a former queen or not. Later I heard from one of her maids that the queen unbuttoned the poor groom's shirt just before he left, knowing her husband would see, and the fool had no idea what she was about. Aye, it was a rash thing she did, aye, it was. For Porfirio's been sacked and yet the admiral still toys with the princess. The queen has taken to her bed because of the upset. I tend to her with my potions, and she is much relieved. My own babe is beginning to show and the queen, being in like manner, guessed my shame. I told her it was Porfirio who brought me down, as he seemed an easy blame, being gone and unable to defend himself. She smiled but a little and said I could stay on, that she could not live without me.

CHAPTER 17

icholas Pigeon was outside my chamber, looking very handsome in a fawn-colored silk jerkin with embroidered guards of Belgian lace. "I've been waiting for you," he said, smiling that dazzling smile. He held out a bundle of beautiful peach-colored silk. I set the books down and took the bundle from him. "I've a warrant for a new gown. You are to be paid ten shillings, and you may embroider what you wish on the fabric. The queen wants to be surprised. Walter Fyshe, the queen's tailor, will complete the gown at the Wardrobe of Robes after you have finished. And if you are in need of fine threads or Spanish needles, you may ask and they will be sent to you."

I stared at the beautiful fabric. My hands itched to

hold a needle, Spanish or no. I looked up at Nicholas and found that he was staring at me, really staring. I stared back. "I do not need to be paid," I said finally, my eyes never leaving his. "If I had to I would spin cloths of gold from gillyflowers for the queen."

Nicholas laughed heartily, and the sound carried down the long hall. "Everyone's paid. That's how the court works. But if you like, I can mark it in the lists as a gift. For the queen is very fond of her gifts. Indeed she is."

"Yes," I said. "A gift." We stood still staring at each other. "The queen spoke of the Wardrobe of Robes. She said I would cause great havoc if I was housed there. Why would she say such a thing? I would be lost in heaven if I could work there. What is it like?"

"What?" He laughed. "I'm sorry; I was lost in your beautiful green eyes."

"The Wardrobe of Robes," I repeated, my ears aflame.

"Full of randy men. The queen is correct in her assessment. You would cause great distraction. I myself wouldn't get any work done."

"But what is it truly like?" I asked, ignoring his comment. "Is it like a great treasure chest?"

He laughed. "Indeed. A treasure chest. Historical

robes, the most beautiful gowns in the world. The best craftsmen, too. Tailors, embroiderers, glovers, hatmakers—anything you can imagine is made there."

"Oh, but I would give anything to see it. Where is it?"

He laughed. "Near the wharf. But it's truly not a place for the likes of you. It's quite a hardscrabble workplace."

"I'm used to hardscrabble. I promise, I would find a quiet corner and you would not hear aye or nay from me."

"There are hardly any women, just the silk women, and they are ugly hags. But perhaps your maid could brighten our work. Did you not say she helps with the spools?"

"Perhaps," I said, my heart sinking, wondering how Anna fared the day.

"And the queen's best embroiderers, David Smith and William Middleton, I tell you, are crying over their needles with the news of this warrant. Not very pleased, I say. But what I would give to see their faces if I did smuggle you in. Exactly what would you do for me?" He grinned. "Perhaps a sweet kiss?" God's me, he was charming.

I glanced down at his lips and involuntarily licked mine. I looked away, blushing. Why had Christian, lying at the base of the pear tree that awful night, suddenly appeared before my eyes?

"I'm sorry," he said with all sincerity. "I was too forward." He cleared his throat.

I turned away and bit my tongue.

"You will be helping with the queen's gowns at the store here. She always maintains a couple score nearby. Several of her ladies are in charge of keeping them aired. Dorothy Broadbelt, I believe, is one. When she's not secretly visiting John Abington under the stairs. He's a mere clerk of the kitchen, you know."

"And why would such news be of interest to you, Nicholas Pigeon?"

"I think it's quite funny, a girl of her stature with a boy like that. But it's mere gossip, and I shan't repeat it," he muttered, embarrassed. "There is a garden just below. Would you care to take a turn with me? One shouldn't linger in this hall, you know."

"Why not?" I asked. I held the precious bundle of cloth up to my chest.

"The ghosts of the dead queens." He smiled, raising his eyebrows.

"Ghosts?"

"Oh, it's all a bunch of tittle-tattle," he said, laughing.

"Just more gossip. Come on, come with me."

How I wanted to. I did. There was so much I wanted to ask him of court, the treasures of the Wardrobe, and most importantly, the queen. And he, indeed, seemed the sort more than willing to talk. I sighed. "I'm sorry," I said. "My maid is not feeling well today. I must see to her."

"Of course," he said, bowing, obviously disappointed. "Perhaps we shall see each other soon."

"Yes." I watched him walk down the long hall. I smiled as he held out his hand to stroke the tapestries that lined the wall. He turned the corner, and a cold chill crept up my arms. And then a tickle on my neck, as though someone from behind blew into my ear.

"Grace?" I called involuntarily.

I opened the door and threw myself in. Anna was nowhere to be seen. I set the bundle of fabric on the floor and turned back to retrieve the books. A servant was standing there.

"God's me, you scared me," I said.

"I'm Anne Twiste, the laundress, come for your dirties. Lawn and linen." I noticed that most of her teeth were gone. "What is it, miss?" she asked as I tried to catch my breath.

I poked my head past her and looked up and down the hall. It was empty. "Did you see someone, just now?" I asked.

"No, ma'am. Everyone's getting their hair done for the banquet tonight. Where is your maid? I came earlier for your things and she was here reading on the bed. Said I must not touch your bag; there was nothing that needed laundering. I didn't quite believe her, for I heard myself you two have just come from the country."

"I don't know where she is," I answered her, looking back over my shoulder. A note lay on the bed. "But are you sure you talked to my Anna? She doesn't read." I picked up the note and read her barely legible scribble. She'd been invited to Lady Ludmore's for the evening.

"Aye, I told myself it was indeed quite queer, a maid reading a journal," the laundress continued, "and so uppity I thought she were, not answering me at first, so enthralled she was in her reading. Then it came to me that she's deaf, deaf as a dead rat, is she not?"

I started to shut the door. "One more thing, if I may, miss," she said, stopping the door with her foot. "Tell her to stay away from my sweet Oliver. He's very much the tenderhearted sort, and his eyes are easily turned by a pretty girl."

"You will have no trouble from her, I assure you," I said.

"Yes, yes, I told myself the same thing I did," Anne Twiste said, and I realized I could count her teeth. She had but five. "For she's not long for this world, is she? I know of a potion, I do, for you see while I stir my great pots of cleaning, I have other pots going, you see. All kinds of cures. Anything for a coin."

"Are there ghosts in our hall?" I asked Dorothy Broadbelt as I sipped my wine at the banquet that evening. The banquet was in honor of a visiting courtier from Scotland, Sir James Melville. He'd been sent by Mary, Queen of Scots, to look over Robert Dudley, Queen Elizabeth's suggested bridegroom for her cousin. Strolling musicians moved between the long tables set up in the magnificent hall. The queen's table was raised on a small platform, and she called up her favorites one by one to sit with her. Currently she sat between Robert Dudley and Sir Melville, alternately turning her head and batting her eyes with great measure at each of them.

"Ghosts?" Dorothy laughed, her hearty, horsey laugh and I noticed a mark at the base of her neck. A love mark, Grace called them, when a man, like a dog, has nipped at a woman. "Not that I've ever heard of," she continued. "Who's been jesting with you? One of the maids said she saw you talking with a yeoman. I must warn you, alluring as you are, it's very dangerous at court. You don't want to be taken advantage of."

"It was only Nicholas Pigeon," I said as I watched the queen. Tonight she wore a French gown of tawny-colored satin. It was embroidered all over with tiny knots, clouds of gold, and furred along the cuffs with sable. Her hair was styled high in a heart shape around her head and I wondered if there were "rats" in there as Maisy had described. The queen touched Robert Dudley's cheek with her fan. James Melville frowned.

"Nicholas Pigeon?" Dorothy snorted. "Don't believe a word he says. He's the worst of the flirts and not the smartest sort, either. And lord's me, he's ambitious. And ambition and naïvety are an unlucky pair for a man at court, my papa says. But not for a woman. I shall do as I please, as long as I find a suitable husband. If Anne Russell can aim high, so shall I."

"I see," I said. "Nicholas has an equal opinion of you. He seems to think you have been visiting the kitchen." And who could blame her? The most wondrous dishes I'd ever seen lined our table. Roast beef, partridge, pheasants, salmon poached in rosemary, venison, artichokes, turnips, even a salad with beautiful violets that one could eat. I picked one up and twirled it around.

Dorothy blushed as red as the wine. "Why, he's lying, the fool. Flat lying. He used to pay me his addresses, you see. Jealous, he must be. I don't know any young men in any of the kitchens," she said, her hand rising to her neck. "Sometimes I'm sent there when the queen requests a sweet. But I don't even deign to look at any of them. Not one," she insisted as she bit into a strawberry that was heavily sugared and fashioned into a little goose.

"Well, I do have to say Nicholas Pigeon was right on one account. I did feel something. Something was there."

"Could have been Lady Mary Sidney, Dudley's sister," Dorothy said, lifting her goblet up high to be filled by a passing server. "She creeps about in the night."

"Why?"

"She used to be a senior lady of the bedchamber. But two years ago the queen came down with the pox and Lady Sidney nursed her, never leaving her side. She came down with the pox herself, of course. Disfigured, poor thing. Her own husband rejected her, as most men would. Lady Sidney spends most of the time in the country but occasionally she comes to court, at the queen's request. No one ever sees her, except the queen, who's quite loyal to those who have been good to her."

My hand flew up to my cheek, thinking of the poor poxed woman. Dorothy continued, "Your hair is awful tonight. I suggest you replace your maid." She sipped from her goblet as one of the musicians, playing his lute, passed behind her.

"No, I can't do that. She's very special to me," I said as I watched the queen, who was now presenting her hand to Melville.

"Do you know of Anne Twiste?" I took a slow sip of the hot wine. It tasted faintly of almonds, ginger, and something else—perhaps honey. It reminded me of a delicious drink Frances Pea made at revels for us when we were children. I closed my eyes. But why think of our vale when I was surrounded thus? Then I noticed Katherine Knevit and Mary Shelton across the table, skewering me with their eyes. They whispered to each other and I looked away.

"The laundress?" Dorothy continued. "Of course. Seek her for any female problem. Not that I have, I tell you. And Oliver Twiste, adorable! I'd go for him myself if I'd dare to sink so low." She burped.

"So tell me, Melville," the queen said now, projecting her voice. "Who has the lovelier hands? Me or your queen?"

Melville coughed. "Why, you, Your Majesty. You, of course."

The queen laughed merrily. "And who is taller?" She turned and stroked Dudley's chin.

Melville appeared to bite his lip. "Queen Mary, Your Majesty, is quite tall."

The queen frowned petulantly and rapped Melville on the head playfully.

"But you are lovelier," he stuttered.

The queen laughed. "Aye, so they do have wise men in Scotland, if not wise women."

"What is she about?" I whispered to Dorothy. "Does she really mean to marry Robert to her cousin?"

"Who knows," Dorothy said, watching, I now noticed, one of the servers intently. He was quite handsome, although short. His eyes never veered her way, and this seemed to vex her greatly. "One ambassador said the queen has a thousand little devils in her. For you see, she has all the ambassadors swinging on cords, she does. She's the craftiest woman you'll ever meet, and smart girls like us have much to learn from her." Still her eyes did not move from the server.

"Do you think she really loves him? Dudley?"

"Oh yes. We've all seen the two kissing, and more, although we do believe she intends to remain chaste. Although she recently gave him apartments next to hers. He's constantly entering, I hear, when she's not quite dressed. But I don't believe she'll ever marry him. He is just her horseman. And there is the stain of his wife's blood on his hands, you see, too. His poor wife, Amy, was found at the bottom of three steps with her neck broken. He was at court at the time, but the world believes his hand was in it."

"And what is so interesting, Dorothy Broadbelt, chattermouth? Hmm?" the queen called across from her table.

All eyes turned on us, and the handsome server dropped his tray. It clanged across the wooden floor.

Dorothy closed her eyes a moment and took a deep breath. "I was just telling Katherine how you have a thousand little angels inside you, Your Majesty."

"See what a petticoat buys me, Melville? Pretty words. Ah, I do like pretty words. Katherine, my pet," she called to me. "Come sit near me and tell me a story. You,

Melville, go sit with our Dorothy, who will fill your ear with much empty talk." Dorothy turned red. All eyes seemed to be on me as I rose slowly from my place.

When I sat down again she said, "And where is your handsome Spaniard?"

"I assure you he is not mine, Your Majesty," I said lowly as others strained to hear.

"Oh yes. You shall never have children, I believe were your words. And if that be so, I should advise you to never take a husband, for the two go hand in hand." She pushed the food around on her plate, seeming to eat very little. "But we are in like mind, are we not?" she continued. "I think I shall not marry either." Dudley dropped his gilt spoon. "Even so, tell your Spaniard to come to court. It's insulting for a lord to be in London and not pay his respects to me." She clapped her hands to the musicians to come to her. "Now, tell me, Spirit," and a strange cold shiver ran down to my toes, "for that's what I have decided to call you. Tell me a good tale."

The queen has finally chosen between two loves—that of her husband and that of her stepdaughter, the Princess Elizabeth. And alas, she has chosen her husband, her love blinding her to the depths of his true deception. The princess and her retinue are to leave at once, after Whitsuntide, and good riddance, for the princess is a cunning girl, the likes I've never seen. But it was her governess who pulled the strings like a Cheapside puppeteer on the whole sordid affair, I tell you. The queen, being the regal lady she is, continues a warm friendship with the princess, and not a cold word has been spoken between the two, although there is a strange undercurrent, a lingering of bad will, since both women know the truth of each other, as women oft do. It's men that are mysteries never to be solved. Today, before the princess climbed into her carriage, the queen slipped a small, gold ring on her finger, a ring she often wore, a gift from her own husband. And as the carriages pulled away, Agnes said to me, "And not a moment too soon, for I hear it be not long before a babe show itself beneath her kirtle." And I thought I should faint, so ill I myself was, and now Agnes has guessed my secret too, and swears she will not speak a word of it. Although she says she thinks she shall murder the admiral, who she rightly guessed was the father. I pray everyone's attention will turn to the Lady Jane Grey, who will come to us soon.

CHAPTER 18

nna was waiting for me when I returned to our chambers. She was standing at the window in her night shift, peering out into the dark night. I went over to her and put my hands on her shoulders.

I turned her chin to me. "Wren, I'm sorry I've neglected you." She turned her head and continued to look out the window. She pressed her forehead against the glass.

"I miss her, Kat," Anna said softly, looking back at me. "Can you believe that? My whole life, I think, I wished to be free, for someone to love me. And now that she's gone, I truly do miss her."

"You're missing home," I said. "Blackchurch Cottage and . . ." *Christian.* Perhaps that's whom she missed most. Did I miss him? I would not think of it.

I walked to the bed and sat down. Earlier in the day I'd pored through the books Blanche Parry had given me. Oh, indeed they were wondrous—full of engravings of creatures and things I'd never seen—sea monsters, and fish of the tropics, and lions and pagodas and exotic flowers. I'd already started a sketch for the queen's gown: a series of intertwined orchids amongst exotic creatures and birds, and in the middle a grand lion, with a golden-red flamed mane.

"Have you looked for her?" Anna asked as she glanced over my shoulder. She showed little interest in my drawing. When we were children she would pull the drawings from my hands, she was so excited.

I looked up so she could see my lips. "Who?"

She sighed. "Mrs. Eglionby," she replied. "But I suppose your head has already been turned by the riches of the court."

I laughed. "But of course it has, little Wren. I cannot even begin to tell you what I've seen. The Lady Wessex had on a brooch tonight in the shape of a ship, its hull a huge oblong-shaped pearl bigger than I've ever imagined. And the queen, you should have seen what the queen wore tonight. I've never beheld such workmanship."

Anna's attention returned to the window. "He's to come for you tonight. In the garden. He has something of importance to tell you," she said.

"Christian?" I asked. "You've heard from Christian?" My heart, to my surprise, was fluttering.

Anna frowned. "Lord Ludmore," she said. "Look. I see him by the rosebushes. He waits for you as we speak."

I walked to the window and peeked over her shoulder. Indeed. Someone was there.

A few moments later, walking quietly, keeping in the shadows, I climbed down the stairs. I crept out into the garden, hugging my arms. The smell of roses, the queen's favorite, lingered in the air. And then, just as I spotted a couple kissing behind a filbert tree, a hand reached out and pulled me farther into the darkness.

Before I could scream, he turned me toward him and put his finger to his mouth. "Shhh." Rafael. It was Rafael.

"What are you doing here?" I asked him.

"What are *you* doing here, a young maid unescorted in these gardens of passion?"

"Anna told me to come to you," I said, lifting my chin.

"It seems you didn't have to be much persuaded." He

smiled then like a wolf, his white teeth showing in the dark.

I pushed away from him, but he pulled me close and kissed me. It only lasted but a few seconds. And much to my own embarrassment, he was the first to pull away. We stood in the darkness staring at each other, so close, so very close.

"Why didn't you slap me?" he asked after a moment.

"I don't know," I said, thinking of what Blanche Parry had read in my palms. "Are you disappointed?"

"No," he said. His head dipped and he kissed me again.

"Is that it?" I asked, breaking away. "Is this why I'm here? For you to seduce me?"

"Yes," he responded.

"But Anna said it was something important," I said.

"Hmmm," he said. "Whatever it was, I've forgotten it now."

"Well, you can tell me the day after tomorrow," I said. "The queen wants to see you. You've insulted her by your absence. There's to be an outdoor amusement. And you are to come."

"Perhaps," he teased.

"We shall not lose you to the queen, shall we?" I asked.

"No," he said. "Rest assured I will not fall under *her* spell," he said. "Have you?"

"I adore her," I answered. "I always have, I think."

He pulled away, his face unreadable in the shadows. "Soon." And then he was gone. As I crept back to the palace, Dorothy Broadbelt appeared next to me on the path, leaves tangled in her hair. I pulled one out and handed it to her.

"Well, now," she said, pulling a rose petal from my own hair. She inhaled it languidly before handing it to me. "You are not so innocent either, are you?"

The next morning I found Anna had risen early and transferred my pattern expertly to the fabric.

"It will be beautiful," she said, her voice flat when I admired it. "The queen will be much pleased when you are finished."

"Yes," I answered, noticing for the first time an addition in the corner. A small wolf under a tree, actually very finely drawn with a determined hand. It added a mysterious edge to the work.

I looked up at her as she busied herself retrieving my needles and threads. She wouldn't meet my eyes.

"What message did Rafael have for you?" she asked

quietly after a moment. She watched my lips, waiting for my answer.

"I don't think there was a message," I answered, trying hard not to hide my smile. I instead bit my lip.

She rolled her eyes. "Is he pursuing you?" she asked.

"It seems so," I answered, taking a needle from her. I looked down at the fabric. The most logical beginning would be to stitch in the background first. Oh, but I was drawn to the lion. It was there I would start, on its beautiful mane.

"I'd have a care, Kat, I would. For I don't think he wants you," Anna said. My sweet Anna, never had an unkind word crossed her lips.

I ran my fingers over the soft fabric. I waited a minute before asking. "What do you mean?"

"Maisy was full of talk. Lady Ludmore is much changed since her son returned home. Seems the lady has been full in her cups by day and full of fear by night. Something about Lord Rafael and his demeanor has not set her at ease at all. Lady Ludmore told me herself that his eyes have changed, gone to the devil, and she fears he will do someone some great harm."

"Lady Ludmore is a strange woman," I said as I drew my first stitch. Oh, how I felt the exhilaration with the movement. I closed my eyes a moment. "And he's harmless," I continued. "A lost soul. There's no evil in being lost, only sadness."

"Are you so sure?"

I ignored her and continued to stitch, working around the lion's mane.

"Have you not thought of Christian and Uncle Godfrey?" she asked after a moment.

I set the needle down. "Of course! Of course I have," I said, over-loudly. Oh, but had I? As I should have?

"No, you haven't. Not if you've let another man in your arms."

I blushed as I poked the needle down into the fabric. "Did you watch us, Anna?" I asked.

"I didn't have to. I know," she said.

It was quiet a good long time. "I'm not welcome here," she said finally. "I feel trapped as though I'm in cage."

"Then come with me tomorrow to the entertainment. Please, Anna, I want you to come."

I couldn't help thinking of the little golden birds in the queen's birdcages. Dorothy told me they often died, so unhappy they were. Blanche Parry had to have them replaced quickly before the queen was aware.

"No, my place is not there."

"Your place is by my side," I said.

There was a tap on the door. Anna opened it. Nicholas Pigeon stood in the hallway wearing an impeccable green cloak over a silk doublet. He bowed deeply, and she blushed.

"And where have you been hiding?" he asked.

She didn't respond but stepped back as he walked into the room, looking her over.

"I have a delivery for you from the Wardrobe," he said, handing me a small pouch. I opened it and poured the contents into my hand. Jewels, tiny but perfect: rubies, emeralds, and pearls shimmering and translucent.

"For your design," he explained. "The queen is very fond of her jewels. These were removed from a former queen's gown, a gown that was not salvageable. Will they work?"

"Yes, oh yes," I answered as I ran my fingers over the jewels. The pearls could be attached to the flowers; the rubies would be perfect for the lion's eyes. I was not sure where the emeralds would go.

"I must be back to the Wardrobe." He bowed. "Shall I see you tomorrow at the entertainment?" He said this to the both of us.

"Yes, yes," I responded. "Of course." He bowed again,

then left us. Anna peered down at the jewels, her pale eyes reflecting their shimmers.

"Kat, your eyes have been turned. Have you not forgotten why you are here?" Anna asked. "You are supposed to ask of Mrs. Eglionby."

I looked over at her but before I could answer, the door opened again. It was Dorothy Broadbelt, dressed sumptuously in yellow, her face distressed. "The queen is having one of her nervous maladies. Quite indisposed she is. No one is to know, of course, but she wants her ladies nearby. Hurry. Hurry. Bring your stitching. No telling how long *this* one shall last."

Grace said once you can never trust a woman who doesn't meet your eyes, for this is how a woman truly shows herself. And when Katherine Ashley sought me out, making a point of sitting next to me on my cushion as I stitched with the other ladies in the privy chamber, she would not meet my eyes, no matter how amiable and sweet her way was.

"Why, it's lovely," she said of the small panel I worked on. I had just given the ladies a short instruction on couch stitching and they were all sitting, working their stitches on fine cambric and lawn, delicate items for the queen's underclothes. It was a dark-clouded day, the birdcages had been covered, the ladies' chatter quiet and subdued. Suddenly Blanche Parry was called into the queen's private bedchamber as two of the maids bustled out. Day, in a new jewel-studded collar, ran after her. Soon he was put out the door, and Katherine Knevit took him into her lap. The rest of us kept stitching. "Oh, but she does love pretty things," Mrs. Ashley continued. "Fastest way to the queen's heart. But where is the special gown you are to make for her?"

I'd left it behind in my room, carefully hidden. "It will be a surprise," I said.

"The queen is not fond of surprises; life has given her too many. Believe you me, she will pull it out of you. How long do you think it will take? She is not a patient woman."

"I'm thinking it will be done by the New Year," I responded. I wasn't sure myself. I'd never undertaken such an elaborate work.

"You'll still be here?" Mrs. Ashley asked, her thin, plucked eyebrows raised. She was what one would call a full-faced woman, yet chinless and thin-lipped, an unfortunate combination. As the queen's top gentlewoman, though, her livery and jewels were the finest at court. But

Dorothy had told me Mrs. Ashley did not have a friend among the ladies, for in Mrs. Ashley's heart there was room only for the queen. "Won't your family have need of you in the country?" she continued. "I believe you came from Gloucestershire or somewhere abouts."

"Yes, Gloucester," I responded, looking at her. But her eyes were now on the chamber door. I'd come to realize her eyes hardly wavered from Elizabeth, no matter if she be behind a door or not.

"What ails her so?" I asked, speaking softly as I pulled up another stitch.

"The queen?" Mrs. Ashley asked. "Oh, but she has always been a sweet, sensitive soul, her nerves always raw. And the crosses she's had to bear! I've borne them with her, I have, unbearable treacheries, some by the ones who loved her most. I'd do anything for her, anything. Even die for her." She glanced at me from behind her lashes. "So no family, my dear, back home? No family at all?" She pulled a knot on the chemise she was making for the queen.

"Just a few to speak of. I was lucky to be taken in by my aunt, Lady Ludmore."

"Your sleeves are lovely. You learned such beautiful work in the country?"

I nodded my head as I pulled up another stitch. Today I wore yet another of my creations, a russet silk gown, the sleeves peach with gold spangles and stitched flowers of pink carnations. The flowers were those I'd seen once growing wild near Blackchurch Cottage. Here they were called lover's pinks. "Yes, I was taught well," I answered.

"And your maid," Mrs. Ashley began. "I hear she's been as long with you practically as I've been with the queen."

"Yes, indeed, Anna is like family," I answered, wondering what question might be next. I looked at her, but still her eyes would not meet mine. Mary Shelton and Anne Windsour, working together on a piece of cambric, had their heads tilted just so, trying to catch our words. Suddenly Robert Dudley burst into the room, startling everyone. He stalked the length of the sitting room before any of the ladies could stop him, opened the door, and walked into the queen's private bedchamber.

Mrs. Ashley jumped up after him. "Out!"

"Out!" I heard the queen scream, and soon Robert Dudley stormed back through, his face purple as a plum above his white ruffed collar. Katherine Knevit snorted with laughter and Mrs. Ashley bade her be quiet. She sat down next to me again.

"The queen has always had troubles with love," she said, sighing. "Trouble seems to follow her around like a dark star. And believe me, I tell you, she is always innocent in the matter. Always. My good queen can do no wrong, that's for sure. She learned early on, poor thing, how a man can manipulate, seduce. Break one's heart. Learned a pretty lesson there she did. Could have cost her her head if it weren't for *my* sage advice." She sighed, looking back to the queen's door. "But here we go again." She waved her hand, exasperated. She'd long since forgotten her stitching. "They had a nasty row last night, they did. Seems he was quite jealous of her playful talk with James Melville, innocent as it was. And he doesn't want to sacrifice himself on the bed of that Scottish mare. The queen rightly put him in her place, and he apparently, in turn, had some unkind words for her."

"Does she love him?" I asked as Mary Howard came over with her own needlework and pointed to a line of stitches. I nodded my head in approval and she giggled and went back to her cushion. Anne Russell frowned at her and threw her own work down in exasperation.

"Of course," Mrs. Ashley continued in a low whisper. "He's one of the few men who have stood up to her, and secretly I think she likes it." She laughed, as one does who doesn't laugh often. "He's intelligent. Smart. Handsome. But she cannot marry him. He's beneath her. Sadly, there are some things a queen cannot have." Her eyes riveted to the queen's door. "And that's why she is now quite beside herself."

"I know a potion," I said quietly as I pulled up another stitch. "For nerves."

"A potion. And how would you know such a thing?" she asked, her head swiveling around and her eyes now meeting mine with great interest.

For Anna. Sometimes Grace had given Anna potions when her nerves had attacked. "Thyme, pig's tail, and digweed," I said quietly to myself.

"Dorothy," Mrs. Ashley softly called across the room. Dorothy put her stitching down and approached Mrs. Ashley, who whispered the ingredients to her. "Go to the kitchen, please and instruct someone to prepare this."

Dorothy's smile disappeared at mention of the kitchen. "Why, Mrs. Ashley," she began. "They don't dare make such a potion for fear if she take a turn, they will be worse for the blame."

"And how would you know the inner workings of the kitchen?" Mrs. Ashley asked, one eyebrow raised.

Dorothy shrugged. "Only what we all know, I assure you," she said and she went back to her stitching.

"The queen will never let her marry her young man," Mrs. Ashley commented, her voice low.

"Is it true the queen chooses husbands for her ladies?" I asked.

"Of course," Mrs. Ashley responded. "We are the closest to her in the whole wide world. It is only natural she should pick our husbands so there isn't a rat amongst us. Not that one doesn't sneak in once in a while. Oh, I've prattled on too long, one of my great faults, I do have to say. So why don't you, dear girl, tell me more of your life in the country."

The queen's door opened. "She's quite distressed," Blanche Parry said to Mrs. Ashley. "I fear for her, I do. She's asking for you."

"I think I know where I can get my potion," I said quietly after Blanche had returned to the room.

"Well then, get it, by all means."

"One more thing," I said as Mrs. Ashley rose, a look of a soldier going into battle on her face. "Have you ever heard of a Mrs. Eglionby?"

She turned her head briefly toward me, her mouth gently falling open. Then she looked back toward the queen's door. "No, never, never in my life have I heard that name."

I gathered some linens in our room. Anna, as was becoming usual, was nowhere to be found. I came across Dorothy Broadbelt in the hall, fetching a blanket for the queen. "Do you know where I may find the laundress?" I asked.

She narrowed her eyes. "Why shouldn't your maid take care of such matters?"

"She's indisposed," I lied.

"She always seems indisposed now, doesn't she? I can't tarry," she said, walking on down the hall. But over her shoulder she said, "Below the stairs beyond the kitchen. Mind no one sees you, for they'll think you have secret maladies."

I wound my way through several long corridors, and down one set of creaky stairs, asking directions at least twice before I finally found the room. A dark cavity it was, like a dark, dank dungeon. Mrs. Twiste stood before two great pots, stirring with a long stick. "Leave it there," she nodded to me without looking up. Farther back in the gloom were two figures laughing as they worked at a long trestle table.

It took a moment to realize it was my Anna with a

young man with curly locks. He looked up at me and I started, so like Christian he was. Anna glanced up slowly, then lowered her eyes.

"Oh, it be you," Mrs. Twiste said as she pulled the long stick out of a pot, a mound of wash wound around it. She flopped it down on the table with a big grunt. "And why would a fine lady the likes of you be down in my lair?" She laughed.

"What are you doing down here?" I mouthed to Anna. She pretended not to see me. The young man next to her caught my eye. I saw now, he was no Christian. He had the devil spark in his eyes. And then I saw a movement behind him, a large cow-faced boy in a red tattered jacket sitting on a stool holding a broom.

"Your sister is assisting me Oliver, that's all," Anne Twiste said. "She needs a little happiness and she gets it here."

My head swung away from Anna back to Anne Twiste. Our eyes met. She knew. She knew Anna was not my maid. And I knew that Anna had not told her. She would never betray me. "She shall not come back. It's unseemly," I said.

"Hmmmph," she snorted. "I think she has more will than you know." She started to lay the garments out one by one. She sighed, the deep sigh of one who has seen too much of the world. "Nay, tell me. What is your need? A babe in the womb? Warts? A herb for your bad breath like that Mary Ratcliff."

"Ratlip." Oliver laughed, and the other boy joined in. I couldn't keep my eyes off him, so strange he looked.

"That be George the sweeper," Mrs. Twiste said, seeing my look. "He means no harm. I found him meself as a baby, left in a basket on the wharf. Poor thing, and I nursed him myself, I did. But he disappears, my boy, usually to the wharf, looking for his real mama, I suppose. And he has eyes for the maids, he do, but they all spurn him, the wenches, and make fun of his queer looks, they do."

"I need you to make a potion for one of the ladies," I said, pulling my eyes away from George the sweeper. Indeed, there was something about him, something hell-born. Perhaps his mother had seen it the moment he was birthed.

"Aye, now you are talking. It'd be my pleasure. But it will cost you a pretty coin."

"I need digweed, thyme, and pig's tail."

"Oliver." She tilted her head. "Go to the market for me." He brushed past me, looking me over, a small grin tilted on his lips.

As we sat stitching for the nursery today, the queen proclaimed her "little knave" must know the work we did for him, for he stirs within her. She bade me come feel, and I reluctantly did so, laying my hand on her belly as it kicked and turned. She laughed, for she finds as much joy in the upcoming birth as I find fear in mine. I have dreamed I shall die and the babe with me, and I tell you I welcome it, as it will be a release from my miseries. I am like a ghost, I am with no home above or below the earth, waiting for the end. The admiral looks straight through me when we pass as though he never knew me, the blackguard. But thank God he hasn't turned his attentions on Lady Jane Grey, who is merely a sweet but whey-faced little child who always has her big nose in a book. Poor thing, for she greatly admires the admiral. And he in turn has named her godmother of the babe to be. And now with the princess gone and me invisible, he's turned his attentions on his wife and the babe. Agnes says a cow doesn't change its spots, and he's probably up to no good somewhere. But alas, we've heard he's spent a fortune preparing a castle in the country for his wife and baby, and we are to leave for this place soon, where she may have a safe and peaceful birth, away from the intrigues and summer plagues of London.

CHAPTER 19

hen I walked into the queen's chamber, Ipollyta was sitting next to the queen's head, like a little harpy bird on a hedge. She gently stroked the queen's temples, chanting some sort of incantation. The queen was still in her linen nightgown, with a quilted silk jacket over it. She lay in a great wooden canopied bed, her hair, natural and full, fanned out on the pillow like a setting sun. The aroma from a pomander—benjamin, sweet cinnamon, civet, and cloves—hung in the air. The queen's eyes opened and lit upon the window. "Someone pull the drapes," she murmured in a low voice, unrecognizable. "I can see it, how it vexes me always, even in the day, smiling at me like the devil." But then she turned her head and saw me.

"Ah, it's my Spirit. I hear you are at work on my new gown. Bring it here. It will cheer me." There were cushioned beds on the rushed floor where her senior ladies slept sometimes, and a delicate dressing table in a corner. On it were several small jewel caskets and a looking glass, and a collection of lidded pots. Dorothy had told me sometimes the queen's ladies painted her face with lead and vinegar to cover her pox marks.

"Yes," I told her. "But I've only just started, and I'd like it to be a surprise, if I may."

She shut her eyes and frowned. "Bah, surprises. They are hardly ever good."

I sat down on the bed, at her feet, holding her potion carefully in my hands. "I think you shall be very pleased. It will be my finest work ever, I promise. But it might take me a good while." I held the potion to her.

"Shall it?" she said softly as she lifted up and drank from it. "And then what will you do when you are finished?"

"Whatever you want of me," I said, "Your Majesty." I took the goblet from her and set it on a table next to her bed.

"Stay with me," she said, taking my hand. "You soothe me." She motioned impatiently for Ipollyta to stop rubbing her temples. Ipollyta got off the bed and left the room.

"Everyone betrays me," the queen moaned in that eerie voice from before, her hand covering her eyes. "Everyone. Cannot I trust anyone?" She gripped my hand and pulled me closer. "Look at me, Spirit."

I tried to pull away, but she held firm. "Can I trust you?"

I looked her straight in the eye, but could not answer. Our eyes locked, and a shiver went down my back.

"Yes," she said after a moment, softening. "I can trust you. Eyes never lie, Spirit." She sighed, pulling her hand from mine. "Tell me another tale. One of young love and happy kisses."

I found indeed I could not lie, not to her, and what I said caught me by surprise. "I think I may have loved once, perhaps, but the life he offered was beneath me. He was a shepherd," I told her.

"Ah, a country lad. Was he handsome?" she turned to me.

"Yes, very," I said, lowering my eyes.

"Gallant?"

"Indeed," I said, trying to hide.

"Oh, how I love a good romantic tale. If I can't have it,

I only truly wish for it for others. As long as I approve, of course. So tell me, Spirit, why are you here and not with your shepherd? Let me guess, the noble Spaniard turned your eye and you came to London in search of him."

I didn't answer. She reached up and tilted my chin to her, and something strange within me turned as she searched my eyes. "Well," she said after a moment, smiling. "You are with me. And here you shall stay. For I don't easily let go of those that are dear to me, as you shall soon know. I am much cheered," she said, starting to sit up. "Where are my birds? And my beloved Day! Someone fetch Robert. Eyes, Eyes, where are you!" she called. Not long after, he rushed in, as though he had barely stepped out of the room. I stood up and backed away. And it was as though I wasn't there. They embraced and kissed, both tearful, murmuring sweet nothings. They loved each other. They truly did.

The next morning Dorothy took me to the queen's store to select a gown for the outdoor feast. Her store was currently in the Tower, where most of the queen's jewels were also, in the Jewel House. My stomach fluttered with anticipation as we walked up the stairs. Dorothy explained that sometimes the store was moved when the queen went on progress or to another palace and it took dozens of yeoman, great leather trunks, and weeks of planning. "Edmund Pigeon stands there with the list, and if anything gets by him without him marking it down, his face turns beet red and he stomps his feet like a child."

"Who's Edmund? Wouldn't that be Nicholas's job as Clerk of the Wardrobe of Robes?" I asked as we continued up the stairs.

Dorothy stopped and looked at me. "Nicholas. What's the little liar been telling you?" She laughed. "Edmund is his father, Clerk of the Wardrobe of Robes; Nicholas is his assistant. Someday, perhaps, he shall inherit his father's position. Someday."

"Why would he lie to me?" I asked as we walked past the guards into the store. It was a circular room the entire floor of the Tower. It was lit by two small arched windows and a low fire. A young maid walked from the back of the room. She stopped and bowed nervously. She sat down in a chair by the fire, her face lowered. My eyes adjusted to the light and I saw that there were many gowns hung on forms, others draped over rods, and stacks of boxes and trunks neatly organized. Rush mats were strewn upon the floor, and there were several carved oak chairs about the room. On a long table was a parchment book—records, perhaps? There was the most sweet smell, like crushed roses and lily water. I inhaled the aroma as my eyes took in with wonder what was before me.

"Oh, who knows. He's very ambitious," Dorothy continued. "He means to marry one of us, and I tell you, as handsome as he is, he'll probably hit his mark. That wasn't, by chance, who you were visiting with in the garden last night, was it?"

"No, I was simply smelling the roses, as you were," I said, smiling.

"Once a week gowns are aired from the trunks and alternated," Dorothy explained as she lifted one off a rod and shook it. "We sprinkle sweet powders, too, to keep them from smelling. The tower is quite full of odors and long-ago ills, I tell you. The queen won't come here; as you know, it holds many unhappy memories.

"This be just a small part of her wardrobe," she continued. "Every other week or so she asks for certain gowns to be brought. That's part of Nicholas's job—to bring them to the palace and mark them in the lists.

The queen possesses a great memory; she can name all her gowns, and she has nearly two hundred. And over a hundred each of kirtles, foreparts, mantles, petticoats, cloaks, several score of jeweled fans . . ."

"Two hundred gowns?" I interrupted, astonished. I walked up to a gorgeous court gown that was hanging on a form, lightly touching the dark plum damask and ruched silk. The stitching was done diamond-wise, couched in gold thread, and set inside the diamond shapes were tiny pearled half-moons. I pulled the fabric closer to me. *Why, miss, you have a mark, a perfect half-moon.*

"That's Italian," Dorothy told me as I dropped the fabric. "She doesn't like that one for some reason or another—one never knows with the queen. That one is French," she said, nodding to another gorgeous square-bodiced gown of dark green. "And there are plenty more in the trunks—fans, gloves, hats, cloaks. The list is there." She nodded to the long table. " Everything must be accounted for. At any given time her tailors might be working on three or more new gowns for her, or reworking several old ones. And of course, there's the one you are sewing in secret." She winked at me. "You shall show me, won't you?"

I ignored her. I was standing in front of the black

and white harlequined gown the queen had worn the night of the masque. "Black. The queen's favorite color along with white," explained Dorothy. "It sets off her jewelry, you see. The white symbolizes her chastity, and the black her sincerity."

The maid by the fire giggled.

"Hush!" Dorothy admonished. "She must be new and untrained," she said to me. Then she pulled me farther into the dresses. "Now let's see, the queen wants to be very fetching for Sir Melville this afternoon."

I couldn't believe my ears. Hadn't I just seen her crying and wretched over Robert Dudley? Dorothy glanced at my face. "She's only trying to impress Sir Melville so he'll send a glowing report back to Mary, Queen of Scots. But she gets double her pleasure in it all, for the jealousy she causes poor Robert." She snorted. "Watch carefully; you can learn a thing or two from her."

"I think I already have," I said.

"But it's a dangerous game, I tell you, fishing for men's souls. It rises passions in them they cannot control. Vain doltheads most of them are." She fingered a gown, stroking the fine cut velvet, then moved on to another.

I lifted yet another one, examining the detail of

embroidered dragonflies and pansies. The dragonfly's wings were not quite correct. Whoever had stitched them had never sat by a country pond on a hot summer day. "Tell me, Dorothy, have you ever heard of a Mrs. Eglionby at court?" I asked casually. "My late mother said to ask of her."

"No, I can't say that I have," she responded as she pulled out a jersey petticoat and held it in front of her.

But the maid near the fire spoke out. "I used to know of a Mrs. Eglionby!"

My head spun around as Dorothy said, "Hush and mind your business."

I dropped the gown and walked over. "You did?" I whispered low.

"Not me, but me mother. My mother used to be in the service of Catherine Willoughby, the Duchess of Suffolk, she did." She pulled up a stitch from her sewing.

"Well then, who was Mrs. Eglionby?" I asked. "Was she also in the service of the duchess?"

"No, I believe she was the governess of some ward of the duchess's. A baby."

"A baby?" I whispered.

"I believe the babe died, though, and Mrs. Eglionby

moved on. Crusty old bat she was, me mother said."

"Where is your mother now?" I kept my voice low.

"Why, she be still with the duchess in the country at Grimsthorpe. The duchess does not come to court anymore. She never got over the loss of her two own sons who died. And she married one of her grooms. Those days are over for her."

"If I were to get a note to you, do you think you could send it to your mother?"

"If I could have a coin or two I could, I suppose."

"And your name?"

"Iris, me name is Iris."

"What are you two mumbling about over there?" Dorothy called as she walked over to us.

She was holding up one of the queen's court gowns, a white satin. She giggled and put her finger to her lip, then held up a fan and posed. "Do I look like a queen?" she asked.

"Very much so," I said. She looked beautiful. She could probably have her pick of suitors, yet she had fallen for a kitchen boy. She opened a trunk and started pulling gowns out. "This one was refurbished from one of her mother's. She can't stand to see it, but she can't stand to part with it either. These gowns all cost a fortune.

They are considered part of her treasury, so worthy they are."

"Does she ever speak of her, her mother?" I asked as I came closer and peered over her shoulder.

"No, poor thing," Dorothy said. "I think she has very little memory of her; she was only three when it happened. Beheaded. Right in the courtyard here. She considers Queen Katherine Parr her true mother, although there was some falling-out between the two at some point. Pure gossip, and the queen never forgave her stepmother for thinking so ill of her. Katherine Ashley knows the whole sordid tale. Chompdown, us maids have nicknamed her, for her name was Champedowne before she married and she has a loose tongue. Prod her with some wine and it will all come tumbling out, although she's been told not to speak of it. Not the wisest one, she is. She spent months locked up here in the Tower, she did, Mrs. Ashley, for her role in the whole affair." Dorothy kept searching through the gowns in the trunk and finally drew out a lovely crimson damask, its flowers and curlicued vines pin-tuckered and spangled with gold beads.

"This will do," Dorothy said, holding the gown up to her chest. "It's alluring, don't you think?"

"Yes indeed," I said, mesmerized by the flame red.

"Try it on, silly," she urged.

"But won't we get in trouble?" I asked.

"Bah." She laughed. "She won't tell," she said, nodding back toward the fire. I peered over the top of the trunk and saw that Iris had disappeared.

"Here. I'll assist you." She helped me out of my own gown and into the red damask. "Now *you* are alluring. If your rose garden admirer could see you now!" She handed me a fan. "My, aren't we the fine ladies," she said with a giggle. But I was suddenly dizzy as images of half-moons and dragonflies flashed through my mind. I glanced back toward the fire. Would Iris find Mrs. Eglionby?

Dorothy pulled my arm. "Come! Come! This way!" she said. "There's a mirror." I followed her. We stood side by side. And then she stepped away so I could peer at myself. I looked regal. Regal indeed.

You can imagine my horror when I learned the country home the admiral was taking us to was Sudeley Castle, the very castle that looms above my father's land. I've kept myself hidden among the stone walls, for I intend for my father never to lay eyes on me again. But one day, not long after we arrived, I was sent out to the fields to gather bitterweed, for my queen was very sickly again, the babe kicking her innards and causing much mischief in these late months. After I had found my herb and picked it, I stood up and locked eyes with my very own brother, Godfrey, not but a hundred yards away. And in that long silent moment, I understood he had known about Papa, and was sorry for it. But by his knowing, and not doing anything, he had betrayed me in the worst way of all. I nodded my head, pulled my cloak tighter, and turned back to the castle. I knew he would not tell, for he would not betray me again. And I heaved a great sigh of relief, until I saw Jane the fool watching me from an upper window.

CHAPTER 20

here was a gift for me when we went back to my room. "Nicholas Pigeon brought it earlier," Anna said as I unwrapped it. It was a fan with a ruby-tipped handle, as beautiful as the ones Dorothy and I had played with in the queen's store. A note read, "For my Spirit, who heals me. Much love, Elizabeth."

"It's from the queen," I said as I fanned myself.

"Of course," Anna said. "There's already been much talk of your sudden closeness with the queen. Where you are from. Who you may be. They say the queen is bewitched by you." She was annoyed, her words jumpy, and it took me a moment to decipher what she said.

"And where would you hear such talk?" I asked her,

irritated. I put the fan down and picked up the queen's gown. I sat and studied the lion. "In the laundry?"

"There is talk low and high of you."

I started stitching. "Oh Anna, people always talk of me."

"But you always cared before. You act like you've no care in the world now."

"I never cared. You know it. And how about you? With that mop-headed fool Oliver Twiste." I threaded one of the Spanish needles I'd received from the Wardrobe.

"He looks at me. He makes me laugh. I deserve a little happiness, do I not?"

"His own mother talks ill of him. Have a care, Anna."

"Do you not think that I deserve love someday?"

"Not in the laundry," I said.

"It's those who are high and mighty who have the farthest to fall. You play with a match that burns on both ends, you do." She straightened my fabric out, kneeling down before me. I rolled my eyes.

"I don't know what you speak of," I said. I plunged the needle in the fabric.

"That Nicholas. I don't trust him, Kat," she said. "No matter how amiable and gallant he acts. You should be wary. And Lord Ludmore. Something deep and dark abides in him. If you look into his eyes, there is nothing there."

I laughed. "Why, Anna, you sound just like Grace."

"Grace was right. No one can be trusted."

"The gossips are saying you must be the queen's long-lost daughter," Blanche Parry said with a little smile as she handed me a marzipan. Made of sugar, it was sculpted like a perfect miniature pear. I held it up a moment, spinning it with my fingers. I popped it into my mouth, where it quickly melted.

"Why would they say such a thing?" I asked, leaning back. We sat under some filbert trees, near the banks of the Thames.

The queen and Robert Dudley floated nearby on her barge, lounging back on golden silk cushions and laughing loudly. Sir James Melville moped in a smaller barge, Anne Windsour feeding him a sugared plum. Other couriers lounged under little pavilions built for the occasion that were decorated with birch branches and flowers from the surrounding fields—roses, gilly-flowers, lavender, and marigold. The queen's servants strewed fragrant herbs along pathways and circulated with trays laden with delicacies—jellies in the shapes of fanciful birds and candied comfits. A warm sweet wine from Anjou was being served, and I slowly sipped it from my goblet.

"Because she's shown you such marked attention. And you do favor each other in many ways, by looks and by temperament." Blanche wore an underdress of russet silk edged in gold beneath her black livery. I wore my gown of carnation silk, stitched with friars' knots and roses, grapes, and leaves intertwined in branches of Venice gold.

I laughed as I ate a sweet wafer. "But I'm too old to be her daughter. Aren't I?"

"A love child can come at any time," Blanche said, her smile fading. "There were rumors once of a child. When the queen was but fifteen and a princess. Ah, here is the handsome Nicholas Pigeon."

I shielded my eyes from the glare of the sun and stared at him. I looked away as he sat down next to me on the linen Blanche and I shared.

"How is the cloak coming, my gift for the queen?" Blanche asked him.

"Soon, it will be ready soon," he said. "Excellent work takes time, does it not, Katherine?" When I did not reply he continued. "I hear your design has monstrous and exotic creatures you've found in a book of evil. Everyone is quite intrigued. The rumors are flying about the Wardrobe. And some say you are a temptress with extraordinary stitching powers bought from the devil. What say you, Blanche Parry, reader of palms? Will the queen like her surprise, or will she be repulsed and have poor Kat thrown in the Tower?"

I frowned. I wasn't sure if he was teasing me or if there truly were such wicked rumors of me.

"Well, as to the book you refer to I can say I've seen it myself and it bears no evil within. And as to the rest, I do believe only the future will tell. Oh, what could Anne want?" Even though Kat Ashley was "Mother of the Maids," it was Blanche who the maids sought, one after another it seemed, for all their worries big and small. Blanche stood up, nodded briefly, and walked away.

I had yet to look at Nicholas. "Well, I see you found your gift," he said softly. He referred to the feathered and jeweled fan, which lay next to me on the linen.

"Yes," I said as I lifted it to my face. "I thought perhaps it was from you till I learned you are a mere assistant to your father." I waved the fan back and forth.

"Oh, I am sorry," he said smoothly, moving closer. "I

guess I was mistaken. For I never took you to be lofty."

I turned toward him as the sun shone on his black curls. "If you only knew how false your words are."

He inched closer. "Then tell me. I will listen to your tale of woe." He smelled of the Anjou wine.

"Not till you tell me why you lied to me."

He leaned back on his arms and sighed. "I'll have it someday. My father's role. I already do most of it. Why, look at my hands," he held them out, his nails black rimmed and stained with ink. "My father's getting on in years. He's never been the same since my mother passed away. I wanted to impress you." He took my hand. I pulled it away. "What can I do to make it up to you?"

"Hmm. Let's see." I smiled. "Perhaps a trip to the Queen's Wardrobe would appease me."

"My, you are full of guile, aren't you?" He smiled. "Father would not be pleased. He doesn't like women about; it causes distractions. And I have to say I agree with him on that account, for you, Katherine, have me quite distracted. I think of you day and night. I truly do."

"Hmmph," I snorted. "Pretty words." I snuck a glance at him.

"Pretty words for a pretty lady."

I looked away. "I've been called many things, but never pretty."

The queen had left her barge and was now walking amongst the crowd. She wore the lovely crimson dress Dorothy Broadbelt and I had retrieved for her.

"I cannot believe no man has ever told you you are pretty. Why, every man you've known must be dumb and blind."

"If you are fishing to see if I've had a love, you will not hear it from me," I said.

"Hmmm," he said as he picked up a marzipan, this one a crimson cherry, and ate it. "Now you have me very curious indeed. Have you ever been kissed?"

His lips were stained with red. I smiled and looked away. He laughed. "I bet you have. Yes, indeed, I bet you have."

"Ha, you are like the blackbird who chides the dark. For I have heard you have kissed every unattached girl in the whole court."

He threw his head back and laughed again. "Is that all? Only the unattached? Not some of the married women, too? I'm losing my touch."

"So it's true."

He sighed and leaned closer. So close I thought

perhaps . . . then he pulled back, but his mesmerizing eyes I could still see very well. Oh, very well indeed. "It's all rumors," he said, licking his bottom lip, wiping clean the red stain of the candied cherry, and I found myself licking my own lip. "I've only kissed two, well maybe three, and one of them I didn't particularly care for. I believe it is she who talks of me."

"And who may that be?" I asked.

"A gentleman never tells."

A large figure suddenly towered over us, the sun against his back. I cupped my hand over my eyes. It was Rafael, wearing a cerulean blue doublet, its guards cut velvet, roses overstitched in gold thread. It was a piece fit for a king. But he looked none too pleased, and I could not pull away from his stare. Finally, frowning, he stalked off.

It was not long before he was surrounded by ladies.

"He looks at you like a papa with an errant daughter," Nicholas said, sipping from his goblet.

"Papa. Ha." I was quick to respond, still staring at Rafael. He was gently stroking a lady's back. She was beautiful.

I leaned back on my elbows and looked at Nicholas. God, he was handsome, his long dark eyelashes framing those beautiful green eyes. "You may kiss me if you like," I said to him.

"What are you up to, Katherine?" he said. "I can't kiss you here and he wouldn't notice anyway; he's quite engaged."

"I have no idea what you are talking about," I said.

"It wouldn't be wise, to tarry with him."

My gaze flew to his face. "What do you know of him?"

"Only the talk," he said. "He's quite the mystery, having disappeared from London for so long. And now suddenly reappearing after all these years . . . and with you."

"I know little of him, even though he's my cousin," I said, my eyes wide. "I barely remember him when I was young. He's been gone for a long time."

"I believe," he said, "as do most of them"—he nodded to the ladies and gentlemen of the queen's court who were strolling by—"that there are no mere coincidences in life."

My laugh was forced. Grace had always said something similar, that God sent us coincidences to warn us a bigger truth was on its way.

"It's no laughing matter, Katherine," Nicholas said,

his eyes twinkling. "If you want me to talk plainly I will. I mean to have you. We'd make quite a formidable pair at court, me with my place in the Wardrobe—you with your knowledge of dress. I'd have to tame you, though; you act like a little child."

"Oh, so romantic, Nicholas." I picked up a pastry and threw it at him. It missed its mark. He picked it up and threw it back at me. We both laughed. "And I think you are a mere boy who doesn't know what he is talking about," I said haughtily.

He looked wounded. "My, you have a tongue, do you not? That will have to be tamed."

"Not by you," I said.

"We shall see," he responded. "Be careful, Kat," he continued. "The queen is suspicious of Lord Ludmore, and I hear she has already had a private audience with him."

"She has?" I asked.

"She's a shrewd judge of character. If she see's anything wanting in him, he'll soon be set packing. Some say you may be her daughter," he continued, looking for a reaction in my eyes. "That it be strange a girl like you, so like her in appearance and temperament, and talented of the needle, has suddenly appeared."

I picked up a sweetmeat and popped it in my mouth. God's me, it left an awful taste, like the sour-tasted, weedy medicines Grace used to sneak in to our food. "I've heard that rumor."

"Some speculate that Lord Ludmore is her long-lost love, and your father." I choked out the sweetmeat, but caught it in my hand. I continued to cough, the back of my throat burning as though a flame licked up from my stomach.

"And is it true?" he asked, handing me his goblet of wine. I gulped as he continued. "You'd be set for life, you would, being a queen's daughter, although she'd never be able to recognize you."

"Nicholas—" I interrupted him, my eyes still watering, my head starting to throb.

He grabbed my hand. "I'm sorry. I've spoken too much."

I broke away and stood up.

"Katherine," he said, his voice low and urgent. And then I saw her—Anna, dressed in one of my finer gowns, walking my way. Beyond her, the queen motioned to me to come.

I felt dizzy. I was going to faint. Ipollyta stood next to the queen, her lips curved up in a gentle smile. She nodded to me like the toad king to the fly. I was aware that Rafael, somewhere to my left, was heading in my direction.

"Katherine," Nicholas called again as I started to walk toward the queen. Anna met me, and I gripped her hand.

"I had a terrible feeling that you were in danger," she whispered. "What has happened?"

"I don't know," I said. "I've eaten something rancid, I think."

"Let me take you back," Anna said.

"No, no, she's calling for me," I said. And now suddenly we were before Elizabeth. Katherine Ashley and Blanche Parry stood behind her. I tried to stand tall, but the world began to spin.

She leaned toward me, a smile on her lips, and then she noticed Anna. The queen's face fell. Anna was beautiful. Too beautiful.

"And who is this creature?" she asked.

"Anna," I barely choked out. The world darkened as Rafael caught me in his arms.

I birthed my baby myself, all alone in my small room on this day, August 30. She was early, a scrawny and ugly little thing with malformed ears and a tuft of snow-white hair. She came into this world barely holding on, mewling like a runty kitten. I hoped with all my being she'd not make it a night, but she did. Aye, she did. But I myself had developed a fever, and was in danger of leaving the world when Agnes burst into my room with the news that my good queen was delivering her own child and was asking for me. I could not go. I couldn't, so weak I was, although I tried. "There, there," Agnes soothed me as she held my little babe. "The queen has the finest doctor and her ladies to attend her. What shall we name your little babe?" I shook my head. "Take her to the stream and leave her. She's malformed," I told her. "Bah," Agnes laughed. "It's your fever talking. She's a beautiful babe, she is." She lifted back the blanket I'd wrapped her in. "She has only a birthmark, a half-moon. If you shan't name her, I will. She will be Anna, me own mother's name. That's the name she shall have." "As you wish," I managed to murmur. "Fetch me wine root and chamomile. I must recover for the queen." "And not for the babe?" "God's death, no," I told her.

CHAPTER 21

month has passed and Anna, my sweet Wren, has left me. I woke up a week ago and found that she had simply vanished, taking nothing with her but Grace's lute. Nicholas Pigeon made a few inquiries, as he never seemed to leave my side now, and found that she was staying with Lady Ludmore.

Things had become intolerable for Anna, for you see, after the outdoor feast the queen let it be known that Anna was not welcome. Dorothy explained that it was simply Anna's beauty, and her beauty alone, that damned her. The queen must always be the shining sun, and if anything were to threaten her, she would strike it down.

Anna never left our chamber, and even when we journeyed to Whitehall, the queen's favorite palace, she would not come. When we returned, her pallor grew more sickly, her spells more frequent, till she hardly left the bed. I felt helpless to make her better, I did, caught between the two, my sister and the queen, who sought my companionship more now than ever.

One night Anna woke me, in delirium she was, insisting there was a ghost in the hall waiting for her. "It's Grace," she cried. "She wants me to join her." But when I looked, shining a candle in the hall, it was Dorothy sneaking out to the rose garden again. "No, Anna," I said. "There's no ghost. It's only Dorothy."

"Promise me, Kat," she had whispered. "Promise me you'll not let Mama take me." And then she had laughed bitterly. "She wants me, for she knows I'm the easiest of us to pull beneath the ground."

"No, no, shhh. You're talking nonsense."

But nothing I said or did seemed to help—none of the herbs or potions I mixed for her, nor my soothing words. She had become impenetrable, lost to even me. The queen, upon hearing of my concern, sent her doctors, but they could do nothing for Anna. And then she disappeared, leaving me afright with worry. When Nicholas found she was at the Ludmores', I inquired of her, and Lady Ludmore promised to send word when Anna had recovered.

Rafael had not spoken a word to me since the day of the outdoor entertainment. He had carried me to my chamber, I was told by Dorothy, and there was much talk, so worried he seemed to be. He had paced up and down the hallway, but when told I had come to, he took his leave. I'd seen him at court, in the arms of a blonde, a woman who Dorothy tells me is a hussy and who has made the rounds of the randy men. He's hardly even looked at me again, and the one moment I did catch his eyes upon me they were so dark and empty, I looked away.

And as to what ailed me that day, I was sure as the sun sets that Ipollyta had tried to poison me, but when I shared my suspicion with Dorothy, she bade me not to say a word of it ever again. "Never make a scene, nor accusation, nor unkindly remark," she advised me. "Those that heed these words stay the longest at court, and those that stay the longest rise the highest."

Strangely Ipollyta seemed to retreat, letting me take her place as the queen's pet, although I did perchance to see a sour look upon her face like a rat who's been denied the larder cheese. And one day a small packet of needles arrived, beautiful fine needles, expertly sharpened, but I tossed them away. I knew from whence they came, poison arrows, I was sure, and who knew what would become of me if I pricked myself?

I'd lost my appetite. Dorothy insisted that her John said it couldn't have happened in the kitchen, as there were yeomen who watched every bit of food that was destined for the queen's table. He said that the sweetmeat had gone rancid in the sun. I'd lost quite a bit of weight, but Nicholas said it suited me, more of a woman I looked now than a chubby child.

It was the end of September, still hot. Since Anna left, I'd spent my free afternoons in my room, the window propped open, stitching on the great gown for the queen. And although she teased me relentlessly about seeing it, I told her she would not until I'd stitched the last stitch, and only then. I'd finished the great lion and sewn the rubies into its eyes. He stared at me, fiery and knowing as I stitched the birds and other beasts with rich threads. And all the while the wolf lurked, waiting for my needle, and whenever I gazed upon it, I thought of my poor Anna. Finally I took some soap and tried to wipe it clean, but it remained like a whisper in the dark. Yes, Anna haunted me, in my thoughts and in my dreams.

The queen was going to raise up Robert Dudley to the peerage and make him an earl. Some said it was in preparation for her finally marrying him. Others said it was merely to keep him at her side, for his eyes had begun to wander. And later after the ceremony, Nicholas was finally going to allow me to accompany him to the Queen's Wardrobe to return the investiture robe the queen would wear that morning.

As I sat stitching and waiting for Nicholas, there was a soft tap on my chamber door. Anna! I put my stitching down and quickly opened the door. But nay, it was not her. Just a shy maid who peered up to me from under a low-brimmed maid's cap.

"Do you remember me, miss?"

I did not. She watched me carefully, her eyes hooded, as though she was memorizing my features.

"Are you Dorothy Broadbelt's maid?" I asked. Since Anna had left, my hair had returned to its former unruliness. Even the queen had noted it, for although she didn't want anyone to outshine her, she didn't want us looking like we have slept in the barn, either. Dorothy had promised her maid would come that morning and work her magic on it.

"No, ma'am, it's Iris." She nodded. "From the Tower." She blinked like a shy goat.

Aaah, yes. It had been dark and she had been sitting by

the fire. And she had known of Mrs. Eglionby. "I have a letter from my mother," Iris continued. "Sorry, miss, but my mother doesn't write, nor I. We both had to seek assistance."

My heart began to beat. She held the letter out and it was a good long moment before I took it. But took it I did, grasping it in my hands. I fetched a small coin for her.

"Thank you." She bowed and retreated, looking me over once more, before turning and running down the hall.

I turned the letter over. I ripped it open.

My Good Lady,

Me daughter tells me you have asked if I ever knew a Mrs. Eglionby. And I thought I'd never hear her name uttered again, so surprised I was. Yes, I indeed knew her. A very long time ago. And she was a good, good governess, who very much loved the little babe, the Mistress Mary who was in her charge. But she couldn't help her, not with the circumstances being as they were. My own mistress is very much aggrieved and sorrowful for her treatment of the sweet little girl and would change things now if she could. It haunts her to this day, the knowledge that the child, a queen's child no less, disappeared under her care. She hasn't heard a word of Mrs. Eglionby in many a year and can't help you on that account. My lady feels strongly that the key to the mystery be with a maid who came with the child's entourage, a maid named Grace, a saucy wench if there ever was one I must say, for I knew her well too. Find this Grace and perhaps you will have your answer.

I ran for the door. I opened it. Nicholas was standing there before me.

"Is everything all right?" he asked as I looked past him up and down the hall. "I rather do like your hair free like that, my country lass."

I discreetly folded the letter behind me.

Dorothy had said once to watch the queen carefully; one could learn everything there was to know about handling men. For in the end, she was always the master in such things great and small.

"She's only giving him a peerage so Queen Mary will think more of him," Katherine Knevit whispered behind me, and Mary Shelton shushed her. Whatever the reason, Robert Dudley was very dignified and proud as he walked around the presence chamber talking with the dignitaries and ambassadors who had gathered for the event. Everyone was richly attired—the councilors in robes and velvets, cloaked courtiers in their finest silks, extra feathers in their caps, doubly thick gold chains upon their necks, the ladies in their most glimmering gowns and costly jewels.

As I strolled about the room with Nicholas, who was neglecting his clerkly duties as usual, I discreetly searched for Rafael. Finally I spotted him, this time a brunette woman by his side. He caught my eye and nodded, but his attention quickly returned to his lady. Chin in the air, I turned to Nicholas. I chatted and giggled and brushed his arm with my fan, just as I had seen the queen do many a time with her courtiers.

The queen sat in a large red damask chair over which hung a crimson velvet canopy and a carved and gilded coat of arms. Sir Melville was by her side, her ladies talking amongst themselves nearby. The queen wore full ceremonial robes of damask silk and a great golden crown with jewels as large as walnuts that shimmered across the room like colorful moonbeams. Her face radiated complete happiness.

The queen's eyes alit on me. "Come here, my Spirit," she called. Nicholas slinked behind a courtier and slipped from the room. "So we've moved from the rose garden into the Wardrobe, have we?" She laughed as I approached her, a puzzled look on my face. "Aaah . . . I know everything, dear Kat, but he doesn't have to slink off like a naughty dog caught with the kitchen roast. Perhaps I would approve of the match."

I bit my lip. I was not thinking of him right now. My eyes darted to Rafael.

"Oh, I see." The queen laughed. "Is that how it is. Where has *he* been, by the way? I'm very offended he's been absent from court."

Her eyes narrowed on the woman. "Lady Marion Huckabee. I can have her banished to the country if you like."

I turned to her. "Nay. I don't know. . . ."

"Just as Blanche once said," the queen mused, "you don't know your own heart. But does anyone? She shall be gone tomorrow. She should be by her own husband anyway. He's an invalid, never leaves their estate. My guess, my dear, is that you could have your Spaniard in a fortnight if that was your wish."

"Do you think so?" I asked her. "He's ignored me for weeks."

The queen let out a hearty laugh. "My dear, you have much to learn in the affairs of men. Much to learn. He's biding his time, as you must too."

"My maid Anna has joined Lord Ludmore's household," I said quietly.

"This I know," the queen snapped. "She was not made for court life, maid or not. I'm sure Lady Ludmore will have her converted before you know it and she will forget you." She turned her head. The subject was closed.

But I could not help myself. "She means much to me, Your Majesty, for we were raised together."

Her face softened. "Well, my Spirit," she said. "Is that perhaps why you've been so forlorn of late? Until this very moment I thought perhaps you were mooning over your poor shepherd."

"No, no," I said all in a rush. "Not *him*." The last words squeaked out of my mouth like a stepped-upon flitter mouse.

"I see." She walked away, a sly smile on her face.

"What did the queen say?" asked Nicholas, who had joined my side again after the ceremony was over. "Does she know of us? Tell me, does she approve?" I glanced around for Rafael, and saw him as he left the chamber with Lady Huckabee.

"I must say, she did not approve," I said. "You shall have to set your sights on someone else. Ipollyta is free, I think."

"Don't tease me so. I think perhaps I'll die of a broken heart," he said, holding his hand over his chest. "You do know I care for you ardently, I do," he said.

I rolled my eyes at him. "Yes, Nicholas, I do know." The crowd started to disperse and I followed the queen's ladies, who followed her out of the presence chamber and down a long hallway.

But before I knew it, Nicholas had pulled me into a curtained alcove and his lips were on mine. God's me, but I let him kiss me.

He started to reach for my bodice and I pushed away and looked at his beautiful face. How could I not love this? "I think perhaps you could learn to love me," he said, his voice low and husky. "I do love you; I have from the first minute I set eyes upon you."

And this made me wonder, why did he want *me* so much, when all the maids swooned at his sight and talked of him endlessly? Why did he want me?

I touched his cheek briefly before running after the last of the queen's ladies into the privy chamber.

* * *

The queen once told me that a woman's intuition always tells her the truth, but only if she will listen. After the ceremony something had tickled up my back until the hairs on my arms stood tall. Something was going to happen. If I'd gone back to my chamber, perhaps, perhaps, everything that transpired that day would not have unwound itself like a spool dropped down Cowslip Hill. But I didn't listen to my intuition. Aye, I did not.

As I entered the privy chamber I saw that several of the maids, including Dorothy, stood at the window giggling and pointing at something outside. It was pouring down rain, and for the life of me I couldn't imagine what they could see in the rain that amused them so. But my attention was quickly drawn to the queen, who for some reason had decided to bring Sir Melville to her private rooms.

The senior ladies of the privy chamber were removing the queen's outer robe. Mrs. Ashley carried it carefully to the doorway, where a yeoman of the Wardrobe waited. This was my opportunity to accompany Nicholas back to the Queen's Wardrobe. In fact, he probably waited just outside the door for me. But I was tired of his pressing his case, aye, I was, and something kept me rooted to the exact spot I had walked to upon entering. Like a fairy-turned-statue I stood, the hair on my arms standing at attention. Still, yet, the maids giggled on.

Sir Melville, embarrassed to be in the chamber, it seemed, busied himself by walking about the room examining trinkets here and there. He came upon a carved cabinet where the queen kept her precious keepsakes. It was usually locked tight. It was Blanche Parry's job to attend to it, but today the doors stood open, like shutters thrown wide on the first warm day of spring.

"Spirit," the queen called. "You are very flushed. Come sit down, I bade you."

I didn't move. I watched Sir Melville take something wrapped in tissue from the cabinet. "'Eyes,'" he read aloud dramatically. He unwrapped the tissue and turned over a small miniature in his hands. The queen was at his side in a second, plucking it from his grasp. Then she snatched the tissue and quickly wrapped the portrait back up.

"Your Majesty," Sir Melville said slyly. "Perhaps this is a perfect gift for Queen Mary. For not only will she rejoice in his new status, but she may look upon his beautiful eyes daily."

"No," the queen proclaimed rather too quickly, and then she took a deep breath, the package clutched to her chest. "It's my only copy, you see, and I can't bear to part with it."

The maids giggled again, their attention still held by something outside in the pouring rain. "I think there is much you can't bear to part with," Sir Melville rejoined.

"Don't be insolent with me," she barked, then softened. "I must undress now, Sir Melville, and unless you want to see the glory of England, it is time for you to leave."

He smiled slightly, blushing. "I bid you good morning." He bowed to her and stalked out of the room.

"Stop that infernal giggling now, I insist," the queen demanded as her ladies began to pull her sleeves off.

"Oh, but you must see, Your Majesty," Anne Windsour said over her shoulder. "It's quite a peculiar sight."

"If you insist." She sighed, slapping away the hands unbuttoning her kirtle. The maids parted as the queen walked to the window. She stood there silent a good full minute as a flaming spark raced up my back. Then she looked back at me, a sly little smile upon her face.

"Spirit," she said, "I do believe your shepherd is a long way from home."

On this same day of August 30, my good queen was delivered of a healthy girl, whom she named Mary. I was not able to attend her, although she called for me, I hear, for I greatly feared for my own life. For you see, I have found, when one faces God, no matter how long one has longed for death, one does suddenly fear it. Agnes watched the queen's birth and said it was one of much joy, despite the fact that the babe wasn't the longed-for heir. The admiral is pleased, for Mary, named after the Princess Mary, is plump and pretty, unlike the scrawny little lump at my breast. I am barely able to feed her, so sick I am. The fever courses its way through me like a hot river, and pulls the blood from my body. Agnes begged me to tell her of a weed to staunch the blood, and when I told her there was only wolf's juniper and it was too late to find it now, she sobbed. But then in the dark night, when I could see God holding his hands out for me and my babe, Jane the fool appeared at my bed, a potion in hand.

CHAPTER 22

hristian. I was at the window before I knew it. It was Christian. Standing in the rain, wearing the silver jerkin I'd made an eternity ago. He stood staring up at the window, his face not flinching when I appeared in his view.

"God's faith," the queen said over my shoulder. "Go put him out of his misery."

"Look at his leggings." Anne Windsour laughed. "And his shoes! He looks quite the rabbit sucker, he does."

Dorothy pinched her. "But look how handsome he is, even soaking wet!" she proclaimed, and all the maids giggled.

"Yes, he is indeed. He could lead my horse, he could," Mary Howard exclaimed.

"As though he would," Mary Ratcliff retorted. "When you stink!"

"You should babble so, you silly strumpet!" Mary Howard replied.

"You may bring him here to warm up. I'd like to speak with him," the queen pronounced.

I stood there frozen, not even blinking. Finally Dorothy nudged me to go.

I turned and ran from the room, through the halls, bumping into people, running down stairs, till finally I reached the garden. I ran to him as fast as my feet would take me, not caring that many eyes watched me from above, and that finally, as I neared him, I slipped in the mud. I flung myself at him, throwing my arms wildly around him.

He peeled my arms away and stepped back, his honey-colored eyes aflame. God's me, how I had missed those eyes. Blinking back the rain, breathing hard, I simply stared at him. He had grown, aye he had, his muscles more shapely and broad, his face more of that of a man. "Christian," I whispered.

"I came for you," he finally said, his voice barely above a sigh.

"Aye." I laughed. "And I'm glad of it." He continued to

stare at me, unblinking, raindrops perched on his lashes.

"Christian," I said.

"I saw you with him," he said flatly.

"Who?" I asked him.

"*Who*? Is there more than one? The fancy boy. Is that what you want? A puffed-up peacock?"

"We are merely friends," I said, "Nicholas and I."

He laughed bitterly. "'Nicholas and I.' My, you do sound lofty."

I peeked over my shoulder and up at the queen's window. She stood there watching, her eyes dark and cold, six female faces surrounding her like rays of the sun. The low beat of the rain seemed to pound in my ears. What was Christian doing here? How long had he been here? And how did he find me? When did he see Nicholas? The questions ran through my mind, but I held my tongue.

"Father has been laid low," Christian said finally.

"Oh Christian, I didn't know." I stepped forward, but he held up his hand. "Why didn't you send word somehow?" I asked.

"I couldn't find you at first," he said, and I looked away a moment, ashamed.

"And how does Uncle Godfrey fare?" I asked him.

"He'll live, Old Hookey says. But he'll never be the same," he said. "It was very bad in the beginning when he thought he was to die. He was fevered and ranting for days. Said he had sinned by not wanting to know, by not doing something, and that God had brought him down. But when he was better and I asked him, he didn't know what he spoke of."

"Was he speaking of Grace and Anna? Of me?"

"I think something further back. His mind frequently returns to the days before we were born."

"But Christian, this could be the key. Can you not ask him more?"

"No. It's too painful for him and I shan't ask him of it." We stared at each other. The rain fell around us on the green grass and on the queen's flowers. "I'll have to work the farm now. That's why I've come. I need you. I want you."

"Christian," I said. "Come inside from the rain. We can talk. The queen . . . she wants to meet you."

He glanced up at the window. "So she can look me over like livestock at market and laugh at me as her ladies have done?"

"They're silly. Just silly maids," I said.

"And now you are one of them."

"No, I am not one of them."

"Look at you." He laughed bitterly. "Even in the rain I can see you've changed." His eyes slowly ran over my body and I shivered. "You're not my Kat anymore."

"That's not true. I'm the same. I am." But I wondered.

"Come with me," he said with such force that his words echoed strangely off the castle wall almost like a howl. "I still love you." The last words were but a long sigh.

I looked up at the queen's window. She was motioning for me to come, her mouth set and firm.

"I shan't ask again," he said, following my gaze. "I won't."

"Christian, I . . ."

"You gave me your answer before, a long time ago. But I didn't believe you. I am the fool. I am."

"I didn't give you my answer," I said softly. "I didn't."

"You did; you left me without a word. My mother always said you were dangerous. That some things couldn't be scrubbed out." He laughed bitterly.

"I need to know who I am, Christian," I said. "That's why I'm here."

"That's a lie," he said. "You're here because you want all of this. And I can never give it to you. Never."

I couldn't respond. We stood there facing each other for what seemed an eternity.

"Where's Anna?" he said slowly.

I bit my lip. "I shall not tell you."

"Where is she?" he yelled, grabbing my shoulders. Two liveried guards appeared in the garden.

"She's at the home of the Ludmores," I whispered, and before I knew it he had released me with such force that I stumbled away from him. He walked away, his shoulders back, his head held high. The guards simply watched him go. I fell to my knees and called after him, but he did not turn back, not once, and I shall forever remember the smell of the roses curling in the rain.

When we were children, I once dared Christian to climb down Puck's Well to see what actually lay at the bottom. We thought it might be a faun, or perhaps a pile of gold. I told him we would use the money to buy Sudeley and live as the lady and lord of the castle. And to my surprise, he actually did try to climb to the bottom, but he got stuck ten feet down. And try as I might to pull him out with a rope, I could not. I finally had to fetch Uncle Godfrey, who fished him out with one mighty heave. "Some things are better left unknown," Uncle Godfrey had said to us before walking off, and Aunt Agnes behind him had slapped me. That was only a precursor to the whipping I'd gotten later from Grace for my imprudent and half-wit ideas.

After Christian left, the queen had me brought to her great bed, where I was stripped of my clothes and put in a soft shift, which had been warmed by the fire. And all the while, the queen sat next to me tenderly holding my hand, her ladies surrounding us with great wide-eyed curiosity. I couldn't speak as tears rushed down my face, and when I looked up at the queen and saw the deep distress in her eyes, I truly did wonder at our connection. Then I was given a draught to drink, and as I sipped it Ipollyta appeared at the end of the bed smiling, smiling like a forest weasel.

Later, much later, sometime in the dark of night, I was moved back to my room. Dorothy appeared by my side, a candle in one hand, a letter in the other: *Christian has taken Anna home with him to Winchcombe—Lady Ludmore*

When I awoke, Dorothy was sitting on my bed. "There now, you've come back to us."

I blinked, my eyelids heavy as lead. Something pounded in my head like the great bell of Winchcombe Abbey. "Is it morning?" I asked her.

She laughed. "The next morning. You've been asleep

for a day and a half. The queen has been quite worried about you. Sat with you for several hours yesterday until she was pulled away by her councilors. She had to bid farewell to Sir Melville. He finally had enough and sailed back to Scotland. The queen is to be summoned as soon as you awaken." She motioned over her head to a maid who stood in the doorway, and the maid scurried off.

"Water," I said, feeling as though I had not had a drop to drink in a year. "I need water." She poured water from a ewer into the goblet that was next to the bed. She lifted my head and I drank.

I looked around for the queen's gown and then remembered I had hidden it under a loose board under my bed, with my other valuables, before I went to Robert Dudley's ceremony.

"She's quite vexed with me, too, I must say," Dorothy rattled on. "For reading the letter to you. Says I'm the reason you wouldn't wake up, for it's only in sleep one finds true peace, she thinks. I'm truly sorry, Katherine. Does it hurt very much? Both of them lost to you?"

I sighed deeply and turned my head. "It doesn't matter now."

"Was he your true love?" she asked, taking my hand.

I couldn't answer her. But my heart felt as though it had

been ripped in a thousand pieces. *Christian gone with Anna.* God's me, I'd be sick, if there be any food to come up.

"Nicholas Pigeon has been here too, pacing the halls until the queen yelled at him for always neglecting his duties. You've been quite the spectacle, you have. Even Mrs. Ashley, who never leaves the queen's side, as you know, came in here to stare at you a good long time till I told her to shoo and be gone."

"And Rafael?" I asked.

"No," she answered. "The queen did not want word sent to him." She grabbed my hand. "You can tell me, Katherine," Dorothy said softly. "Anything. You know my secrets. Most of them, anyway." She smiled. "I may talk a lot, but I'm no tittle-tattler like Katherine Knevit."

I looked at the window and took a breath. "I am not Katherine Ludmore. I've come here to find my mother. My true mother. There are two letters there, hidden underneath the drawer." I nodded to the bedside table. Dorothy's eyes raised as she quickly pulled the drawer out and ran her fingers underneath. She plucked them out.

"Perhaps this is what the queen was looking for. She was very determined, she was."

"What do you mean?" I asked, my skin prickling.

"I saw her," Dorothy whispered. "Going through

everything. She was even on her hands and knees looking under your bed. It was quite a funny sight, I tell you, to see her so ill-composed."

I smiled, relieved. "She was looking for the dress I'm stitching her. Did she find it?"

"No," Dorothy said as she opened one of the letters and read it. It was the letter from Iris's mother. "Well, it's simple," she said after a moment. "It says right here all you need to do is find this Grace."

"But she's dead, Dorothy," I told her. "She's the one who raised me in Gloucestershire."

"Well then, she won't be much help, will she now?" she muttered, looking over the letter again.

"Read the other one," I told her. She opened it up and read Grace's letter to me. Her eyes opened wide. "Is this the same Grace mentioned in the first?"

I nodded. "I think so. And she bades me to stay away from the queen. Is not that a clue?"

Dorothy smiled. "Everyone is warned to stay away from court, everyone high and low. That is what she must have meant, especially with a face like yours."

"Grace told me as I was growing up that I wasn't wanted."

Dorothy nodded. "Aye, girls are never wanted, that's

true. I was a great disappointment to my father." She sighed, then picked up the first letter again. "There is nothing here to say you are *this* Mary, even if there was a maid named Grace mentioned. And as to the name Mary, why that could be anyone in all of England. There are lots of Marys about, named after Mary the queen's sister before anyone knew how bloody brutal she was."

"But it says in the letter the child Mary was a queen's child, no less."

"So you think perhaps you are a princess come to take your throne?" She snorted with laughter. I thought of showing her the necklace, still sown into my skirt. But something told me no, this was better kept hidden, even from Dorothy.

"MS. I believe my initials are MS."

"Well, that's something to go on indeed. And who is this duchess?" she said reading the letter again.

"Under the bed," I said as I lifted up and sipped the water. "I've hidden a bundle of things there under a loose board."

She was on her hands and knees in a flash. A moment later she pulled it out and opened it. Her eyes grew wide. "Costly things," she said, lifting up the crimson counterpane. She held up the wooden cup. "The painting is fine, as good as one of the court painters." She lifted the unicorn horn, raised her eyebrows, and dropped it back in the box. Next the little gold rings. "Cramp rings to cure the morning pains. I've seen Catherine Carey wear them many a time, as I have the lowliest of maids." Next the little silver goblets. "Very fine." Then lastly the little pillow with the initials. "Ah, no royal crowns for you, poor Kat. The queen's surname begins with a T. Tudor," she said, laughing. I coughed and sputtered, my eyes wide. Dorothy quickly slipped the bundle under my coverlet.

"Ah, my Spirit is back." It was the queen, regal and splendid in a crimson gown with a high, silken diaphanous collar that fanned out like a setting sun in my doorway. Her smile was warm and generous. Crimson. My mother had loved crimson. I smiled back weakly. She was my family now. The court my home. I'd no longer think of Anna and Christian, oh God, I couldn't. They were gone forever.

Why is it set in nature that when one life is saved another must go? I recovered and will live, but my good queen Katherine Parr has fallen into a fever. I came to her this morning and knew when I saw her that she will not last beyond a week. No matter what I do, God has a tighter hold on her now. Poor thing, she whispers nonsense to me that our babes will grow together and be like sisters, and made me promise to watch over them. Her ladies are much aggrieved and tearful, even climbing on her bed to be near her. And to my great surprise, the admiral is beside himself with grief and cannot bear to look upon her. Finally he came to her this morning and held her hand tenderly, but she much berated him for his cruel words of long ago and other things she whispered to him low.

He called her sweetheart and love, but she cried that he wished her sickness on her and if he had chosen a better doctor she'd be well. It was a sad sight indeed, and I felt very aggrieved for her. And when her husband left, she begged me to give her something that would give her peace and her sense back, and God help me, I did. And then she was calm and recited the Lord's Prayer and told her almoner Miles Coverdale her wishes, that her husband have all her worldly goods. And then she pulled me close and made me swear I'd watch over her little Mary and I said yes, yes I would. And then it was mercifully over. She died at two in the morning, not but a week after her little babe was born. And now I have two little babes at my breasts, sisters now, in more ways than one.

CHAPTER 23

rom that day forward I became as indispensable to the queen as she became to me—like two halves of a copper coin we were. And I felt it had always been so. I provided the potions, with Mrs. Twiste's help, for her nervous attacks, for they worked better than most, aye, they did. I mixed new creams for her poxed face, and stitched lovely gloves for her hands, and offered a gentle ear for her many woes. And she in turn kept me busy and entertained and merry, for she knew I mourned my loss although we never, ever spoke of it. And I was content. What did it matter who I was now that I was in the lap of the queen? I was content. I was. Any girl in the whole kingdom would take my place. Except for Anna. But I willed myself not to think of them.

But Grace was right when she said the human heart does not lie, aye, she was. For I woke up in the middle of the night screaming of ghosts and beasts and fierce creatures of the sea. But the image that is burned in me forever from the day Christian came in the rain is that of the queen standing in the window quietly watching with her dark eyes, her hands clasped in front of her. Yes, the heart does not lie. It was telling me to be content, and not question my soul. And so afraid of sleep I was, like Grace, that I started staying up late at night, stitching and stitching the queen's dress, for hours on end, until I'd finally nod off in my chair.

But like the village shrew, fate has its way of interfering. One day not long after Christmas I found myself alone with Mrs. Ashley in the wardrobe store, and I couldn't help but feel she had engineered it that way, for it wasn't her usual duty to be there. Iris had long since disappeared. Dorothy forever plagued me to try to locate her, but I ignored her. We had just argued about it again, when she was called away in search of pins. I was mending the seam of one of the queen's French hoods.

It was but a moment before I realized I was being

watched. I looked up to see Mrs. Ashley standing in the doorway.

"Yes?" I asked her.

"I was thinking that in the firelight you look like him. The slant of your cheek, the spark in your eyes. You very much embody him, you know. I knew the instant I saw you."

"Who do you speak of, Mrs. Ashley?" I asked, tying off a thread. I threaded another needle.

"I loved him," she said, and I quickly looked up. "But alas, every woman did. Including your mother, the poor soul."

"You knew them? Both of them? Who are they?"

"You do not know?" she asked, a small smile turning at the corners of her mouth.

"No" was all I managed to utter.

"Good," she murmured. And then she was gone.

"I don't like the quiet," the queen once told me. "It makes me chew upon the past." But here she was in the garden, the next morning, tucked behind a rosebush, reading a small prayer book with not a soul to attend her. In all the time I had been at court I had never seen her alone or still. I'd come to sketch. Strangely, it reminded me of home, being there.

"I've given them the slip," the queen said when I approached her, referring, I knew, to her ladies. She wore a simple gown of blue satin. "I do adore them, I do, Spirit." She sighed. "But sometimes I do tire of their endless chatter." She patted the bench where she sat. I joined her, putting my sketchbook to the side. "Dorothy." She smiled slightly. "God's me, I don't know how you abide her sometimes." I looked away, fingering the friendship ring the queen had given me the night of the masque. "Hints and allusions, tiptoeing and whispering." The queen laughed. "Why can't anyone ever be honest with me? Why does everything have to be danced around? I do have a kind heart, I do. If she'd just ask me for her kitchen boy, perhaps I'd give her the answer she wanted."

"Would you?" I asked, quite surprised.

"Not now, no." She sighed. "I don't like making decisions. Decisions are for another day." Just then one of her councilors, Lord Burghly, walked across the garden at a rapid pace, his eyes swiveling about. "Oh, why do my councilors have to harangue me so? It never ceases, never. I can't have a moment's peace." She glanced down at my sketchbook.

"What do you draw, Spirit?" she asked.

"Where the true beauty of nature lies," I said. "The stem of a flower, the vein of a leaf. There is much to see if one looks carefully." I pushed the book away discreetly. But I needn't have worried; her mind was elsewhere.

"Ah, Spirit," she mused. "I think I shall never marry. Not if I can't have him." She sighed as deep as a last breath. "I do love him, you know, but as a woman, not a queen."

I indeed knew, for I saw it a thousand different ways all during the day.

She took another deep breath. "Do you think perhaps a loved one forgives once they are laid beneath the ground?"

I shook my head. "I think perhaps," I offered, "that it is only God one can seek for forgiveness."

She laughed. "A queen does not seek forgiveness. Not from anyone. Ever."

It was quiet a moment longer. "Tell me, Spirit, do you know what they say of us?"

"That I am your daughter, Your Majesty." I continued to finger the ring she had given me. I could not meet her eyes.

"But isn't it ridiculous? Why do you not jest? Do you

think it true? As though I could conceive at fourteen? Ha. Now that's a silly story, and there have been many of them through the years, believe you me."

"Can a heart fall in love at fourteen?" I asked in wonder, peering at her. And then I thought of Christian. Had I loved him from the beginning?

"Yes. But a first love is always false, Spirit. Banish him from your heart, as I have banished him who deceived me." And before I could respond, she announced, "Meadowsweet. That's what this garden needs. I shall tell my man to plant some tomorrow. My mother loved the scent. I have very few memories of her, but I do remember that. It's strange how scents can evoke memories. Have you heard of it, Spirit?"

"Yes, Your Majesty. The berries can be used to soothe the nerves."

"Ah yes, the nerves." She laughed. "You've been the only one who has ever eased me on that account. Oh, how they've plagued me. If I were a man, perhaps my life would have been easier. A man's heart is made of steel, I think. A man is never brought down by love, that is the God's truth."

"I'm glad I can be of help, Your Majesty," I replied.

"I hear that Anne Twiste assists you with my potions.

Can a simple laundress be trusted?" she asked. "There's not a chance I should suddenly be found dead, sleeping at peace, my face raised to the Lord?"

"No, Your Majesty, no," I told her. "I make everything for you. I promise."

"Well then, my life is in your hands, Spirit," she said, pulling a winter rosebud over to her face and smelling it. "When you may be executed at any moment, your whole being changes," she continued. "You never forget or feel calm again. Ever. When death has almost reached you, it never leaves. It lingers like the ghost of an old friend, around the corner, beckoning with one long, curled finger."

"No one wishes your death, Your Majesty," I told her. "You are beloved. Indeed you are, by everyone." I could smell the rose she held.

"Ah, you are naïve, my dear," she laughed. "And that's why I adore you so. You remind me of myself when I was young, before, before. My own sister wished for my death, Kat, and when one's sister wishes that, you know there is no surety to one's life ever. A king is never safe. A sword hangs above his head at all times. God, I smell juniper; I told him to remove the juniper, I did. It stinks."

I smell wolf's juniper, Grace had said that day, the day

the dwarf arrived. The day everything began.

"I think it is quite pleasant," I told her, for I had always loved the smell of juniper.

She closed her eyes a moment and smiled. "Any of my ladies would have agreed with me. Only you would dare to disagree."

"Juniper has many pleasing qualities," I said. "It can be used to—"

"Oh spare me," she interrupted. "I don't like it and you shan't change my mind. It reminds me of my stepmother." She clutched the prayer book to her chest protectively as though she held a baby bird.

"And this brings unpleasant memories, Your Majesty?" I asked very quietly.

"Only regrets," she murmured. "Just regrets. She's the only one who truly loved me, you know. She brought me back to my father. He had rejected me. Declared me a bastard so my brother could inherit the throne. But my stepmother brought me back to him, made him see reason. I wouldn't be the queen I am today without her. She was the kindest, most intelligent woman who ever lived. And the only mother I ever had." Tears began to well in her eyes.

"Your ladies love you," I said.

She snorted. "Yes, they do. Blanche Parry is my rock. And Katherine Ashley has been imprisoned for me twice, did you know that? She'd lay down her life for me, she would. But she also led me astray once, and I shall never forget it."

"Astray?"

She waved her hand dismissively, and I knew I had gone too far.

"You shall be by my side always, won't you, Spirit? You won't leave me, will you? You do know there is no going back, do you not? Your shepherd married your maid, I'm sorry to tell you." But when I looked in her eyes, I did not see sorrow, only a shadow tinged with cruelty. She was lying. She had to be lying. I thought I could not breathe, and the ring upon my finger seemed to burn. I quietly took it off and held it in my hand.

"And what of your great friend Lord Ludmore?"

Rafael. I peeked at her from the corner of my eye.

"He is not for you," she continued. "A girl of uncertain birth, mysterious, marrying such a man. Let him dangle for quite a long time, and then cut the string."

I turned away, but she grabbed my hand. The ring fell down between us, clanking like a lamb's bell. She picked it up, slid it back on my finger, and continued, "Don't be ashamed, Spirit; it's your humbleness I most admire. It's the highly born ones I must most suffer. For they have the most to lose."

"But Lord Ludmore has a mysterious past too," I said quietly, thinking of him as a minstrel the night I had seen him at the revel and all those years he was missing.

"Yes," she said, closing her prayer book and attaching it back to a fob at her waist. I noticed for the first time that there was a sapphire shaped as an eye in the middle of the jewel. "And I want you to find out why he has returned after all these years. Do so, to set my heart at ease. Perhaps he has a secret wife, lowly born, in the country, or made friends with my Scottish cousin, or perhaps he's made visits to Spain. And he has not come for you at all these weeks. He's courting three different ladies and spends the night hours at the brothels, I hear."

She broke off the rosebud and handed it to me just as Blanche Parry and Katherine Ashley appeared at the garden gate, gesturing at us. "Ah, I've been found out at last." She stood and walked toward them, but then she turned back. "The gown. You will finish it someday, Spirit?" But it was not a question and she did not wait for an answer.

I pulled off the ring and rubbed my finger. I held it up to the light. The ruby glinted in the sun like old blood. Something caught my eye, an inscription. I brought it closer and read: "I hold what I have." And next to the words a mark—a tiny half-moon.

That night at a feast to welcome yet another ambassador, a most curious incident occurred. Ipollyta, dressed in a simple gown of gold, appeared at my side as I watched the dancers spin elegantly about the room. My mind wanted to put things together, to search, to seek answers, to think of Christian, but I drowned it all out with sweet, warm wine. The queen tapped her feet in cadence with the dancers while she flirted with the ambassador. Robert Dudley sulked at her side. I kept my eyes away from her, but I knew hers were frequently upon me; I could feel her attention as an insect wrapped in a web knows the spider is nearby, waiting, watching. I could only focus on Ipollyta's little gold gown. It reminded me of another dress, a dark night, wolves, sickness, and death.

"You know I wish you no harm," Ipollyta said, planting something in my hand.

"I think perhaps you do," I replied, wincing in fear

that it was a needle. But it was only an old gold coin, foreign, with a wild-looking queen set upon it. "In fact, I do believe you wish me great harm." I tried to return the piece, but she had put her hands behind her back and wouldn't take it.

"My mother came to this land many a year ago. She was told the royals here fancied little people such as us. My father was a normal man, I hear, a groom much loved among ladies. Porfirio was his name."

"Why are you telling me such things?" I asked, the room starting to spin.

"Because your heart wants to know, as does mine. Perhaps we can help one another. My mother's name is Jane. Jane the fool."

Jane the fool. I should have guessed it. I focused on her lips, what she was saying to me.

"But it's shameful even for a fool to have a bastard. I was hidden. Given away. Did you ever hear of my mother? She has been long lost to me and I seek her. I'm told she roamed the country looking for a stolen fortune. Did she ever come your way?"

Jane the fool. Aye, she had come our way, briefly, that dark night. And she had taken Grace with her. I took another long drink of my wine, for Grace always said it helped one lie. Aye, I knew where Jane was. As for the fortune she sought—it was sewn into the hem of the dress that I had worn to London and hidden with everything else under the bed. But I did not trust Ipollyta. She had tried to poison me. That I was sure. I closed my eyes.

"No," I said. "I never heard of her."

"You might change your mind," I heard her say. "And someday perhaps I may help you in kind." She turned and walked away. I dropped the coin and it rolled under feet and legs, and amidst the roar of the room, I heard it rotate and clamor before coming to a peaceful rest.

I arose in the dark and looked out my window into the night. A few minutes later I was down in the garden, my sketchbook in hand, sitting in the moonlight on the bench the queen and I had sat on. Her roses had different hues at night, and I started to sketch. A few minutes later a tall, dark figure walked toward me. I stood perfectly still. It was a man. The figure came directly up to me and stopped. Rafael.

"There you are," he whispered. "I didn't even have to come to you."

I sat unmoving, my heart beating.

He pulled me to my feet, and when our eyes met, he blinked a moment, startled, and then smiled.

"What is it?" I whispered. "Why are you here, Lord Lordmore?"

He leaned into me, his eyes boring into mine. "Rafael. My name is Rafael." I blinked and then I hiccupped. "I just wanted to look upon your face again," he said, handing me a rose. He was teasing me, and it felt good to hear his voice again.

"You are not leaving to become the wanderer again, are you?" I smiled. "Will you think of me often?"

He stepped closer. "Perhaps I already think of you day and night," he said with that wolf grin.

"I doubt that," I said, smiling. "I hear you have been very busy day and night."

"So I've made you jealous?" he asked, pulling me to him. "Then I have succeeded." I lifted my eyes to his, but I saw only a deep emptiness, like a bottomless sea. Then a cloud covered the moon and his expression was lost to me. He leaned down to kiss me, but I pushed away. Something turned in my stomach.

I held the rose up. "This was not for me, was it?" He didn't answer and I dropped it. "Why did you come back, Lord Ludmore?"

"To reclaim my inheritance, seek a wife. Make my mother happy again."

"And did she tell you to pursue me?"

"Nobody tells me to do anything." A bird called out softly in the darkness as the moonlight again shone on the dark planes of his face.

"Why do you play with me, Lord Ludmore?"

"I do not play with you," he responded. "I have intentions."

"Intentions. To marry me?" I asked.

"That is for me to ask, little heartbreaker." I could see his white teeth flash in the dark. "I do love you."

I suddenly knew with a great clarity that he lied. "I don't believe you. I think perhaps you are the one Grace warned me of my whole life."

Suddenly there was a movement in the bushes, and a female figure darted for the doors. I picked up the rose. "I think one of your loves has lost her rose."

She lay in her bed for many hours, no one having the heart to remove her. Her husband, I hear, did not see her again, but locked himself up in his room, crying like a lost child. When I came to her, I caught Jane the fool snipping a bit of her hair and quickly pocketing it. That evening, while Agnes watched over the babes, I helped the queen's ladies lay her out. I rubbed her body with preserving oils and gently brushed her beautiful red hair. Then we wrapped her in cerecloth, between layers of melted wax and tar. The final image we had was that of an angel before the last cloth was laid across her face. Mary Odell and Elizabeth Tyrwhit were very lamentable and stayed with her during the night. I could not. I had two babes to feed—

little Mary, usually so quiet, seemed to sense her loss and howled like a wolf the whole night, and Anna, my own, followed suit. The next morning Agnes watched the babes so I could attend the funeral, which was held in the chapel. The coffin was brought in followed by the chief mourner, Lady Jane Grey. The admiral did not attend. The queen was laid at the front, the coffin surrounded by lit candles. The queen's almoner, Miles Coverdale, gave a good and godly sermon commending her many virtues and then a choir of children sweetly sang "Te Deum." After, they laid her beneath the floor without nary a marker or stone.

CHAPTER 24

The next day, after visiting Anne Twiste for a draught for a headache, I decided to seek out the library that Blanche Parry had told me to find months ago. I had finally finished sketching all the beasts, monsters, and exotic flora I was interested in, and no longer needed the books she had loaned me. After stitching into the wee hours of the morning, I'd sat with my sketchbook and pored over pages and pages of my early drawings. And I'd come to know that as fanciful and wondrous as my copies might be, nothing could match the beauty of Christian's pears, the grasslands of Belas Knap, even the wild wolves of Humblebee Wood.

The books were kept in a room near the queen's

private bedchamber. Blanche was dusting, her back to me. It was a dark, low-ceiling room with nary a window. Yet it smelled wonderful—perfumed with sea, spices, and faraway lands. There was a small desk covered in purple velvet, embroidered with gold. A silver inkpot and parchment papers and letters were scattered on top. In the corner, Day, finally finding his night, slept upon a satin pillow that I had seen the queen herself embroider for him.

"What you see here is the finest collection in all Europe. The queen is quite fond of her books," Blanche said over her shoulder. "Reads every morning and before she goes to bed. It soothes her." I put the books I held on a long drawing table. "Although she doesn't have the time as she once did," Blanche continued. "When she was young her tutor said she had the finest mind he'd ever seen, male or female. She really is quite brilliant, you know. I think if she hadn't been a queen and she'd been a man, she'd have been a great scholar."

"What was she like when she was young? Was she very beautiful?" I asked, sitting down on a high-backed oak chair. I wondered if this was where the queen sat when she read.

"In her own way, I suppose," Blanche answered. "I'd

say she was alluring, like you. And what made her alluring was her vivacity and her intelligence. She speaks five languages, you know. She could write in Latin when she was seven. My own aunt Lady Troy was in charge of the royal children's education—taught them their letters till royal tutors took over."

"Was she happy, ever?" I asked.

Blanche took a book off a shelf and dusted it with care. It seemed to be bound in white velvet and embroidered in gold. "Why, that's an odd question. I never really thought about it, I suppose. Can a queen be happy? Can a woman ever be happy? I think not. We just do what we must do to survive." She put the book back and pulled out another richly bound tome. "That is what our world is about Katherine—survival. And those that know it last the longest."

"When you read my hand that day, what was it you saw?"

She looked up quickly. "Do you truly want to know?"

I nodded.

"You have very similar lines to the queen's, very similar, as though you were . . . sisters, I should say. It's uncanny. Like the queen, you shall live a long life, but a hard one fraught with many difficulties."

"Will I marry?" I asked.

"Yes. But do not ask me who, for that I don't know."

"God's me, I won't have children, will I?" I leaned my head on my hand. My head still throbbed. Aye, it did.

"God will give you children," she answered. "Two boys."

I lifted my head. "Bah. Two boys. I will not have one child, much less two. Did the queen ever love young?" I asked, looking up from under my lashes.

"Yes, and it almost ruined her forever. She fell in love with Thomas Seymour, lord admiral of the high seas. He was quite a seducer, and she was caught under his spell. She was but fourteen, poor thing, and had never had the attentions of a man. They were both high-spirited, you see, drawn together like two stars," She walked over to her desk and sat down, going through some of the papers, then dipping a pen in the inkpot. "Mrs. Ashley had a hand in it too, I must say," she continued, "hoping they would marry someday and pushing them together whenever possible. I was there, but just a face among many of her servants. Not high enough to offer goodly advice." She sighed.

"Well, why didn't they marry?" I asked. "If they loved each other."

"Well, for the usual impediment. He was already married." She did not look up from her work.

"Oh, I see," I said.

"Don't judge her, Kat," Blanche said, raising her head. "She only did what every other woman did from ten miles around him. Fell in love. The scoundrel. Even Mrs. Ashley carried a torch for him I hear." *Your father was the greatest scoundrel the world has yet seen.*

"Where is Thomas Seymour?" I asked.

"Why, executed for treason many a year ago. At the Tower. The very same Tower where the queen's dresses are kept." She held out a small treat for Day, who had awakened. He ran over, snatched it from her hand, and ran back to his cushion.

"Katherine, are you ill?"

"I stayed up most of the night," I told her.

"Aye." She laughed. "But I think something also troubles you. I hear candlelight is seen under your door at all hours of the night. You have the night circles under your eyes."

"Who talks of me?" I asked.

"Why, everyone talks of you," she said. "The young maids of honor, mainly."

"They do not like me much, do they?"

"They are jealous of anything that catches the queen's fancy, whether it be a bauble, or a pet, or an alluring girl with a mysterious past. There is much to hate."

"Will I be tossed aside like Ipollyta?"

"Ipollyta has done well for herself. The queen only turns on those who have already turned on her. And you will not hurt my queen, will you? Deep down she is only a scared little girl who was abandoned by those she needed the most." *Scared little girl.* It was something Grace had said of me, despite my bravado. Blanche tilted her head in contemplation. "She seems to need you for some reason. What is it?"

"I do not know, myself," I said.

She dipped her pen back in the ink.

"Blanche, but is there any way, any way at all that the queen had a child by him, this Thomas Seymour?"

"No child," she murmured. "There were rumors as such many years ago. But there've always been rumors surrounding the queen. I know her better than almost anyone in the world, and I can tell you she's never been with child. Although not always as close as I am now, I have never left her side."

"But do you know that for certain?"

"I would know such a thing. The queen wears her heart on her sleeve."

"What has she said of me?"

"Only that she adores you with all her being. She would be crushed if you ever left her."

"And why should she fear such a thing? I have no intention of ever leaving her."

"The queen trusts no one. Everyone betrays her eventually." Day ran over and jumped into her lap. "Even you, little Day," Blanche said, petting his head. "Even you. He nipped the queen's finger and has been banished from her sight for now."

"And will I? Is that what you saw upon my palm that worried you so?"

"No. That is something only you know, my dear."

I sighed. "Who was Thomas Seymour married to?"

She laughed. "Why, the good queen Katherine Parr, that's who."

"Katherine Parr of Sudeley? She died after childbirth, did she not?"

"She did, poor thing, of the childbed fever."

"And what of the child? The babe?" I asked leaning forward. "Was the babe a boy or a girl?"

"Why, I do believe it was a little girl."

"A girl, I see. Was she raised at Sudeley, do you know?"

"No, I believe after Thomas Seymour was executed,

everything—jewels, properties, money—was seized by the crown for the young King Edward. The queen's child was left penniless, then sent to live with the Duchess of Suffolk."

"The Duchess of Suffolk?"

"Yes. But the duchess didn't want her. Wrote pitiful letters to my cousin, William, Lord Burghly asking for money from parliament to raise her. No one wanted her, the poor child, a queen's daughter no less. Not one of her living relatives stepped forward—a penniless queen's child is quite costly, you see. Elizabeth looked for her—she would have been her stepsister. But she was powerless to help her. She was under house arrest at the time."

"And what happened to the child?" I asked, the hairs on my arms rising.

"She died, poor thing," Blanche said. Day looked up at me from her lap, yawning and showing his tiny sharp teeth, then lowered his head to sleep again. "The duchess's letters to Lord Burghly stopped on the eve of the child's second birthday. And after a time he became worried and wrote to her. She replied that the child had died along with several servants in a fever that swept the household."

Died. If the child had died and I wasn't the queen's child, than who was I? "And Blanche," I whispered. "Are you certain in your heart your queen has never had a child?"

"Is anyone ever certain of anything? Let these matters rest, I tell you. Let it rest, Kat."

Grace used to say it was only the vain who sat for a portrait, and it was far better for loved ones to remember someone in their hearts than from some false image. But I said *fa* to that, for the only image I had of Grace was her contorted face in death. In my dreams, when I did sleep, that death mask transposed onto every memory I had of her, so that I could no longer bear to think of her, or really any of them, those who had left me. It was a bitter pill to swallow it was. Aye, it was.

I was summoned to the Queen's Wardrobe on a special errand a few days later, "a grand surprise," Nicholas said in the note, and we decided to walk the great gallery, for although I'd rushed by it before, I'd never lingered. Nicholas chatted away as though we were on best terms, as I looked at the portraits of the queen that hung alongside her ancestors and those who had ruled before her. Her face never changed from portrait to portrait, the same determined eyes, the aquiline nose that was actually more beaked in life, the snow-white complexion that hid her slight pox marks, the gentle smile that masked her brilliance. In one portrait I noticed she wore the ring she had given me.

"What do you think the words 'I hold what I have' may mean?" I asked Nicholas. "It was written on a piece of jewelry of the queen's."

"Ah, it describes her well," Nicholas said, laughing. "For she clings to the things she loves with much abandon and will never release them."

Suddenly I stopped. A different portrait, not of the queen but another woman, regal and royal, kind. But it wasn't her face that caught my attention, at least not at first. It was what she wore—a loose gown of crimson satin with even deeper crimson velvet banding embroidered in gold and lovers' pinks. At the base of her neck the woman wore an ornate rubied and sapphire necklace surrounded by pearls. My necklace. I froze.

"What is it?" Nicholas said behind me. I could not be related to this woman; no. This was the face of a sweet person, not a hasty-witted, foolish girl. She didn't look at all like a woman of high passions and rash impulses.

"Who is she?" I asked, although I knew. My eyes

slowly traveled up even farther, to her coif. I could see just a hint of red hair. *You inherited your red hair from your mother and your high spirit from your father.*

"Why, that's Queen Katherine Parr, the old king's last wife. My father knew her well. She loved her finery, she did. Shoes especially. In one year forty-seven pair were made for her at the Wardrobe. The shoemakers called her Old Smelly Foot, for all the trouble."

"Will I meet your father today?" I asked, my eyes lowering to the necklace, then back to her eyes. Ahh. Yes, I had seen them before. So long ago, when I was a little girl. It was her, the ghost in Humblebee Wood.

"If there is time, perhaps. He has good days and bad. Come on, we are late," he said, taking my arm.

We left the palace by the west gate and walked through throngs of people, the aroma of salt and brine from nearby Puddle Wharf permeating the air. Nicholas kept up an incessant monologue about the superiority of silk over sarcenet while I went through all the clues I gathered in my mind. Could I be *this* queen's daughter? Nay, for Blanche had said her child had died of a fever. Perhaps somewhere there was a lie in the story I had been told. No, Blanche would not tell a lie. But could someone else have?

"Why, there's Mrs. Miniver!" Nicholas said, pulling me out of my thoughts.

I looked across the road, and saw her, her arm locked snugly in that of a tall, long-necked man who rather resembled a sad giraffe, one of the beasts I'd seen in the *Animalium* book. Just as they disappeared into the crowd, it crossed my mind that the man she was with could be Mr. Bab, *the* Mr. Bab. I turned to call after them, but Nicholas pulled me short. We were at the Queen's Wardrobe.

It was a long wooden-beamed building, two stories high with a tower in the middle. Two black-velvet-clad yeomen in livery guarded the entrance. Many smaller buildings surrounded the main building; the area resembled a small village. The small buildings housed the craftsmen who worked at the Wardrobe, Nicholas explained. An old parish church from the time of Edward III remained on the grounds. "When I was underfoot in the Wardrobe as a child, father brought me out here in front of St. Andrew's to run and play on the church green," Nicholas said fondly.

Then he pointed to the doors of the main building. The Queen's Wardrobe. "It houses the Removing Wardrobe of Beds, the Stables, and the Wardrobe of

Robes, of which Father and I are in charge," he said with great pride. One of the yeomen opened the door and Nicholas gestured for me to proceed him. I held my breath and stepped forward.

We walked into a huge great room. Liveried men bustled about, moving sumptuously dressed beds, tapestries, carved chairs, and cushions. I recognized a cushion I had sat on the previous day and remarked on it. "The Removing Wardrobe of Beds is in charge of removing her furniture when the queen moves from palace to palace, or when she just has a whim and wants to see something new," Nicholas explained.

A distinguished-looking man with heavily embroidered livery barked orders to the workmen. "Who is that?" I asked.

"John Fortescue, Keeper of the Queen's Wardrobe, an entitlement he has for life, unfortunately," Nicholas said caustically as he led me to the other end of the great room. There were bolts and bolts of rich fabrics—velvets, damasks, silks, taffetas, and satins in every color imaginable! My eyes greedily took in the treasures as men delivered new rolls on their shoulders, red-faced and huffing. "Straight from the wharf," Nicholas explained. "Ribbons from Cologne, guards from Burgundy, silk from Persia, taffeta from Spain, gold threads from Venice. We import the best in the world." In a corner two clerks weighed laces and spangles, beads and large pearls, and recorded them in books. They would be locked in chests and presses until they were needed.

Nicholas nodded his head in the direction of an old man who stood at a tall angled desk, bent over a large parchment. "My father," he whispered, something unreadable in his eyes. "Old before his time." Mr. Pigeon dipped his pen in ink and continued to write. "It takes a lot out of someone. The Warrants. Everything must be recorded and recorded correctly and accounted for," Nicholas said somberly. "One begins to hate the smell of the ink." His father never even looked up from his work.

We continued on to a room where the great robes were stored—rows and rows of them lined up—scarlet coronation robes, mourning robes, robes for Parliament, and robes for the Most Noble Order of the Garter, a fig-brown mantle worn over a crimson kirtle. There were grand leather cases with gilt decoration for some of the older pieces, Nicholas explained. I ran my hand over an ermine-lined robe.

"King Henry the Eighth's," Nicholas said, his smile

returning. "He wore it for his investiture." Another liveried man walked past, frowning at Nicholas for the way we tarried. "Come"—Nicholas nodded to me—"the best is ahead."

"And who was that?" I asked him as he hurried me away.

"Ralph Hope, yeoman of the Robes. Cruel man, he is. Wishes to work my father to his death, and then me afterward." I looked over my shoulder and began to wonder just how many men were above Nicholas in the rank of the Wardrobe and just why Nicholas did not have the livery they had. I opened my mouth to ask, but he pulled me forward to yet another series of rooms—the menders. Why, there were more than two score, all of them sewing away at different pieces of livery and various garments, big and small. One man worked on a petticoat that I was sure was one Dorothy owned, perhaps torn in the rosebushes?

Next Nicholas showed me the queen's artificers—cappers, hosiers, shoemakers, skinners, locksmiths, and then the queen's tailors. Nicholas made me peek from around a corner at the tailors, for Walter Fyshe, the main tailor, was very brisk and mindful of strangers who might poison his cloth. He stood before a long wooden table littered with parchment paper for patterns, pins, chalk, a pressing iron, and thimbles. He held shears and was very carefully cutting into a long length of emerald velvet. And just beyond him, two men sat cross-legged on the floor sewing. Above them hung wooden rods from which various garments were draped. Nicholas pulled me on when Walter Fyshe looked up from his work.

At long last—the embroiderers. My stomach fluttered, then dropped as I peered into the room. Men, all of them men, I was disappointed to see, even though I knew that would be the case. They worked in rows, sitting before large frames where the fabric had been pulled taut. I opened my mouth to ask a question, but once again, Nicholas pulled me along. The embroiderers never even acknowledged us as we passed through. "You're as dangerous in here," he teased me when we were back in a dark hall. He kissed me quickly on the lips. "That is for what I've shown you, Kat. And after, when you have seen it all, you shall give me more."

"Nicholas," I said as I leaned away from him. "Why do you not have the livery your father and the other distinguished men have?"

His smile faded. "You know how to lower a man, do

you not? I've worked my entire life for it, and I shall get it. And someday soon, too. Come," he said, pulling my arm once again. He opened another door. "The Queen's Wardrobe."

I held my breath and clutched his arm. Several clerks sitting at desks near the doorway looked up from their work. Stretching to the back of the room were elegant trunks with embossed leather bandings, stacked, some open with gloves and cloaks hanging out. In the back hung gowns, hundreds of them, in the French, Italian, and Flemish styles, in every fabric imaginable. I stood frozen a moment, not believing what I was seeing, not believing I was here. Then I ran down one of the aisles, skimming my hand through the luxurious fabrics, while Nicholas laughed behind me. I walked more leisurely up another aisle, stopping now and then to pull out a gown and study its cut, or the embroidery, or the richness of the fabric. Nicholas followed, his hands clasped behind his back.

"Oh Nicholas, I could not have a better gift." I laughed as I spun around to him. "Thank you for bringing me."

"This isn't all, Katherine," he said, crooking his finger. I followed him to an antechamber. A low fire cast an amber glow around the small space. Draped across a chair was the most magnificent gown, bejeweled, tufted, and ruched in an iridescent peach and tawny silk. The stomacher was embroidered with butterflies, lilies, strawberries, and eglantine. I did have to admit to myself that her embroiderers were indeed talented, although I imagined that what I worked on late at night would put all the dresses to shame. Nearby lay a ruff, sleeves, a forepart, and gloves. Even her jewelry had been laid out, and her prayerbook still attached to the "eye" fob. I bit my lip and turned to him.

"You are to pose for a portrait," he explained. "As the queen herself. She doesn't have time for such things. They take hours upon hours, and as you know she doesn't have much patience. She actually only sits for but a few of her portraits. So her ladies take turns. The queen's face is painted in later with a pattern."

"Nay, you are jesting with me," I said, holding the gown up to my chest, smiling perhaps the biggest smile of my entire life.

"Indeed I'm not. The queen herself asked for you. Says you resemble her the most anyway. Dorothy, the cow, is not very happy. It would have been her turn."

Later, when I was dressed, I sat before the painter,

holding my chin up regally, a scepter in one hand, the other across my waist. I had dreamed of a day like this—dressed so nobly like a queen. Bejeweled and resplendent, wearing the finest things in the world. But as I sat, my heart began to sink. I had rather be in the other rooms, standing behind Walter Fyshe, looking over his shoulder as he cut, or with the embroiderers, asking of new stitches they had learned, and from where they got their fine needles. And then a vision passed before me, Anna and I working at home in Blackchurch Cottage, the door thrown open for fresh air. I could feel it as though it were real, the smell of honeysuckle floating in, sparrows calling in the distance. But the moment was spoiled when I glanced in the long mirror placed against a far wall. I saw a mere girl, buried in false finery staring back at me, and beyond her, a more curious sight—Nicholas and a young maid, a servant girl, locked in an embrace.

And now I am sure of it. The man is the biggest scoundrel the world has yet seen. And even more, a man with not one whit of wisdom. He couldn't leave well enough alone and be content with a queen's child and all that would entail for the future, but has thrown all over and risked everything. He's frequently away, and we are in fear what mischief he's up

to. And now word has reached us he's visiting his nobles at their country estates in hopes of forming a coup to take the protectorship of the young King Edward from his brother. In the meantime, Agnes and I worry for our own futures, for although the queen left each of us a milch cow in her will, neither of us have a farthing to our name beyond it. And the new governess for the baby Mary, Mrs. Eglionby, has taken a particular hatred toward me. I'm allowed to nurse Mary and then she is taken from me until she is hungry again and brought back to me. How I ache for her when she is gone. . . . For it is more than the affection I had for the queen that I have for this child. I love her more than my own being, more than my own child, God help me. Not yesterday, I was caught in the babe's nursery watching over her, and Mrs. Eglionby declared me a witch and ordered that me and my bastard would leave on the morrow. But by my word, the next morning Jane the fool came to me and said all was fixed and that I owed her my life—twice now, for she had saved me before. I do not know what sort of devil potion she gave the governess, but it was declared I could stay.

But alas, bad news has hit us again. On this day of 17 January, our fears have come true. We have learned the admiral has been arrested and taken to the Tower on charges of piracy and high treason. And it was a dog who brought him down. The admiral was trying to kidnap the young king and one of his little dogs woke up and barked. It is not likely he will live, they say. We are to be sent to the admiral's brother, the very same man who plagued my poor queen with worries and intrigues and kept her jewels and lands from her. God, what will become of us?

CHAPTER 25

here's always a price to pay when one is given something costly," Grace used to say at Christmas when there were no gifts for Anna and me at Blackchurch Cottage, just a goodly meal of shepherd's pie and a warm fire provided for us by Uncle Godfrey.

Dorothy's maid Beatrice finished my hair as I stared at my reflection. My hand fingered the necklace, freed from its hiding place, hanging at my neck.. Its weight was heavy and mighty under my fingers. I wondered if this was the only reason Jane the fool, sick with death, had come to Blackchurch Cottage. And why Grace had let her die rather than give it to her.

Dorothy appeared behind me, her hands on my

shoulders. "My, my, you are gorgeous! Why, it's the gown you tried on when we played at the store!"

"It's from the queen, a gift for Christmas," I said, running my hands down the deep crimson fabric. It was of a Flemish design, cut low, my breast almost tipping over the bodice. It had been left for me on my bed. I'd found it when I came home from the Wardrobe, my feet and back aching.

"And the necklace?" Dorothy asked, one eye raised up.

"Lord Ludmore," I lied.

"So poor Nicholas." She laughed. "He's lost you for good."

"Yes. I guess you could say that. I saw him kissing a maid. So much for his undying love for me."

Dorothy let out a long, hearty laugh. "Why, that is nothing new. Men like to have their crumpet and eat it too. You are simply to turn your head and abide it. It's the way of things, I'm afraid."

"And if your John has his crumpet, what shall you do?" I asked her.

"Kill the whoreson with my own hands, I would." She laughed. "Really. Let Nicholas have his dalliances. If you were to have a man who didn't partake as such, there'd be no one left to choose from, 'cept the old men who we might have to have anyway. But maybe perchance, your Lord Ludmore is such a man," she said, and I smirked to myself, thinking of his bastards. "When a man gives one such a gift," she said, lightly touching the necklace with her fingertips, "and a woman receives it, she knows there is a price. Rafael has won you for good."

"No," I insisted. "Nothing is settled."

"I think I feel sorry for Nicholas," she said, taking my arm. "Poor thing, there are no ladies left for him to court. We've all discovered his ways."

The feast of Twelfth Night was a favorite of the queen's, and no expense was spared. The tables, still strewn with evergreen and holly, were laden with roast beef, goose, and stuffed turkeys, and even roasted swans and peacocks, their feathers gilded with gold leaf. Sweet melons and apricots, plum porridge, and minced pies were served as courtiers sang carols accompanied by the low sound of pipes and drums. Later there was to be a play.

I sipped mulled wine, its warmth tickling my mouth, as I watched the queen. She was feeding Lord Dudley an apricot, giggling and laughing loudly.

"You truly love her, don't you?" Rafael asked, appearing by my side. I turned to him and his eyes were immediately drawn to the necklace, a look of puzzlement crossing his face.

"And what if I do?" I said. He was looking at the queen, his eyes, for a moment, sharp as daggers.

"What do you know of love, Heartbreaker? You are but a child," he said, finally meeting my eyes, his own eyes soft now.

"You know there are brides younger than I." I took another sip of my wine.

"I shall never marry." He looked away again.

"Ha. Then why come back to court?"

"Hmmmm." He ran his finger along my arm. I hissed and pushed his hand away.

"Well, I shan't marry either," I proclaimed.

"We're a lot alike, Katherine," he said, and I realized he had never said my full name before.

"Except for our feelings for the queen," I replied, glancing around in time to see Dorothy slap her John Abington and run from the room. A nearby maid watched her go, with the look of one trying to hold back a smile. And then just beyond them I spotted George the sweeper with such a sorrowful look of longing on his face that shivers went up my back.

"Actually, my sweet, love and hate are the same."

"What do you know of love, Lord Ludmore?" I said just as a lady walked by, a look of longing aimed at Rafael. "Ahh," I said. "Let me guess. She's missing a rose."

Rafael's face darkened and I could see beads of sweat on his forehead. He stood. "They are starting to dance and I shall go find a partner, a suitable partner who doesn't talk."

He bowed and walked off through the dancers and soon I saw him happily spinning the rosebush girl around.

Suddenly Dorothy appeared, her eyes rimmed with red. "Come," she said, leaning down and helping herself to my wine. "Let us dance and forget our men." She pulled me by both my arms, laughing, into the crowd.

"What's happened between you two?" I asked, my voice low.

"He's long wanted me to ask the queen if we can marry," she said over her shoulder. We joined a group of dancers. We were each spun around by a courtier, coming face to face again a moment later. "As though I would, and ruin my chances at court," she continued. "My father would kill me." She was spun away from me in another direction. I was whirled around again, just as she said, "And now he threatens to tarry with that fat-rumped slut. But I'll show him tonight, I will."

And just then I was spun around again and suddenly I faced the queen, who smiled at me genuinely, until her eyes alit on my necklace. She froze, grabbed my arm, her nails sinking into my skin like daggers, and pulled me out of the dance and away. The music stopped.

We walked through the room, quickly, our arms linked together, our hands clasped in a death grip. If she hadn't held me, I thought I should fall as the room had begun to turn. "Smile," she whispered through clenched teeth as we swept past the astonished courtiers. I managed a stiff smile. Tears stung my eyes. The music began again.

A moment later we were under a stairwell, her face half obscured in the dark.

"Where did you get that necklace?" she hissed, her fingers gripping my arm painfully again.

"Do you know it? Is it yours?" My heart raced in my chest.

"You do not ask a queen questions!" she roared. "Where did you get it?"

"It was my mother's!" Aye, it was hers. I knew it with all my being.

She stood back and looked at me, her head cocked like

a cat examining a cornered mouse. "I wasn't sure," she said. And then, "I didn't know where you were. I didn't. I looked, but I couldn't find you."

My stomach sank down to my toes. "I saw a portrait, Your Majesty. Of Queen Katherine Parr. She was wearing this necklace. Can she be my mother? Can she? I do not resemble her in any way."

"But you're the spitting image of your father," she said, cupping my chin and turning my head side to side. "You have his eyes. His allure. God's death, but he was my first love. One never forgets that kind of love. But he could not be trusted. He betrayed everyone. Even you. He died for his own mistakes and left you alone."

"I don't believe it. I don't believe any of this," I said, suddenly wishing I was back home, back at my real home, Blackchurch Cottage. *Christian*. A sob rose in my throat.

She reached down and pulled up her fob, this one elaborately jeweled with a half-moon crescent on it. She opened it, and there was a small portrait. She held it up for me to see. It was of a strikingly handsome man, thin faced, emerald eyes—sea-green eyes. It was like I was staring in a mirror.

"I called him 'Moon,' for he was the moon and stars

to me, and for other more private reasons," she said as I held the portrait even closer. *You have a mark, a perfect half-moon,* Ava had said to me. It didn't prove anything. I dropped the fob. Nothing proved anything. "But he was quite the disappointment, I must say," the queen continued. "And our tryst parted me from the only mother I ever had."

"Did he betray you, Your Majesty?"

She looked away. "I was young, naïve."

"You were just fourteen."

"I knew what I was doing," she said. "I just didn't forsee the consequences that would ripple through the rest of my life."

"Are you my mother, Your Majesty?"

"What does it all matter, my Spirit?" she said, looking at me clearly. "You are my daughter *now*. And you will never leave me; I will hold you to me forever. You can spend the rest of your days on my gown. I don't have a care for it, only you." She smiled.

I tried to smile back at her.

She pulled me close, hugging me so tightly I couldn't breathe, and I swore to myself I could smell juniper. Even if it be ever so faint, it was there. I knew it.

* * *

Later, back in my room, I found myself sobbing, for what I knew not. Finally I wiped away my tears, pulled out the queen's gown, and examined my work. It was very fine, fit for the most royal, and it was indeed superior to anything in all the Queen's Wardrobe. I knew it was. But something wasn't quite right; something was missing. I ran my hand over the area where Anna had drawn the wolf beneath its tree. Yes, something was needed there.

There was a soft knock at my door. "Dorothy?" I called.

"No, ma'am, it's me, Maisy," a voice with much urgency whispered.

I ran to the door and opened it. "Lady Ludmore has sent for you," she said, her face pained and scared. "She's sick . . . and Bartolome, too." She burst into tears. "They're in a very bad state, very bad I tell you. I fear very much for their lives. Can you come?"

I grabbed a cloak, a bag of herbs, and followed Maisy down the dark hall.

An eternity later, we arrived at the Ludmore home. It was dark. Maisy opened the door and I followed her in. Immediately I was struck with the smell of death, vile sickness, and vomit.

Maisy lit a candle. She walked to the stairs and pointed. "Where is Ava, the kitchen girls, the grooms?" I whispered.

"Some fled. Others downed with the sickness. It came of a sudden." She peered up the stairs. "It's mighty powerful, I tell you. Unstoppable."

"What kind of sickness?" I asked her.

"The pox, ma'am. I'm sorry. I should have told you, but I was so afraid. So afraid you wouldn't come. We couldn't get anyone to help us, not even the doctor or the herb woman from Downs Street. I remembered you had a talent with potions."

I took the candle from her and went up the stairs, my feet heavy, so heavy as I walked down the dark hall. I pushed open Lady Ludmore's door. The room was lit by several tapering candles, guttering away—"Prepare the winding sheets" Grace would have said. A low fire cast an amber glow around the room. There were two figures in the bed. I walked closer. It was Lady Ludmore and Bartolome, blistered and pustuled, their faces barely recognizable. Oh, God's me! I took a deep breath.

"Where's Lord Ludmore?" I asked.

"Down the hall," Maisy answered. "When he came home from the feast, he was already in a fever. It's those that get it last that go down the hardest, I'm afraid."

I listened for Lady Ludmore's breath. It was there but faint, like small wavelets over a dry river. Bartolome's breath was more even and full.

"Can you help them?" asked Maisy behind me.

"I don't know," I said. I opened my bag and took out clary wort and galyntyne. "We can only make them comfortable. Perhaps Bartolome has a chance. Boil this with honey and goat's milk, white pepper, and cloves. I have but a little bit. If we had time I'd get more. But pray me, there's no time."

Maisy started to cry. "Oh, stop that blubbering, girl; I'm not dead yet," Lady Ludmore suddenly said. Maisy startled, and crossed herself. She took the herbs from me and ran from the room.

"Lady Ludmore," I said, taking her hand.

"So I shall die, shall I?" she asked me. "Perhaps you shouldn't come near, child."

"Nothing in life is certain." I looked away.

"Except death. Don't lie to me, girl." She coughed. "Should I be praying for my soul?"

I looked straight at her. "Yes."

"Thank God I won't be joining Luddy," she said with a laugh that quickly turned into a violent cough.

"He's down in hell for what he did to my boy."

I dipped a cloth in the basin near the bed and put it on her brow. "No," she said. "Tend to Bartolome. Give him everything. All of it. You must save him at any cost." Oh, God's me, she didn't know Rafael was sick, too.

Maisy came back with my potion in a steaming pot just as I placed a cloth over Bartolome's face. He didn't stir. Still, though, his breathing was even, and I was glad of it. I dipped a second cloth into the pot and started to rub the mixture over his body.

"She's gone," Maisy said suddenly, falling to her knees. I looked up. Lady Ludmore's eyes, still and fixed, rested on Bartolome.

Aye, and he did meet a ghastly end, for it took the ax man two whacks we hear, this day the 20th of March. And it be no day for celebrating, for both my babes have lost their father, and little Mary now be an orphan, and a poor one to boot for her mother rashly gave all her inheritance to him, and now that he be executed for thirty-three counts of treason the crown has seized it all. Lord Seymour the Protector is a cruel man, and his wife even more so. She has not even looked once upon the babe, not once, for she sees her as a rival in rank to her own newborn child. But God have mercy on us, for we have good tidings. We are sent to Catherine Willoughby, the Duchess of Suffolk, the good queen's old friend. I pray she be a kind and righteous woman who will love the queen's child as her own . . . as I do. The Lord Protector promises to send the child tapestries, and rich plate, and later to restore lands and jewels her mother inherited from King Henry. This is the child's only hope. But I see the man is wicked, more so than his brother, a thousand times he is. We are sent away, a dozen of us, with barely a thing, just the linen upon our backs, the two milch cows, and a few paltry nursery items. But I have something, aye, I have, something that the queen's child rightly is due. It will be her inheritance, her safety. Jane the fool predicts an ugly end for all of us. God's precious soul, do not forget us. . . .

CHAPTER 26

e was lying in his bed, in the dark. I walked slowly forward, a candle in hand, till I reached his bedside. His eyes were closed, his breathing labored. The pox and pustules were just beginning to form on his beautiful face. I moved the candle down to his open nightshirt, revealing rivers upon rivers of snarling pink scars. I pulled back his shirt. I held my hand over my mouth to keep from screaming. Scars flamed up and down his torso.

"So this is what it takes to get you to my bed," he said hoarsely.

"What madness is this?" I gasped as I held the candle above his stomach.

"How is my mother and the boy?" he asked.

"They are resting comfortably," I lied.

"Will they live?" he asked. "I've grown rather fond of the boy."

"He's your son," I said as I felt his forehead. A high fever that had little hope of breaking, not without a miracle, not even if I had a full basket of my herbs.

He blinked. "Why would you say such a thing to a dying man?" he asked, but in a way that indicated he knew it was true.

"A blue-eyed beauty in Kent, I believe was Lady Ludmore's description of his mother."

I ran a cold cloth gently over him, his face and chest.

"Your mother cared very much for you," I said.

"Not when I was younger," he said, sounding like the child he had been. "She let him, she let my father hurt me. So I left determined that I would never marry, determined to let the Ludmore name die out forever. It was my revenge."

"Then why did you come home?"

"I spotted a beautiful lass I couldn't forget." He smiled. "And I found out she was headed for London."

I smiled, too. "And saw many more beautiful women in London."

"No. Just one," he said.

"Stop teasing. You didn't care to see your mother again?" I asked.

"I cared." He sighed. "I cared too much."

"Rafael," I said. "What is all this?" I asked as I ran a finger up his chest. He winced.

"Many years ago, after I left. A small town in Yorkshire. I happened upon it," he closed his eyes a moment before speaking again. "Someone was being burned at the stake and I tried to save her." He smiled slightly, looking up at me. "Perhaps I do have a heart, Heartbreaker." He closed his eyes again, trying to gather a breath. Then he continued, "It was a young girl, so very young. I couldn't save her, and in turn was burned myself. I can still feel the flames."

"You said your scars were a gift from the queen," I whispered, a feeling of horror rising in my throat.

"It was by order of your queen that this girl was being burned to death, for little more than her words," he spat out.

I could not believe it. "No," I said. "She's kind. She would not do such a thing."

He laughed bitterly. "You are naïve, little one," he said.

With shaking hands, I dipped a clean cloth into the bowl of water near the bed and wrung it out. He caught my arm. "If I live, I will kill her."

"Is that the true reason you came home, to do her harm?" I asked, tears filling my eyes.

"I thought perhaps there was hope for me. But it was too late. I died a long time ago. Let me go, Katherine; it will be a mercy," he said.

"Live," I told him. "Live for your son."

"My son," he smiled, faintly.

I managed a smile just as Maisy brought in the pot of herbs. Her eyes grew big when she saw Rafael. "There's just a bit left; perhaps it could help him." She backed out of the room.

"What is that, a potion to save me?"

"It might, if there is a will to live," I said.

"Save it," he said. "Use it on Bartolome."

Later, after I'd closed his eyes and turned the sheets over him, I went and peered out the window. The sun was rising, and just beyond the rooftops, a line of trees glimmered like emeralds.

I had long judged Grace, indeed I had, for letting Jane the fool die. But was I any better? Would I rot in hell someday like her? I did not know nor care. Maisy met me at the bottom of the stairs.

"Ava has passed away also, but Bartolome, his fever broke," she said woodenly.

"Is there any money in the house?" I asked, breathing deeply. Hot, I felt so hot.

"A coin or two perhaps, hidden in the larder," she said. "How is the master? Will he live?"

"He's gone too," I said my voice cracking, and she fell to her knees. "We need money to pay the gravedigger." I walked to a chair at the table, hoping the movement might bring me relief, but if anything, I felt hotter, like I was burning alive.

"Lord Ludmore, poor soul, he never did anything right in his life," Maisy said. "Lady Ludmore forever worried about it. The crown will seize everything. There is no true heir. What will we do? I have no family, no one."

I rose, gripping the back of the chair. "Listen to me very carefully. You are to stay here until Bartolome is better. I will send you more coins, enough to bury everyone. Once that is done, you must send Bartolome to Blackchurch Cottage in Gloucestershire. Anna . . ." I choked out. "Anna will want him. Then you are to come to me as my maid, do you hear me?"

"Yes, yes, I will," she sat down on the stairs and sobbed. "You will not forsake us, will you?"

"No," I told her. "Now take your dress off and give it me. I'll sell the one I wear. And I'll come right back."

God's death, but how can it get worse? The duchess hates the queen's child too and spends, it seems, every minute of the day scheming of how she may be rid of all of us. She wrote many a letter, I hear, to a lord of the Parliament, asking that the child's inheritance be restored to her, but to no avail. Even the child's living relatives cry poor mouth and turn their backs. And the Lord Protector has yet to send the things he promised, and I know we'd sooner get blood from a turnip than any kindness from him. I've had to hide my poor Anna—the duchess can't abide any of us, let alone a bastard—and the other servants cover for me, for they have grown to love her. She is a scrawny, ugly little thing. But thank God above for her malformed ears, for she seems to be deaf as a doornail and never much makes a sound. We all pray that someone, anyone, will come for the child and relieve us of this woman. I hatched a plan to save us, sending Agnes back to my home with her cow and a gaggle of ducks I bought with a coin to ready a place for us. But the nitwit married me own brother Godfrey, she did. And now I am left to bide my time and seize the right moment, and it is tonight, for Mary is very sick, and I know in my heart that something is amiss. I start to pack right here and now. This is the moment, I know, but Jane the fool catches me carefully packing the babe's nursery things and I bravely tell her, "Aye, and I shall leave in the night with my two babes." And she begs me to never do such a thing for fear of the reprisal for the rest of them, and I tell her, "Who shall look for this queen's child? No one, not one gentle soul has come for her, nor will. They've all forsaken her." "Well then, leave, and I shall come for it someday, in payment for my silence," Jane the fool says to me, and I knew not how she guessed of the queen's necklace I took the night the queen died.

Later, much later, I heard it told that the duchess let it be known that the queen's child died in the night and was buried in the churchyard, and in a sense she was, for from then on she was Katherine, named for her mother. But no one here shall ever guess, for I keep her close to the cottage and her hair bundled. No one will ever wrench her from me.

CHAPTER 27

floated in a dark world of ghosts. Rafael was there, smiling at me. He told me I had put him out of his misery and then he slowly drifted away. And Grace was there too, laughing and beckoning me to come to her, but when I tried to flee I found I had no legs. And then Jane the fool offered a golden goblet of wine. I sipped it while mystical beasts, grotesque and fanciful, roared around me, baring their sharp teeth. And a dark-hooded figure sang to me like an angel, but when I tried to lift her hood she backed away, pulling my hand, and the world became bright, so bright I had to close my eyes again and I cried and cried. And it seemed I had been here in this dark world forever.

"Hush, hush," came a calm, sweet voice. "There, there now. It's time to come back to us."

My eyes fluttered open and there before me was the ghost, the ghost of my dreams. Only her hood was pulled back, her face scarred, deformed, like the ugly beasts of the world below that I'd seen in *Cosmographia*. But her eyes, blue like a clear winter sky, were kind and glistening. I had seen her before, aye, I had. She was Lady Mary Sidney.

"You took care of me, didn't you?" I asked a few minutes later when the world was more clear. My throat was parched. I looked about and saw I was in a sumptuous bed with embroidered counterpanes. Along the borders, cast in black and gold, were the beasts I'd seen in my dreams. A low fire roared in a nearby fireplace, and above it hung a portrait of a handsome gentleman. And by a far door, a maid sat. I blinked a couple of times before realizing who it was. Iris.

"No one else could," Lady Sidney answered, bringing a golden goblet to my lips.

"How did I get here?" I asked, falling back on my pillow.

"You were brought to the palace," she answered. "By a man who said he found you lying in the street near a millinery shop. He disappeared before anyone could inquire of him further. The queen had you discreetly brought to me."

"Where are we?" I asked wearily.

"In the palace. I have hidden rooms as I do not mix with society anymore. Beyond that door there is a secret hall that leads to the store."

"And Iris, she's your maid?" I asked.

"Yes. She's my family here—here in the dark. My children are mostly kept from me, but I am glad of it. I want them to live, to enjoy the outside world."

"And the handsome man in the painting, who is he?" I asked, my eyes glancing again above the fireplace.

Lady Sidney sat back in her chair and took up her stitching. She sighed deeply before answering, "My beloved husband. I was the fairest in his eyes one day and the foulest the next. He now seeks the arms of a younger woman. This the man who said he'd love me till death parted us. And I believed him. Women, we are always the fools."

I tried to lift my arm but it fell limp and heavy like a fallen branch. "How long have I been like this?"

She looked down to her stitching, a small panel of delicately worked rainbows and raindrops. The work was beautifully done. "Over a fortnight. You barely survived, my dear. The court moved to Richmond upon news of the pox in London. They returned yesterday. Everyone was told you are recovering at the Ludmores. Dorothy has been beside herself with worry, I hear, but of course hasn't ventured a visit. She has her complexion to worry of. And Ipollyta brought you a drink, just last night. She somehow knew you were here."

"And I drank it?" I asked, coughing. "She's poisoned me before. Oh God, I shall die."

Lady Sidney laughed as she pulled up a stitch. "You shall not die. In fact, I think it was Ipollyta's drink that saved you. It's everyone else who wishes your death."

"Who? Who wishes my death?"

"Practically half of the court, my dear. Everyone is very jealous of your closeness with the queen. Even my brother Robert Dudley is wary of you and not pleased I have nursed you."

"Does the queen know you are here?"

"Of course. She had the rooms built for me and visits me often."

"Has anyone else visited?" I asked, wondering if the queen had come for me.

"No, I'm sorry, the poxed are short of visitors,"

she said. "I should know." A feeling of terror coursed through me, hot down to my toes. I tried to sit up.

"God's me," I cried. "Where's a mirror?" I stared at her crippled face and a strangled cry came out. Then I slowly raised my hand up to my own cheek. Poxed, I was poxed; I could feel several on my cheek.

Lady Sidney did not look up from her stitching. "They will fade with time," she said quietly. "As all things do—love, loyalty, hate. You are lucky to be alive, my child. Very lucky. And it's not nearly as bad as mine. You are still beautiful. You will marry, live well. Although its unlikely you'll have children. I'm sorry."

I held my hands over my ears. "God has forsaken me for I have sinned."

"No, my child, God has given you a gift, a gift. You live."

I rolled over to my side, as tears ran down my face. "Has the queen come to see me?" I asked.

"No," she answered.

"Not at all?" I asked.

"She's a queen. A queen cannot risk getting sick. That's why the court moved to Richmond."

"She left me?"

"You couldn't be moved, my dear. And she could not stay. It's as simple as that for a queen."

"But she had the pox before, did she not?" I asked, then realized my error. Lady Sidney had gotten the pox while nursing the queen.

She continued stitching. "Hers was a mild case. It's conceivable she could take sick again. She inquired of you, of course, but she couldn't come." *I'd do anything for you, I'd die for you,* Grace had said long ago. But the queen would not. I reached down and felt the ring upon my finger. *I hold what I have.* Except for me.

"Rest, my dear. Rest."

Everyone has a streak of cruelty in them, and those who can't resist it but ask for forgiveness, will be granted God's blessings. But those who were willingly cruel often didn't even know it, and those were the ones to be most pitied, for they had the fastest route to hell. But what I couldn't comprehend was how a mother could be cruel to her own child as Grace had been. A true and good mother could never be cruel to her own. I'd heard Father Bigg preach that more than once. But this was something I'd never face myself now, would I? Blanche Parry was wrong; I would never have a child.

When I awoke again, the queen was at my side, sitting on the bed, her face expressionless. She was wearing a resplendent crimson gown, the stomacher embroidered with roses and leaves. Curiously, a jeweled serpent wound its way up her arm. She tilted her head, studying me. "Now what are we to do with you, child? How are you to find a husband now? Even Nicholas Pigeon, callow thing, with news of your condition, turned tail and ran. He's courting yet another of my poor maids." A slow smile, hued with something more—perhaps victory?—tilted at the corners of her mouth. "You will always be at my side now, Spirit."

"Am I that horrible?" I asked, tears forming. I wiped them away, my fingers treading lightly over my face. I did not want her to see me cry. I noticed Iris, quietly dusting a cabinet, ears perched back like a nervous horse.

"No worse than mine." The queen smiled as she got up from the bed. She walked over to the fireplace and stared up at Lady Mary's husband. "But I am a queen. There is a lot a man can overcome when one is a queen. He does visit her sometimes," the queen said, tilting her head up to the painting. "Once a year or so, but only in the dark of night. And she actually welcomes him."

I turned over and hugged my pillow. It smelled of lilies. I started to cry, but tried to muffle my sobs. "And I hear," she continued, "your shepherd is quite persistent. Proud thing too, I do have to say that for him." I listened quietly, my face still in the pillow. "I sent a gift of several lambs, of course, but the gardener found the three little buggers eating my favorite roses this morning."

"Was *he* here?" I whispered.

She didn't answer. I looked up to see that she was examining her hands front to back. Then she nibbled on her thumb. It was a childlike habit I'd seen before, when she was deep in thought. "You are better off with me, my Spirit," she said finally. "You were not made for country life."

Had he come? Oh God. Christian.

The queen stood and stared at herself in a long mirror. Nearby were long dress forms and sewing tools I well recognized from the store. "Crimson," she said quietly. "Crimson always becomes a redhead. My stepmother loved the color, you know. She was not particularly pretty, oh but how I adored her.

"I had a very austere life when I was young, Spirit," she continued, still looking in the mirror, holding the sides of her dress and turning this way and that. "And now I very much enjoy beautiful things. As you do. You were not made for the country—dust, death, filth, mud. You were made for better things, beautiful things, the things you have longed for your entire life. Things you are entitled to. And I can give you everything as long as you stay with me."

Rafael had said once I was not made for the court life. And now he was gone, God save his precious soul. God's me! Bartolome! I'd forgotten. And I'd promised Maisy. I rolled over and sat up the best I could. Iris ran over and propped some pillows behind me.

The queen turned. "See now? You are quite recovered, you are. I want you back by my side as soon as possible. All the ladies have asked about you."

"Your Majesty," I began. "Lord Ludmore left behind a son, a little boy who survived the sickness."

"A son?" she asked, her eyebrow arching. "A bastard, you mean."

"I was wondering if you could see fit in all your compassion to provide him with some of Lord Ludmore's estate."

"What estate? I know nothing of what you talk about." She had moved to the window. She casually lifted the curtain and stared out. "We all live in cages, don't we—some more gilded than others."

"I was told you would seize the estate. . . ."

"I? I?" She smirked. "If anything is done, it's only in

my name." She waved her hand. "Things are done all the time. I can't worry about these kinds of matters. It's already been bestowed upon someone else anyway."

"But you have the power—"

"Hush! Didn't that country cow teach you anything?" She turned back to the window and took a deep breath. "I was a bastard too, once. But I made my own way. So shall he." Then she turned to me. "I've left you a gift. Be back in chambers promptly tomorrow." She picked up her skirts and opened the door. Lady Sidney was standing just on the other side. She curtsied, and the queen walked on.

Iris picked something up from the end of the bed. She handed it to me. It was a small book, wrapped in ribbon. I pulled away the ribbon and opened it. It was the prayer book, the one the queen often wore at her side. My mother's book. I held it to my heart.

I slept again. When I awoke, Lady Sidney stood near me, Iris behind her. "Who is Bartolome? Was he your Spanish lover?" Lady Sidney asked.

"No, he is Lord Ludmore's bastard son who has been left with nothing," I said. Suddenly an image of that night came to me. My hand went up to my throat. "Was

I wearing a necklace when I was brought to you?" I doubted it. Whoever brought me to the palace had certainly sold it and pocketed the money.

"Yes, a quite beautiful one, I must say," she said. "I've kept it here for you." She motioned to Iris, who quickly went to a cabinet. She brought it to me and I turned it around in my hands, admiring its beauty.

"Could you do something for me?" I asked Lady Sidney. "Can you send Iris with it to my room? Under my bed there is a secret place with some things I have concealed. Have her hide it there. She will find a small pouch of gold coins the queen gave me at the New Year. Tell her to buy passage for the boy. I'll write directions. He is to go to my sister Anna at Blackchurch Cottage in Gloucestershire. I know she will not turn him away."

"Did a young man with long locks come for me while I was sick?"

Iris was helping me dress for the first time. The queen had sent three new beautiful gowns along with new gloves, cloaks, and fans—glorious things a princess would wear.

"Yes and it was quite a sight, I tell you," Iris said. "The queen's guards kept him from coming inside the palace and threatened to throw him in the Tower, but didn't for your sake. Finally someone took pity on him when it was clear you'd live and told him. Then and only then did he leave."

I looked upon the heavily curtained window, where a tiny sliver of light teasingly shown through, like a pathway to another world.

CHAPTER 28

hen I nearly died those many months ago, I came to realize that I loved Christian and would love him forever. But I discovered I could find some sort of happiness at court by the queen's side. It was a different kind of happiness, a dull contentment, the kind one has when sipping something hot on a wintry night. And what more can a young woman ask for but contentment, and lovely clothes, and festive parties, and the love of a good queen? I can't think about Christian.

Death came near, but I have scared death away for a long time, Blanche Parry says. She still insists I shall live a long life and I jest with her how wrong she was that I would marry and have children, two boys! God's me.

Two boys. And she laughs that fate has a way of turning when we least expect it. Dorothy tells me there are some men who could look beyond a pox or two, especially on the face of a favorite of the queen such as me, but a barren lass cannot be borne, for a man needs an heir—no matter his station in life, high or low, an heir must be had.

So although death shall not find me for a while, it still comes for others as it often does in the heat. We've had an unbearable hot summer, with winds that seem to foretell a hellish winter. One morning near the end of July, I was called to the bedside of Mrs. Ashley, who had been wasting away for quite some time. She had refused my potions, but little matter, for there is no stopping the wasting disease, and when a soul wants to leave this earth, there is no stopping it. The queen, as she often does when full of heartache, had taken to her own bed. I'd had to leave her side to attend to Mrs. Ashley's strange request.

Her maid sat by her side weeping. The windows were propped open, to relieve the heat of midsummer, but still it felt like the inside of Mrs. Prim's oven. I crept toward the bed and I was surprised when I saw that she was still alive, so worn away she was, like cleaved bones in a night shift. But her senses were still intact; I could see that in her eyes.

"You know who your mother is, don't you, girl?" she said, breathing heavily. Her voice was strong, but low. She nodded to her maid to leave. "I thought you'd come to do harm to the queen, and I couldn't abide that."

I didn't answer her but waited as I stared at the veins in her clawlike hands. "But you look more like your father, you do," she continued. "Although I love my John Ashley, there was always a man above him. Thomas Seymour. The queen would have done well with him if fate had worked the way I'd hoped. 'Moon' she called him, did you know that?" She gripped my hand, and her hand was cold, so cold. She was already not of this earth I knew, but only hovered here like a fine morning mist. Her voice was very faint now; I had to lean near her face to hear her. "You have his eyes. I was quite startled when I first saw you. Those eyes." She laughed softly. "How they knew how to flatter, seduce, and torment.

"The queen adored him. He was her first love, he was." She sighed. "And God forgive me, but I encouraged them. But it went too far. And when I saw that, I tried to put an end to it and confronted the admiral. But do you know what he said? 'By God's precious soul,

I mean no evil and I will not leave it.' And he would not. The queen had to make the decision for him. It didn't turn out well, as it never does for a first love. There were consequences to be paid."

"What are you trying to tell me, Mrs. Ashley?"

"That I'm sorry for what I did to your mother."

I let go of her hand. "And what do you know of my mother?" I asked. I leaned forward.

"That she wanted you very much. She longed for you. He wanted you, too. Of course you were to have been a boy. A former queen's daughter is mighty powerful, but when the queen dies, the power dies with her. And you were not wanted after that." *No one wanted you. But I did.*

"I don't see any of Katherine in you. All I know for sure is you have *his* eyes. That man could have sired many a bastard across the entire kingdom. He had flirtations with those high and low. There was one—pretty little thing, as I recall. Didn't know her place." She paused a moment, her breathing becoming more labored, her voice more faint. ". . . Tried to win the queen with her witchcraft . . . you so like her . . . ingratiating yourself into the queen's heart . . . stitches and potions . . . the both of you. Vexed. I was very vexed with you."

"What was her name, do you remember?" I asked, lifting her hand again.

"Grace," she whispered. "It didn't fit. A lass from the country with little grace she was."

"And you think perhaps she had a child by him?" My heart was sinking.

Her voice rose. "Yes! For we heard of it at Cheshunt, we did, and the princess was not happy, but her mind was quickly turned with the news of the queen's death. When guilt is mixed with grief, it makes a mighty potion. Mighty indeed—took to her bed for a week. To cheer her, I told her that perhaps now she could have her man, but she said she had little care for it, for he was a man of much wit, but little wisdom." She managed to laugh a little. "And he had cost us much, the devil. Elizabeth might never have been queen for all the trouble. She was thrown in the Tower, and me with her, and questioned about the whole affair. But Elizabeth kept her wits about her, as she always does when she is on the point of a precipice. She prevailed as she always does."

A hot breeze came into the room and her eyes started to flutter. Death had come for her, buoyed on the wind. It would be very soon.

I stood to leave, but she spoke one more time. "I'm sorry, girl," she said. "For what I did to you."

"What do you speak of?" I said, turning to her.

"I told Ipollyta I needed a potion to kill rats," she said. "I didn't want you to die. I just wanted you to leave. And Ipollyta nearly killed me when she figured out what I had done. I thought she'd be grateful. You see, my child, I just couldn't look upon those eyes anymore. It was like *he* had come back from the grave to tease me."

After Katherine Ashley passed away, the queen mourned her dearly. A light had gone from her eyes, although she appeared to the court to be as merry as ever. I stayed with her constantly, never leaving her side, as she seemed to cling to me now more than ever. But I wasn't true with her, not completely. When she held my hand, I did not pull it away, but I didn't grasp it either. And when I was able to steal away, I went to visit Lady Sidney, and we quietly did our needlework together. Here people did not stare quizzically, counting how many pox there were beneath the white paste. What does the queen see in her? I know they ask themselves. Here there was only companionable silence. Except for Maisy and Iris, who had become fast friends, and who were always chatting away in a corner.

One day when Lady Sidney had dozed off and I had sent Maisy on an errand, Iris asked me, "Do you ever wonder, ma'am, what would have been?"

"Pray me, what do you mean?" I responded, dropping my needle and having to pick it up again. I was very near finishing the queen's dress, thousands of hours I'd worked on it, it seemed.

"Lady Sidney has not betrayed you in any way," Iris said. "I figure things out on my own. Me own mother said if perhaps I'd been born higher, I could have gone far. So I always wonder, I do, what if. What if I had been born a queen's daughter and then it had been taken away from me. And what if it was possible to seize it all back?"

"And what if it wasn't possible?" I responded quietly as I drew up another stitch. "To have it all?"

"I don't know, miss," she said. "I think perhaps I'd choose love. If I couldn't be a queen's daughter, I'd choose my true love. If he'd have me."

"No one will have me now, Iris," I said. I realized I'd done a row of crooked stitches. "My true love cannot be had anymore."

"I heard he has dumped Anne Windsour. And he let it be known that he was thinking of you again despite your affliction."

I laughed. I laughed very hard. "I wasn't thinking of him, Iris," I said.

"Then your shepherd?" she asked, smiling. "Can it be that the shepherd is your true love?"

I didn't answer and continued to stitch. Grace had always said stitching soothed the soul. Aye, indeed it did, and always would. But there are some things that cannot be stitched away.

Iris stood up, went to a cabinet, and brought me a letter. "Lady Sidney was keeping this for you till the time was right. It arrived several weeks ago."

I took it from her and opened it up.

My Good Katherine Bab,

As I never learned to write me letters, good Father Bigg has transcribed my words and here they be. Our dear, and yours more, Anna Bab was laid to rest on Whitsuntide next to her mother Grace. You must find joy in the fact that Anna was happy these last months back in Blackchurch Cottage, although I must say, she spent many a night looking out the window toward Nutmeg

Farm, but he only felt kinship for her, not what she hoped in her heart. A fortnight ago, a fever overtook her. I did the best I could, I tell you, but God took her from us on a moonless night, most easily I must say, for once in her delirium, Anna drifted away quickly. And when I laid her out I found a most curious thing, a mark above her ear, a little half-moon, and I was very sure the devil himself had put it there after taking it from the sky. And I did wonder, I did, if all those old stories about Grace Bab were true. Katherine Bab, I beseech you to come home. Come home, lass. That wide-eyed little imp who Anna lovingly took to her heart needs a mother, and I'm too old. Bartolome, he be called. Strange doings indeed. But Old Hookey will not tell a soul all I know. Come home, my sweet, come home.

Yours, Nan Love

CHAPTER 29

nna. My sweet Anna. I mourned quietly, privately, not telling a soul. The queen noticed, of course. She was fearful, indeed she was, of my heartbreak and what it might bring. I could see it in her eyes. But she did not ask. I think she did not want to know what troubled me. And then her fear changed to compassion. She must have made inquiries. New gowns, gifts, trinkets, appeared daily.

"A queen knows everything," Dorothy had told me once. "Be wary." Only Elizabeth did not know my heart. She could only guess of it.

My dreams were of the hills above Belas Knap, of Humblebee Wood, and Puck's Well, running with Christian through the long grasses and laughing under the pear trees. But then he would be pulled away from me as though a mighty wind had come, and the last thing I'd see were his eyes, and my poor Anna, howling as she died. And then I'd wake, and Maisy would have to soothe me till I could fall back asleep.

One day as we were stitching in the privy chamber, the queen strolling with Robert Dudley in the garden below, Anne Windsour announced, "There is to be a new lady of the privy chamber to replace Mrs. Ashley." And in walked a stout lady, with a severe lumpish face, like unkneaded bread dough. "Mrs. Eglionby," she said. The lady nodded to us and Dorothy pinched me hard. I ignored her.

It was several agonizing hours before the opportunity presented itself for me to approach her. I was giving yet another embroidery lesson to the ladies as Katherine Knevit played for us on the virginals. The queen was with her councilors. I approached Mrs. Eglionby and sat next to her, slowly and carefully as to not attract attention. She nodded. "Nicely done," I told her, looking at her needlework. "There, pull the stitch up tighter."

She glanced up at me as she did so. "I've seen many a face I have in my time, and I feel I know you from somewhere."

"Where were you before the court?" I asked.

"I was a governess to Lord Eastbourne," she said. "I've always been in charge of babes, I have. Highborn and lowborn, it did not matter, I loved them. But I'm tired of that work, I am. Lost too many along the way."

"There," I said, pointing to another of her stitches. "That one would look better as a satin stitch. Pull the needle up to the left."

"Why, you're right," she said, smiling. She looked down at my own cloth, a panel of crescents and rolling hills, a picture of a land I knew long ago. "Why, yours is beautiful. Gorgeous. The last time I seen stitching that beautiful was when my good Queen Katherine Parr stitched her nursery things for the baby."

"Ahh," I said, quietly, my stomach lurching. "Katherine Parr. Was she a good lady, Queen Katherine Parr?" I asked.

"Yes, pious, sweet, good-natured," Mrs. Eglionby said. "The most noble of them all. She had everything, but what she wanted most was a little babe. Poor little Mary. Nothing went right for the child. A queen's daughter, no less. Perfect in every way she was when she was born. A full crop of red hair she had." She laughed. "And a half-moon mark above her ear! Oh, but the poor queen died she did, of the fever."

"And the child, what became of the child?" I asked casually, as my stomach continued to flutter. I looked up at Dorothy, who nodded at me from across the room.

"Stolen she was," she whispered, looking around. "Although I was sworn to secrecy by the duchess. The duchess never cared for little Mary. And when the child got sick and disappeared, the duchess never even looked for her. Why would she, now? She'd been relieved of a very costly burden. She just let it be known about that the child had died."

"But who took the child?" I asked.

"We all knew," she stated flatly, then lowered her voice again in a whisper. "For the three of them were simply gone." I leaned in to hear better. "But I knew for sure, and kept my mouth buttoned up. On the night she disappeared, it was dark as hell, it was. Strangely hot, too, for it was the end of summer, very near the child's second birthday. I was at the window opening the shutters and I happened to see the maid Grace leaving with her milch beast, and carrying two little bundles. And that harpy swag-bellied fool seemed to be helping her get away. I couldn't see very well since it be a moonless night, so I'll never know for sure if Grace carried the babes with her or not. It was simply too dark."

"Why did you not sound the alarm the next day when the queen's child was gone?"

"I figured it was better this way, you see," she said. "For I had overheard, just two nights before, the dwarf talking with the duchess about making a sleeping potion that would make the little girl rest forever and put us all out of our misery." She pulled another stitch up. "It was the dwarf's idea, but the duchess didn't say aye or nay, and I knew this did not bode well for the child. Oh my," she proclaimed, holding her hand over her mouth. "I always did have a loose tongue. I've gone too far, haven't I?"

"Oh no," I said, my voice lowered to a whisper as well. "I'll never tell a soul. And what would it matter? No one wanted the child and the fortune was already lost, wasn't it? And what happened to Jane the fool?"

"Who?" she asked, looking at me strangely.

"The dwarf. Swag-bellied you say. Was she with child?"

"I thought so, I did," she said. "There were rumors she met a groom somewhere in the woods. And not long after Grace and the queen's child disappeared, Jane the fool, aye, that was her name, indeed it was, disappeared too on a dark, windless night. And it was said she'd turned herself into a wolf, for the most ghastly howls were heard in the woods that night."

"Perhaps she was birthing her babe," I suggested quietly.

"Aye, perhaps she was. And her babe runs with the wolves now."

A century or so ago, near Winchcombe, a small child drowned in Old Simon's duck pond. It's not the ghost of the child who lingers there now, but its mother waiting for it to come home. "The lingering," they call it, the feeling that something is there but cannot be seen. I did not appear in the queen's company for two days, and strangely she did not call for me, but I knew, aye, I did, that something waited between us. I took her gown to Lady Sidney's rooms, and I stitched and stitched away as it was pinned around one of the forms, finally determined to finish it. Lady Mary Sidney helped with some of the stitches.

"I'll be leaving soon," I told her one afternoon. The heat was searing, so her curtained windows had been propped open, letting a curious light into the room.

She looked up at me, the light bestowing a special beauty upon her poxed face. "I know," she said. "And I'm happy for you. For your escape. But the queen will not let you go; you will have to sneak away in the night. You do know this."

"I can't do that to her," I said.

"It's beautiful," came a quiet voice from the doorway. It was the queen. Lady Sidney nodded, then retreated to her rooms.

"It's my gift to you."

"A parting gift," she said as she walked around the form, running her hand across the peach fabric. She stared at it a good long time, stroking the great lion, whose ruby eyes glimmered on the stomacher. She touched the delicate orchids entwined with curling vines, the exotic beasts from faraway lands stitched in Venice gold, a sea monster in green silk swimming along the hem. Puckered all over the gown were hundreds of luminous pearls set within truelove knots. I waited with indrawn breath to see if she would notice my final touch. But if she did, she didn't comment on it. "Magnificent," she finally said, her eyes still on the dress. "You've given me everything. Almost everything."

I did not answer her. I couldn't. "Come with me," she said quietly. She led me down the staircase and along a short hall guarded by two yeomen. They bowed and opened the door. I followed her. Jewels, boxes and boxes of jewels, everywhere. The Jewel House. Blanche Parry had told me of it once.

"Some of this is yours," she said, throwing her arms in the air. "Some of your things went to relatives; some were seized by the Crown when your death was reported. I cannot give it all back to you intact. But you can take whatever I have. It is yours. I do not care."

Rubies, diamonds, emeralds. I put my hand inside an ebony coffer and let my fingers pass through the gems. They felt like river pebbles.

"But I do not want any of this," I said. "I don't!" Tears ran down my cheeks. I turned back to her. Her face was unreadable.

"So you shall choose love. A man's love," she said. "Over your own stepsister."

"When did you know, really?"

"The very first time I laid eyes on you," she said. "It was like seeing a ghost, for we were told you had died when you were two. I wasn't completely sure for quite a long time. I would have loved you regardless. You are the daughter I'll never have." I stepped forward to embrace her, but she must have read what was deep in my eyes. She stepped away from me. "Go now, then. If you've made up your mind, go to him."

"I very much doubt he will have me," I said.

"I think perhaps he will." She smiled.

"No," I said. "And I can't bear to lose him again. What would you do, Your Majesty, if you were in my shoes?"

"I'd give the world to be in your shoes," she said. "To choose love. Real love." She had turned from me, her voice royal and commanding. "We can have no further contact. If I were to give you anything, if we continued to speak, they'd for sure know there was a connection. I can't recognize you for who you really are and have that particular scandal stirred up again. I nearly lost everything for tarrying with your father. They'd only assume you were my daughter, anyway. There were rumors, so many rumors. I'm sorry, but we will never see each other again."

A sob caught in my throat as I started to take off my ring. "No," she said quietly. "Keep it. It has only sad memories for me, but will have good ones for you." I stepped toward her again. She held up her hand. She looked at me one more time, then walked from the room.

When I made it back to my chamber, my court gowns and things had already been taken away. On the bed was a gold coin, enough for a journey into the country. I quickly got down on my knees and searched my hiding place. God's me, but my things were still there—the nursery items, and the necklace. And something else—hidden underneath it all—a journal. I flipped through the pages quickly. In Grace's own hand. A note fell out. Barely legible, Anna had scribbled, *I thought I'd lose you.* I opened to the first page of the journal and began to read.

> *The Good and Rightful Remembrance of Grace Bab in the Year of Our Lord . . .*

CHAPTER 30

knew where the chapel at Sudeley was, indeed I did, even though I'd never been inside. Tucked behind the castle, with a turret and spikes and stained-glass windows that glowed at night like jewels, it was a miniature version of the big castle. Many a time I'd spent at Belas Knap wondering what it would be like to live there.

I'd come here first after walking all the way from Gloucester, one bag in hand. I couldn't go straightaway to Nutmeg Farm. Not yet. Grace always did say that despite my high spirit, a scared little girl resided in me. And I knew now, beyond a doubt, who I was. My mother lay in there somewhere. I stood at the entrance to the chapel, my heart racing. I pushed open the heavy wooden door and crept in.

I slowly made my way up the center aisle. Wooden pews lined the chapel. The altar was elaborately carved, and behind it a magnificent alabaster wall lit with candles eerily cast a glint of white gloom about the room. I peered around, looking for any sign of a tomb. But I saw none. I made my way to the alabaster wall, gingerly running my hands over the smooth marble. She was here somewhere in this chapel, but where?

I took one of the lit tapers and knelt before the alabaster, shining the light into the dark shadows. Behind me, I heard the chapel door creak open. I looked back over my shoulder. A small, stooped man, with a long white beard that nearly touched his belly, was walking up the aisle.

"And who be you?" he asked. "One of the Winchcombe rats come to plague me?"

I sat still, for I had long heard tales of this man who scared away miscreants in the night. I slowly stood. "I'm not a rat, sir. I'm a lass. And I've come looking for my mother."

"Your mother be not here," he said. "Go home now before I fetch my—"

"My mother, sir," I interrupted him. "She died after giving birth to me. Here at Sudeley."

He was silent a good full minute before walking to me. He came within a foot of me, and I had to hold my breath, so foul-smelling and goatish he was. He turned his head this way and that, giving me a good study. He settled on my eyes. Then nodded his head.

He shuffled to the candles. "And how old are you, lass?" he asked as he slowly started to extinguish them one by one with a long silver snuffer.

"Nearly seventeen," I answered. "This August."

"August thirtieth," he said.

I blinked. "You know of my mother? Queen Katherine Parr?" I asked him.

He moved to another set of candles. "Of course I knew of her. I came shortly after her death. I've looked for her myself the best I could without digging all the stone up. She's waiting. She'll show herself to us someday when she be ready." The old man extinguished more candles, leaving but two. Then he tottered back out the chapel without saying a word.

I felt the lingering, a hush of air like a ghost's whisper circling me. Aye, she was here. I could feel her. I knelt back down and ran my hand across the alabaster in the far left corner, till I felt a place of warmth. I laid down on top of it, hugging my knees, letting the heat run through my body like a long embrace. I lay there for a long time feeling at peace, like I could sleep forever, and when I opened my eyes I saw an elegant figure in crimson float down the aisle and through the wooden doors.

One of Christian's lambs, loose from his enclosure, followed me up the path to Cowslip Cottage, his bell sweetly tinkling. Did I imagine that he frowned at me? What would his master do? When I reached the door, I found I could not go in, my heart beat so. Instead I sat under one of the pear trees watching birds go by, butterflies swim in the wind, insects circle the sky. It was late afternoon, the sun sinking like a great gold coin. When I was young, Agnes would cook an early dinner for Uncle Godfrey and Christian when they came in from the orchard. But everything was different. I had no idea what they'd be doing now.

Finally the door of Cowslip Cottage opened. I sat up. God's me, but it was Bartolome. He was heading somewhere, but he stopped when he saw me under the tree.

"It is you," he said shyly, with little expression.

"Yes, it is me," I told him. "Is Christian at home?" I asked, a tingling rushing up my spine as I spoke his name.

"Yes."

"Can you tell him I'm here waiting for him under the tree?" I asked.

He grinned wide, turned, and ran inside. An eternity later, the door opened again. I stood and brushed off my dress. But when I looked up shyly, it was only Bartolome running back to me.

"Well, what did he say?" I asked, my heart falling down to my feet. I leaned back into the tree.

"Nothing at first. Old Nan told him to stay where he was, that you should come to him, with all you've put him through, and so he just be sitting there. And then Uncle Godfrey said, 'Go,' and still he be sitting there, his face white as linen, and Nan Love had to fetch him some ale and he drank the whole cup down in one gulp." Bartolome laughed.

God's death, he didn't want me. Of course he didn't want me. I looked up at the pear tree, my eyes filling with tears. I was too late. I leaned down to kiss Bartolome and pick up my bag to go, but just as I did the cottage door opened. It was Christian. Christian standing tall, proud, unsmiling in the doorway.

I started to walk to him, and then to run, and finally he began to walk toward me till we met in front of Agnes's old herb garden. I threw my arms around him, tears running down my face.

"I love you, Christian," I said, my face buried in his chest. "I just didn't know how much." He still hadn't said anything. He lifted my chin and ran his thumb over my face, his eyes full of something I couldn't identify.

Then he picked me up, and carried me across the field, away from the cottage. I nuzzled my face on his shoulder, taking in the deep aroma of wool and sandalwood. I didn't care where we were going. I was with him and he hadn't turned me away.

But soon he was carrying me through the village. And soon a gaggle of boys was following us, then others, emerging from their cottages, even the old creatures.

"Christian," I said, my face aflame in embarrassment. "What are you doing? Put me down! Christian, say something!"

But still he did not speak. We passed the town green, and Winchcombe Abbey, and the churchyard. And the next thing I knew I was in the duck pond dripping wet, from head to toe. And Christian was already walking away as I made my way out of the pond, water pouring from my dress, my hair loose now and soaking wet.

I ran after him, my shoes sloshing and squeaking as

Frances and Piper Pea and Alice Ogilvey laughed. It was a long way back. But he walked all the way to Cowslip Cottage, never acknowledging my calls and pleading.

"Christian!" I called once more as he walked up Cowslip Hill.

And finally he stopped. "Am I good enough for you now, Kat?"

"You were always good enough for me. Yes, Christian," I said. "I love you. I love you." He leaned down, his lips hovering just above mine until finally I moved forward. His lips were warm and soft. I thought my heart would burst.

"Well, you have the rest of your life to show me," he said, turning back toward the cottage. "Come," he said quietly.

We walked hand in hand up Cowslip Hill over the centurion, the setting sun sending fiery streaks of golden red across our beautiful valley, the last one God made.

EPILOGUE

saw the queen again many, many years later. She came on progress to Sudeley Castle in the year of our lord 1592. Although Christian bade me not to go, as he was much worried for me, I did go with the other villagers. Our son Miles, born like a God's miracle twenty years into our marriage, came along with me, excited of the day. Bartolome had long left, living the life of an adventurer like his father. Uncle Godfrey had passed and was buried next to Agnes. I tended the graves, all of them—Grace's, Agnes's and Anna's. I had buried Grace's journal and my necklace back with her, for such secrets belonged under the earth.

We stood with a throng of people lining Sudeley

Lane. I was near the back, only hoping to get but a small glimpse of her, the queen—my sister. "Is it true like Papa says, you knew the queen long ago, Mama?" Miles asked. He pushed himself through the crowd, dragging me along with him.

"Yes, I knew her," I said. "And it was indeed long ago."

And then suddenly there she was, high atop a white horse in her procession, her bearing as regal as ever, although there was many a line upon her face. She was wearing it, the gown I'd spent so many months stitching. Even from here, I could see my wolf, its emerald stare boring straight through me.

The queen and I locked eyes, both of us frozen in the moment, her face not changing, unreadable. And then she slowly nodded her head. I returned her acknowledgment; her procession moved on. She never looked back.

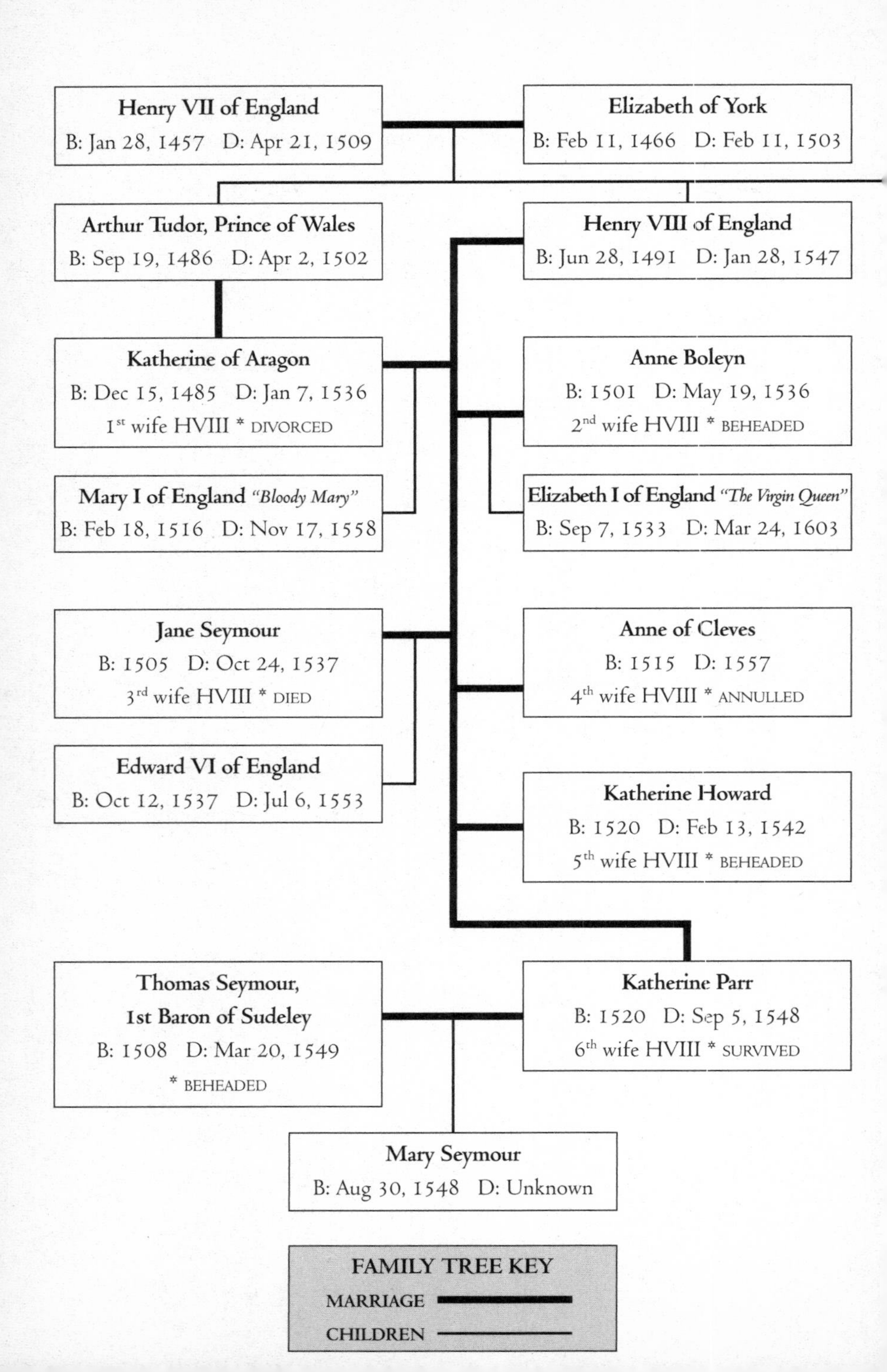
Henry VII of England
B: Jan 28, 1457 D: Apr 21, 1509
Elizabeth of York
B: Feb 11, 1466 D: Feb 11, 1503
Arthur Tudor, Prince of Wales
B: Sep 19, 1486 D: Apr 2, 1502
Henry VIII of England
B: Jun 28, 1491 D: Jan 28, 1547
Katherine of Aragon
B: Dec 15, 1485 D: Jan 7, 1536
1st wife HVIII * DIVORCED
Anne Boleyn
B: 1501 D: May 19, 1536
2nd wife HVIII * BEHEADED
Mary I of England "Bloody Mary"
B: Feb 18, 1516 D: Nov 17, 1558
Elizabeth I of England "The Virgin Queen"
B: Sep 7, 1533 D: Mar 24, 1603
Jane Seymour
B: 1505 D: Oct 24, 1537
3rd wife HVIII * DIED
Anne of Cleves
B: 1515 D: 1557
4th wife HVIII * ANNULLED
Edward VI of England
B: Oct 12, 1537 D: Jul 6, 1553
Katherine Howard
B: 1520 D: Feb 13, 1542
5th wife HVIII * BEHEADED
Thomas Seymour,
1st Baron of Sudeley
B: 1508 D: Mar 20, 1549
* BEHEADED
Katherine Parr
B: 1520 D: Sep 5, 1548
6th wife HVIII * SURVIVED
Mary Seymour
B: Aug 30, 1548 D: Unknown
FAMILY TREE KEY
MARRIAGE
CHILDREN

The House of Tudor

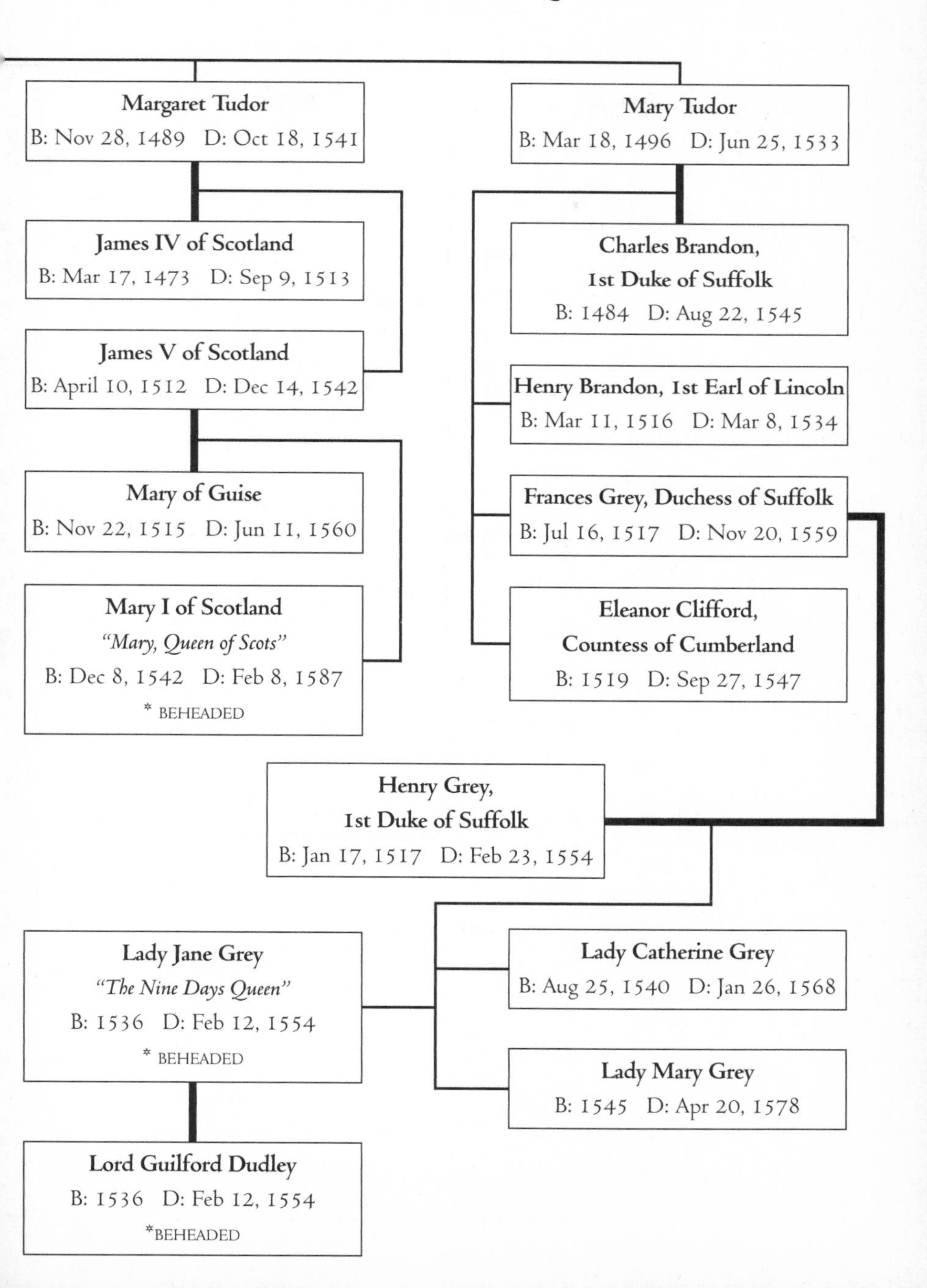

AUTHOR'S NOTE

There are various accounts of what happened to Queen Katherine Parr's coffin, and who eventually discovered her. It is generally agreed that she was forgotten for more than two hundred years, until her coffin started to rise to the surface in the decaying chapel at Sudeley. One story has it that a Mr. John Lucas dug up the slender steel coffin and found the former queen completely intact—moist, her face beautiful as though she had just died. Two years later when her coffin was found amidst some rabbit holes by yet more curiosity seekers, her face had turned to bone.

Queen Elizabeth did visit Sudeley on progress in 1592, twenty-eight years after my story ended, ostensibly to celebrate the anniversary of the defeat of the Armada, but also to escape a particularly bad summer of the plague in London. A three-day celebration included a rich feast and pageant of mummers, bear baiting, and jousting.

Dorothy Broadbelt did indeed get her man—she married John Abington, clerk of the kitchen, in 1567. Nicholas Pigeon, along with his father Edmund Pigeon, Clerks of the Wardrobe, worked tirelessly in the Queen's Great Wardrobe, keeping extremely detailed records down to the location and price of pins. Among these records are generous gifts of clothing from the queen to Ipollyta the Tarletan, "our woman," including a velvet hat, a caul of gold and silver, and a clout of Spanish needles. The last time Ipollyta is mentioned in the warrants is 1569.

Family legend says I'm related to Lady Jane Grey, godmother to Mary Seymour and chief mourner at Katherine Parr's funeral and, later, the tragic queen of nine days. My mother's ancestor John Gray, a one-armed pensioner of the British navy, came over to America in the seventeenth century. His great-grandson James Gray fought alongside his father and father-in-law during the American Revolution.

On the list of Mary Seymour's nursery items of rich bedding, "good and stately gear," and other necessaries that were to be sent to the Duchess of Suffolk were two milch cows for maids who would soon be marrying, three silver goblets, an embroidered scarlet tester (a bed canopy—likely embroidered by Katherine Parr), and a lute. In an inventory of a jewel chest owned by Katherine Parr, the following items are found: twelve cramp rings (for morning sickness) and two pieces of unicorn horn. Mary Seymour's governess was indeed a Mrs. Eglionby, and a Mrs. A(E)glionby did replace Kat Ashley after her death at court, but it's my own conjecture that they are one and the same. The real Mary Seymour disappeared from history on the eve of her second birthday. It is interesting to ask, if she died as a child, as most historians believe, why wasn't the death of a queen's child noted somewhere? Perhaps it was, but is lost to us in history. Or perhaps, perhaps . . .